to Claim

AN ENEMIES-TO-LOVERS OMEGAVERSE

DANI LOUGHARY

ALSO BY DANI LOUGHARY

THE HEARTS OF VALINE

Embers of Fate
Flames of Change

Signed copies of all books are available on Dani's website:

Cover & Interior: Juniper Hartmann (@TheRedFoxCreative)
Character Art: Tess (@Fishbone.Art)

Motion to Claim

AN ENEMIES-TO-LOVERS OMEGAVERSE

DANI LOUGHARY

For all us ice
queens hiding a soft
cinnamon roll center

CONTENT WARNINGS

- Explicit Language
- Spicy scenes
- Sexual Assault (off page, not detailed)
- Eating Disorder (in recovery, but discussed)
- Murder (off page, hinted at)
- Mention of pregnancy (non-major plot point)

PLAYLIST

Welcome to New York
Taylor Swift

Bad Idea, Right?
Olivia Rodrigo

Wildest Dreams
Taylor Swift

Hailey's Comet
Billie Eillish

Illicit Affairs
Taylor Swift

Beggin'
Måneskin

Need You Now
Lady A

Simply Irresistible
Robert Palmer

Rewrite the Stars

Zack Efron, Zendaya

The Prophecy

Taylor Swift

Cold as Ice

Foreigner

This Is Me Trying

Taylor Swift

This Love

Taylor Swift

I Don't Wanna Live For ever

Zayn, Taylor Swift

Stay

Rihanna, Mikky Ekko

Only Love Can Hurt Like This

Paloma Faith

All of Me

JohnLegend

Listen to the offiical playlist here:

AUTHOR'S NOTE

If you're coming here from my Hearts of Valine series and you're not familiar with the omegaverse, you'll probably want to read this all the way through before continuing. If you already know the ins and outs of the genre, feel free to skip ahead and get the party started, you lil' freak.

The omegaverse originated in the fanfiction world and was almost exclusively male/male, with heavy infl uence from shifter romance. Over time, it's branched into a few subgenres. Classic omegaverse is still primarily M/M and often includes male pregnancy.

More recently, heterosexual omegaverse has become popular, especially stories where packs of male alphas form around a female omega. Either way, the genre tends to explore how society treats women, either by subverting expectations with a male omega or by placing a female omega at the center of a group of devoted alphas.

So what exactly is the omegaverse?

Essentially, it's an alternate universe very similar to our own, except for how biology works. In addition to gender, everyone has a secondary sex designation: Alpha, Beta, or Omega. Everyone also has a unique scent profi le that signals their designation to others.

Betas are everyday humans like you and me and make up most of the population. Alphas tend to be physically stronger, more aggressive, and natural leaders. Because this is a secondary designation, alphas can be male, female, or non-binary. They also differ from betas physically, most notably through the presence of a knot.

At the base of either the penis or the clitoris (technical terms here for clarity, don't worry, I won't kill the vibe in the actual story), an alpha has a large knot. During sex with an omega, the knot swells during orgasm and locks them together until it defl ates. Whether a beta can take a knot is up to the author. In my universe, they can't.

Last, there are omegas. Instead of regular menstruation, omegas experience heat cycles, usually two to four times a year. During a heat, an omega's body temperature rises sharply and they experience intense discomfort or pain that can only be eased with alpha pheromones and, yes, copious amounts of knots. Their scent becomes far more potent during this time and can drive nearby alphas a little feral.

Often, the concept of mates also comes into play. These are fated partners who feel an undeniable pull toward each other from the moment they meet.

Bonding is something that can happen even if an alpha and an omega are not fated mates. It is essentially like a marriage of sorts, with the alpha biting the omega or beta during sex to "claim them," and the receiving partner can either accept or reject the bond. In many versions of this, a bond comes with the ability to sense each other's thoughts and feelings.

In this universe, biology infl uences behavior, but it doesn't erase agency. Consent and choice still matter. Alphas don't get a free pass to be monsters, and omegas aren't always weak. Power dynamics exist, yes, but they are meant to be examined and challenged. At the end of the day, this is still a romance book. Messy feelings, bad decisions, yearning, growth, and love are still very much part of the deal.

If any of this doesn't sound like your thing, this is probably not the book for you, and that's okay! But if you're down to try something new, you're in the right place.

Now that I've done my due diligence and you're been suffi ciently informed, let's go.

1

Ava

I hate his face.

Well, that isn't exactly true. It's a devastatingly handsome face that I quite enjoy looking at, so long as he doesn't realize I'm looking. Right now, he's smirking at me as we're called to the judge's bench, so I have to refrain from stomping on his foot with my stiletto. I'll mentally wax poetic about the square line of his jaw and the dark, neatly trimmed beard some other time.

I'm pissed at myself for walking into his trap, letting him swipe at me just enough to get me to rise to the bait and snap at him, knowing that Judge Reynolds has no tolerance for our bullshit. I'm normally better than this, but I'm running on little sleep and nothing but an energy drink. Oh, and a banana that my assistant Shelby shoved in my hand as I made a mad dash from my office to the courthouse.

This case is a doozy. My client, Joseph Simmons, is completely guilty. Everyone in the courtroom knows it. I only hope to prove that the police fumbled the chain of evidence, but it's not clear yet if that'll be enough for a win. If I'd been going up against one of the assistant prosecutors, that would have been a different story, but Mark Taylor now oversees any of my cases that land on the docket in his borough. He knows nobody else stands a chance against me if the prosecution's case is shaky.

After I made partner, I started to get higher-profile cases in Manhattan. So now, it feels like the majority of every day is spent going toe-to-toe with Manhattan's youngest district attorney.

"You've both been warned about your attitudes in my courtroom," Judge Reynolds leans forward to hiss at us. He's an older beta, with graying hair receding to balding, showing off a few age spots along his scalp. His eyes are fixed in a seemingly permanent angry squint, but today they seem extra narrowed.

I wince.

Shit. He's really mad this time.

"I don't care if we are filming for the mayor's illustrious NYTV or not. I don't have the patience for your behavior today." He turns to look directly at Mark. "Wipe that grin off your face, counselor; I saw you set her up for that. Behave, both of you, or I'm calling a mistrial and throwing you in a cell to cool off."

"Yes, Your Honor, sorry," we both say in unison. I shoot Mark a glare, but quite enjoy the flush around the collar of his shirt. He's embarrassed for getting called out.

Good.

Shithead.

I walk back to my table, offering a sunshiney smile to my client, a hulk of an alpha that I've had to bend over backwards to make look less scary to the jury. I might lose his case, but he doesn't need to know that. Panicked clients are a pain in my ass. They whine and start questioning everything I do, not understanding that criminal law is a lot like chess. It isn't only strategy but also anticipating the moves of your opponent. Additionally, this particular client is almost certainly part of the Italian Mafia, and I do try my best not to piss them off.

The problem is that Mark is genuinely a damn good lawyer. We run right at about 50/50 on wins when we go head to head. There's a betting pool at both my office and the police station over who will win at the end of the year, the viper or the tiger.

The police, unsurprisingly, are not fans of mine, hence the viper nickname. I've yet to uncover how Mark got the tiger moniker.

Clearing my throat, I straighten my suit jacket and turn back to the witness I'd been questioning. "I apologize for that interruption. Detective Stephens, could you please answer the question regarding the gap between when you logged the evidence into the system at 10:32 p.m. and when it was officially signed over to the crime lab at 7:15 a.m. the next morning?"

"I don't remember your original question," the detective says coolly, his face carefully neutral even as his eyes flash with loathing.

Liar.

I smile sweetly at him. "Understandable. I'm sure it's hard to remember minor details when you work as many cases as you do."

I hear Mark cough, and I bet he's choking to death on the objection stuck in his throat. But he won't risk pissing off the judge further, and he can't technically object to me being a bitch.

"My question was, do you have any explanation for this gap?"

I already know the answer. I've gone through all the records with a fine-tooth comb during discovery.

"No," Detective Stephens says, "but I assume—"

I raise my hand to cut him off. "You aren't here to testify about assumptions. With no documentation of the evidence's exact location or who might have had access overnight, can you, without any doubt, swear under oath that its integrity was preserved the entire time?"

"Objection—argumentative. She's badgering the witness," Mark says loudly.

I give the judge an innocent look and wait for his reaction. I totally was, so it's a fair objection.

Judge Reynolds looks at us both with annoyance and then over at the witness. He chews on his answer for a moment.

"Overruled. It's a fair question, if worded more argumentatively than necessary."

I manage to refrain from grinning in triumph. But just barely.

Our first recess starts at noon, and I tell my client to enjoy his lunch. I gather up my things. If I hurry, I might beat the rush to the hand-pulled noodle place a couple of blocks away for some of my favorite potstickers.

"Glad to see you can rein it in when the judge is on your ass," Mark says, leaning against my table as if he doesn't have a care in the world.

I frown and "accidentally" move my briefcase so the corner catches his hip, stifling a laugh at his wince. "You're the one who got us yelled at in the first place, but sure, you can blame me if it makes you feel better about being chastised. Male egos and all that," I say, rubbing my temple with my middle finger.

"What's the matter, Ms. Kendrick? Not feeling up to your normal antics today? Does the viper need a nap?"

I glare at him. "If anything, it's dealing with your childish nonsense and inept police force that's giving me a damn headache. Honestly, it's no fun when you just keep handing them to me. Now get out of my way so I can go get some lunch."

"Yes, I'd hate to see you hangry," he says with a laugh before walking out ahead of me, whistling as he goes.

I try—and fail—to not watch the way the muscles in his ass and thighs bunch underneath the fabric of his tight slacks as he walks away. Alone in the courtroom, I allow myself the small indulgence of a frustrated whine. God, that man infuriates me.

I find my spot at the little noodle shop, tucked at a corner table with a plate of steaming dumplings and my case file spread out in front of me. The server doesn't even blink anymore, she's seen me do this too often.

I pop the dumpling in my mouth with my chopsticks, keeping a mental tally as I chew. Six dumplings on the plate; I'll allow myself four. Around four hundred calories, give or take, plus the noodles I'll pick at later. Add that to the banana and the energy drink this morning, and I can still comfortably have dinner with something green to round out my macros while staying under the number I allow for myself.

It's better now than it used to be. At least I eat within a mostly healthy range and try to focus on getting plenty of proteins and veggies, even if the caloric amount is lower than my brother Jack would like. I've struggled with an eating disorder since I was a teenager, and watching me go through all of it—the dieticians, the personal chefs, the hellscape that is inpatient therapy food—inspired him to become a registered dietician. Jack is a big, dumb golden retriever about ninety-nine percent of the time, but not when it comes to food. That, he takes seriously, and he's helped me more than anyone. I'd be lost without him.

So I mostly follow his plan, keep up on my therapy, and I'm at a healthy weight. Counting is a habit I haven't been able to shake, try as I might. Like a little ghost that lingers, despite all the attempts to exorcise it.

Balancing a dumpling in one hand, I scan the evidence log in front of me again, trying to think of any other angles I can take. I know there isn't one, but it never hurts to be sure.

The courtroom hums with low chatter as everyone filters back in after recess. Mark strolls in last, which gives me pause. He's normally in before everyone else. His tie is looser, not enough to make him look unprofessional, but I notice it. What was he doing on his lunch break, and why do I care?

I force myself to turn back to the bench as the bailiff calls us to order and Judge Reynolds returns. "Ms. Kendrick, are we ready to resume?"

"Yes, Your Honor," I say smoothly.

The detective shifts in his seat as I return to cross-examination. Perfect. He already looks like he'd rather swallow glass than face me for another round, which is exactly how I like a witness for the prosecution.

"Detective Stephens," I begin, "earlier you testified you collected the evidence yourself, logged it into the system, and delivered it to the lab. Correct?"

"Yes."

"So, can you explain this decidedly elegant signature on the sign-in sheet? It doesn't match your signature on the original report." I push a button on my laptop and cast a picture comparing the two in split screen on the large monitor facing the jury.

Stephens freezes, and I watch the color drain from his face.

"Objection," Mark snaps, already on his feet. "Assumes facts not in evidence."

I tilt my head. "The lab's report and sign-in sheet are in evidence. Pages forty-three and ninety-two."

The judge waves a hand, impatient. "Overruled. Answer the question."

Stephens hesitates, fumbling for an answer, and I wait him out, calm as a cat watching a cornered mouse. "I, uh, my partner ran it down to evidence for me."

"Reasonable enough. However, why did she sign your name? And why did you testify *you* took it?"

Stephens looks to Mark as if he could save him. I glance over my shoulder at my opponent to see if he has anything to add. Mark's face is blank and his body language is relaxed, but he's tapping his pen against his paper—a tell I've become familiar with. I grin triumphantly, catching his eyes with mine. His hand freezes, his eyes narrowing.

"Actually, Your Honor, I don't need that question answered. I'm finished with this witness," I say, turning back to the bench.

"Mr. Taylor, I'm assuming you would like a chance to redirect the witness?" Judge Reynolds asks.

"Yes, Your Honor, though the prosecution requests a chance to review the evidence for the redirect and reconvene at a later date."

"Agreed. We will resume tomorrow morning at nine." Reynolds bangs his gavel, and we are all dismissed.

Mark is out the door before I can gloat, and I smile to myself, pleased at the outcome of the day. Outside the courthouse, the city is in its usual chaos—horns blaring, people yelling, the smell of street food mixing with exhaust. I should have my driver take me to the office to prepare for tomorrow. Instead, my body betrays me and angles towards the coffee shop across the street.

I'm not really a coffee girlie, but I'm a sucker for all things caffeinated and fruity. The barista whips me up a sparkling energy drink with a medley of sugar-free flavors, the bright colors melting together in my cup, and tops it with a generous heap of vanilla cold foam. I take one blissful sip and start unwinding, only to see Mark walking in the door.

Because of course.

"Stalking me now?" I ask coolly.

He smirks. "Don't flatter yourself. This is my spot."

I want to argue, but the barista greets him by name. Traitor.

Mark orders, then has the audacity to sit at the table next to mine instead of keeping his distance. For a moment, neither of us speaks, and there's only the sound of keyboards clicking from the students nearby and the hiss of the espresso machine.

Then he leans back lazily, every line of his body screaming unbothered alpha. "I gotta hand it to you, Kendrick, I thought this was going to be a slam dunk. You certainly know how to keep it interesting. Even if you might let a murderer for the mafia walk free."

I blink. The insult I was used to, but the partial compliment with it was new. "I'm sorry, I thought my client was on trial for armed robbery and resisting arrest. I don't remember anything about murder."

He snorts. "You know damn good and well what I'm talking about."

"I know that if you had enough evidence to bring those charges, you would have."

He chews his lip in thought, and I brace myself for a fight. He'll probably question me about how I can sleep at night. The usual shit that all defense attorneys get.

"You're a royal pain in my ass," he sighs, "but we need people like you to keep us on our toes. Bad policing affects everyone," he admits, surprising me. "I may not like it, but you're just as important for our legal system as I am. The constitution says so. We just need to work harder to get the big charges to stick."

For one dangerous second, I forget to hate him.

I mask it by sipping my drink. "Glad to know I provide a needed public service. Now, if you'll excuse me, I have actual work to do."

He raises his cup in a mock toast. "Until tomorrow, counselor."

I open my phone, typing a few quick texts to Shelby, but a familiar heat coils low in my belly, and I freeze. My pulse quickens, and I try to remember what time I took my suppressants this morning. I know I took them—I never miss them, since that would risk everyone figuring out I'm lying about being a beta. They shouldn't be fading this early. It's not enough for anyone to tell, my scent neutralizer will prevent that, but my omega senses are kicking into overdrive. I shift in my seat, crossing my legs tightly, and press my hands against the table for a moment while I take a deep breath.

The café feels too warm, and all the sounds are amplified. The smells—god, the smells—are all suddenly so strong that it feels overwhelming. Particularly the leather and whiskey scent rolling from Mark. My omega is drawn to it like a moth to a flame. She wants to roll in it, on him. Preferably with no clothing.

Warning bells sound in my mind. I need to get home, or to the office. Fast. If I don't, the desire to touch Mark Taylor will grow into an ache, and before I know it, if the suppressants have worn off enough, slick could drip down my thighs. And there is zero chance that even the scent neutralizer will prevent an alpha like Mark, not to mention every other nearby alpha, from noticing *that.*

I snatch my phone back up and text Tony, my driver, that I need to leave ASAP, dropping him a pin to my exact location.

I steal a glance at Mark, hoping he hasn't noticed my sudden distress.

He hasn't, but the glance doesn't help the battle with my omega side. All she wants to zone in on is the way the sunlight is catching the hairs on his forearms, now revealed from his rolled-up sleeves. When he moves to lift his coffee cup to his full, sensual lips, the muscles tighten and flex, and I wonder what they would look like pinning me against a wall.

Shit. I appear to have exited the "need to leave soon zone" and ended up in the "danger zone."

I quickly gather my things and eye the exits of the coffee shop. Ideally, I can make my way out without having to move too closely to Mark. I'd prefer not to get a bigger dose of his scent, lest my omega lose her damn mind.

Luck is on my side. His phone rings, and the signal is spotty here in the old stone building. He frowns and steps outside to answer it, and I take my chance to exit.

I duck out a side door and force myself not to glance back for a last look at him. Tony pulls up to the curb, and it takes more control than it should for me to not throw my things and myself into the car and demand he take off like I just robbed a bank.

My heart is certainly pounding like I did. That was a bit too close for comfort, and an excellent reminder of why I need to stay the hell away from Mark Taylor.

2

Mark

Ava is there before me when I enter the courtroom, standing at her table and speaking with her client. Her hair is down today, tumbling in long red waves around her navy-blue suit jacket. She rarely wears it down, and I briefly wonder if her head is still bothering her. I noticed her rubbing her temple yesterday.

I shake my head and question why the hell I care. If anything, a headache benefits me. Maybe she'll be distracted. Though that feels like a cheap way to win. Not really my style.

I should hate her. God knows half my colleagues think she's the devil wrapped in Dior. But what I told her yesterday was true—she helps the system work the way it's supposed to. The NYPD has been forced to take shit far more seriously since she came on the scene. So, I respect the hell out of her. Not that I would tell her that part.

Though my tendency to watch her hips sway in her tight pencil skirts isn't based on respect. I'm certain most people would find how frequently my thoughts turn to wondering what her juicy, plump peach of an ass would feel like in my hands downright *dis*respectful.

Ava Kendrick. Manhattan's most ruthless defense attorney, my personal nemesis, and the only woman who has ever made me want to strangle and kiss someone in the same breath.

I wonder sometimes if we'd have been friends under different circumstances. Possibly even date, since I'm obviously attracted to her. From all the times I've caught her looking, I think it's a fair bet that it's mutual. Not to mention we're both "prodigies" in NYC's law scene. I'm the youngest elected district attorney in Manhattan's history, and Ava has to be one of the youngest women partners at any of the major firms in the city.

Fate placed us on opposite teams, though, so we are forever stuck being adversaries. She is decidedly unpopular in all the circles I'm in. The cops hate her for the number of cases she wins, especially since she got a cop killer freed earlier this summer. My attempts to point out that she'd won because they'd mishandled evidence and ignored interview protocol tended to fall on deaf ears. To them, she's the viper. Nothing more.

The fact that she's become one of the loudest champions in the city for omega rights hasn't gained her any favors either. Takes on pro bono cases no one else will touch for them—workplace discrimination, custody battles, you name it. And because she's a powerhouse of a lawyer, she almost always wins.

The more conservative alphas that run the city do not appreciate this. And those are the ones I have to butter up if I have any hopes of them donating to my eventual mayoral campaign. I just can't figure out why it's so important to her. She's a beta, and so is her entire family other than a couple of alphas somewhere back in her pedigreed family tree.

She lifts her head, green eyes meeting mine, and I have to look away. No more distractions; I need to focus on beating her. I do have a reputation to uphold, after all.

After the bailiff calls us to order, Reynolds looks to me and nods. I clear my throat. "The prosecution calls Detective Marisol Vega."

"Objection, Your Honor! Surprise witness," Ava says sharply.

I spread my hands. "Merely following the path the defense set up with her questioning of Detective Stephens, Your Honor."

He nods. "I'll allow it, though keep the scope within the chain-of-command questioning, or I will allow Ms. Kendrick time to prepare for the witness." There's an unspoken threat in his wording that annoys me. As if he's saying, *you don't want to give her that, do you?*

It's not incorrect, which annoys me more. The more time Ava has to prepare, the likelier she is to find something to attack.

Vega takes the stand, and it's obvious she is flustered and nervous, which actually helps what I'm attempting to do.

"Detective Vega," I say evenly, "you are Detective Stephen's partner, correct?"

She nods. "Yes, sir."

"And how long have you been on the force?"

Color stains her cheeks. "I've been with the NYPD for seven years."

"At the time of Mr. Simmon's arrest, how long had you been a detective?"

"Objection, Your Honor! I thought we were sticking to the chain of command, not going over Detective Vega's resume," Ava says.

A fair objection, but it's early in the day to be so sassy, especially with Reynolds already annoyed with us. A little off her game today.

The judge shoots her a warning look, and I suppress my grin. He looks at me and raises an eyebrow. "I'm assuming there's a point to this, Mr. Taylor? Let's move it along."

I nod and look back to Vega to await an answer.

She sighs. "It was my first day as a detective when we arrested Mr. Simmons."

I give her a gentle, understanding smile. "First days on the job can be overwhelming. New responsibilities, new expectations, new paperwork. Fair to say?"

She lets out a small, nervous breath. "Yes, sir."

"Despite that, though, you were still a trained NYPD officer with seven years of experience in the field."

"Yes."

"Please explain how the evidence got to the lab and what state it arrived in."

"Detective Stephens logged the evidence into the computer, but before we could take it downstairs, we were called to an emergency scene. I watched him seal the bag and initial the tape before locking it into the evidence locker near our desks. In the morning, I unlocked it and took it downstairs."

"So you followed standard NYPD protocol during the transfer?"

"Except for the signature portion, yes, sir. That was the only mistake."

I wish I'd had a little more time to prep her for the stand. She needed to learn to only answer my questions and not offer anything additional. I made a mental note to have my assistant reach out to her captain to set up some training time. If she is going to remain a detective, she needed to be better prepared to face off with Ava.

"Explain what you mean about the signature."

"I read the sign-in sheet incorrectly. I thought it was asking for the name of the officer who had logged it into the system, not who was bringing it to the lab. So I signed Stephens's name. I—"

I cut her off before she can continue adding on. "At no point was the evidence unsecured or able to be accessed by anyone but law enforcement?"

"No, sir."

I nod once, letting it settle into the jury for a moment. "Just to be clear, the discrepancy the defense highlighted yesterday reflected only who physically transported the sealed evidence, not whether the evidence was compromised. Correct?"

"That is correct."

I glance toward the jury, then back to her.

"No further questions."

I keep my expression neutral, but my mind is already running through the angles Ava will take during cross-examination. She'll likely attack Vega's inexperience and poke holes in whether there is any proof to back her claim. Insinuating this was damage control, which it was.

But the jury should hopefully see it for what it is. Stephens misspoke, and Vega clarified that a simple first-day-on-the-job error occurred.

I give Ava a quick wink as I head back to my seat.

The case finally wraps for the day, Judge Reynolds practically shoving us out with threats of contempt if we so much as breathe too loudly in his courtroom tomorrow. My staff flies out ahead of me, discussing catching up on paperwork.

When I step out on the courthouse stairs, the late afternoon light is dappling between the heavy gray clouds. It looks like rain. Probably if I were home, it would smell like rain too, but here in the city, you aren't able to catch that.

Ava is ahead of me, waiting on the curb for her car. Her phone is to her ear, voice clipped, and it's the same voice she uses when she's cross-examining. Business, then.

I should keep walking. Hail a cab and get back to my office. Yet my feet betray me, and I'm by her side before I know it. Even in her ridiculously tall heels, I still tower over her, and she has to tip her chin to look up at me. The wind blows a tendril of hair across her cheek, and I have the strangest urge to wrap it around my finger just to see if it feels as silky as it looks. This close, I should be able to scent her, even though betas have muted scents, but Ava always wears a heavy-duty neutralizer. I don't know what she smells like, and it bothers me.

"Kendrick. A solid attempt at a win, but I think we both know how this one is going to go," I say, unable to stop myself from baiting her.

She lowers her phone and smiles at me, but there's no sweetness in it. Her eyes are sharp and sparkling, the black cat-eye liner around them making the deep emerald green pop. "Don't get too comfortable, counselor. The jury is smarter than you give them credit for. They can smell a rushed cover story."

I can't help but smirk. "I guarantee everyone on that jury has fucked up on their first day on the job at some point."

Her car pulls up, long, sleek, and black. "Can't relate. I don't make mistakes." She opens the door, casually tossing her hair over her shoulder. "Have a good night, counselor."

My grin widens despite myself, and I give a sharp salute with my fingers as she pulls off.

The mayor had invited me to a dinner event he was hosting at a private club downtown, which clearly meant I was expected. It's all mahogany walls, leather chairs, the faint smell of cigars baked into everything. A place that prides itself on being exclusive. Men in tailored suits stand around cocktail tables, talking too loudly and laughing even louder. A few are sprawled in the large chairs, clouds of smoke hovering above their heads. Servers weave between them with silver trays, keeping glasses full so no one has to stop bragging.

Almost all these guys are alphas—old money types. A few have brought their omegas with them, but they all hover together, far away from everyone else. To be honest, I'm envious of them. I wish I could avoid talking to most of the men here. I don't particularly like them. If I'm very lucky, I can make myself visible and only manage small talk with the ones that are tolerable while flying under the radar of the ones I can't stand. They have a habit of slapping me on the back and talking down to me like I'm a child, which to be fair, they also do to the omegas.

If I were a better alpha, I wouldn't stand for it, but the testosterone-laden posturing never came naturally to me. I prefer to win an argument with words. Not that I can't beat the snot out of someone if they push me—I grew up on a farm, after all—it's just not my go-to.

Back home in Missouri, I didn't grow up around many alphas or omegas. My folks are both betas. I was the first alpha in the family in a couple of generations. Most of what I know about designation dynamics I picked up from textbooks, case law, or the occasional news story. At UCLA, I didn't have time to think much about it. I was too busy clawing my way through law school. Even now, in a room full of other alphas, I still feel like an outsider.

It doesn't matter. I need to get and stay on these guys' good side. If that means playing the game and letting them think they are bigger, badder men than me, so be it. Campaigns aren't built on strategy alone. They need connections, handshakes, and money.

In an ideal world, this would not be the case. But this isn't an ideal world; it's America, and this is the system we have. If I want to make real change in this city, I have to get to the top. Which unfortunately means I have to "talk less, smile more," as Lin-Manuel Miranda so eloquently put it.

I spot Harold Harvey holding court over by the fireplace. His silver hair is slicked back in a valiant but doomed effort to hide the bald spot. He's skinny for an alpha, but he makes up for it with enough dominance and swagger that being near him too long feels like a low-grade migraine. It puts my inner alpha on edge.

He catches me looking at him and immediately beelines my way.

I suppress a groan. *There goes flying under the radar.*

"Mark," he says, clapping a hand on my shoulder, "glad to see you could make it tonight. I know how hard you work for the borough."

"Of course, Mr. Mayor. I wouldn't miss it," I reply with a practiced, easy smile.

I'm taller than him, and it makes me think of Ava. She never seems bothered by our height difference, just tips her chin up and looks me square in the eye as if we are evenly matched. Harvey, on the other hand, hates having to look up at me. You can see it in the set of his jaw and the way he takes a step back to make it less noticeable. He could learn a thing or two from her. Hell, all of us could, really. No one has as much confidence as Ava Kendrick.

"How are things going down at the office?" he asks. "That Kendrick girl still a thorn in your side? Your win record was a lot better before she came along." His grin doesn't quite reach his eyes, and I recognize the jab for what it is—an insinuation that I'm not doing my job properly.

"She's tough," I admit. "Sharp as they come. Runs circles around almost every attorney I know." *And she'd skin you alive without ruining her designer shoes*, I add silently.

"She's trouble," Harvey corrects flatly. "Mark, if you have aspirations past this borough, you'll want to watch how often you lose to her. Voters don't like a man who looks weak against a woman. Especially not one who spends half her time grandstanding about omega rights."

"Luckily, I win as many as I lose," I counter, polite smile still in place, "which I've heard is doing wonders for the ratings on your NYTV project. A great idea, by the way—bringing the average citizen into the inner workings of our justice system."

I leave off the part about how Harvey's office carefully selects which cases go on air. The cases with Ava pull the best numbers, but they also tend to make the NYPD look bad; therefore, they're limited.

For just a second, Harvey's expression tightens, as if he isn't sure if I just complimented him or needled him. Then he lets out a smooth laugh, loud enough for others to hear, and claps my shoulder again, harder this time.

"Gentleman," he booms, steering me toward a circle of older men in expensive suits, "you all know Mark Taylor, correct? Our sharp young DA. A hell of a fighter for the people of this city."

As I shake everyone's hands, I recognize a few of the faces. There's Robert Hargreeve, the chair of Public Safety. Victor Langston, a real estate developer and major donor of Harvey's. Franklin Otero, head of the Police Benevolent Association. And the one I'm most interested in, Martin Kline—a venture capitalist that I've heard is growing dissatisfied with Harvey and has a history of bankrolling campaigns.

A couple of men nod, a few grunt something about good work. I've been in enough rooms like this to know most of them don't give a damn about me, they just want to see where Harvey's putting his chips.

"New York needs powerful men willing to stand together," Harvey says, putting his hand on me and squeezing to stress the line. "Men who understand the responsibility that comes with being an alpha in this city."

The group hums in agreement, a couple of them raising glasses. I take a sip of my drink, mostly to keep from saying something I'll regret. The responsibility of being an alpha? What the fuck does that even mean? My inner alpha practically recoils from the posturing.

Harvey squeezes my shoulder again, and I glance sideways at his hand. If he doesn't knock it off, I'm going to rip the damn thing from his arm, future mayoral run be damned. I'm not sure if he senses it or not, but he drops it back down to his side.

"That's what I aim for, mayor," I say firmly. "Strength. Integrity. Doing right by the people. As an alpha should."

It's a bullshit line. We all know it. But it gets the polite chuckles and nods I'm aiming for and reminds Harvey that I can play the game too. He bristles, and I hide my smile.

"Mr. Mayor, a picture?" one of his staff members says to our side, and we both turn. When the camera flashes, I know the picture it captures isn't the truth. Harvey and I front and center, smiling and looking like we are cut from the same cloth. He'll use it against me later when I'm running against him. Nothing to be done about that now.

I became a lawyer because I grew up watching people get left behind and told it was their own fault. No jobs to speak of, no industry, you drove thirty minutes to work or the grocery store, the school was underfunded, and the message from every direction was that this was just how it was. I got out. A lot of people I grew up with didn't.

I moved to California, then New York, thinking things would be different. In a lot of ways, they are. But some things hold true from sea to shining sea. Families priced out of their homes by greedy landlords. Kids in the Bronx in crumbling classrooms with outdated books, same as back home. Parents choosing between childcare and rent. The details changed, but the overall pattern didn't.

That's why I want the mayor's office. Not because New York is the biggest stage, though it is. If you can fix it here, you can prove it's fixable anywhere. Freeze the rent on stabilized units so families aren't one lease renewal away from losing everything. Put real funding into childcare so a parent can hold down a job and advance their career. Hold the police accountable instead of just defending them on principle.

I know what it looks like when a system decides people aren't worth the investment. I grew up in it. I'm not interested in presiding over another version of it.

So I'll play Harvey's game. For now.

3

Ava

There's a firm knock on my office door, and I lift my head from the file I've been reviewing. "Come in," I call.

Shelby opens the door, guiding in a woman slightly older than myself—mid-to-late thirties, I'd guess, with red bags under her eyes like she's done a lot of crying recently. She clutches her purse strap so tightly, her knuckles are white, and she looks around my sleek corner office as if she's stumbled into a different world.

"Maya, this is Ms. Kendrick," Shelby says softly, lowering her voice like she always does with other omegas. "She'll be handling your case personally."

Maya blinks at me, clearly thrown. "I—I thought you'd hand me off to someone else. I didn't figure you..."

"I don't trust anyone else with these kinds of cases. Not the ones that matter," I say, gesturing toward the chair across from me. "Please, sit."

She perches on the edge, body tense. Her scent, probably normally a pleasant light lavender and linen, has sharpened into something bitter, fear and exhaustion burning it at the edges. It makes me want to hide her away, and I'm not even an alpha.

Shelby raises an eyebrow at me, and I shake my head. She closes the door behind her, leaving me and Maya alone.

"First thing first. You can call me Ava, not Ms. Kendrick," I say, leaning forward and opening my body language so she knows I'm on her side. "When I take a case like this, I want you to think of me as your meanest best friend. I'll fight like hell for you. The cops like to call me the viper." I grin.

A hint of a smile loosens her face, and her shoulders drop half an inch.

"Start at the beginning. Tell me what brought you here."

She bites her lip. When she finally speaks, her voice trembles. "I left my alpha, Daniel, six months ago. I broke our bond and left with the kids. Now he is filing for full custody and wants to strip my parental rights."

I wince but maintain composure even as anger flares beneath my ribs. I don't know the facts yet, but it's a story I've heard often enough. I slide a box of tissues closer to her.

"His lawyer claims that my heat cycles make me unfit," she continues. "That I'll either be bringing random men to our home or abandoning the kids to go to a clinic to get my sexual needs met. He says it would be inappropriate for them to witness their mother being a... a whore."

My jaw tightens until my teeth ache. "Let me guess, this motion came shortly after you brought up child support and alimony because you need help to pay the bills?"

She nods.

"It always does." I let out a breath. "Okay. These are some questions I have to ask everyone, so please don't view them as offensive," I say carefully. "Do you have a history of violence or neglect? Anything he could point to besides your biology?"

She shakes her head, hard. "Never. I stayed home with them, and he never had an issue with how I parented until now. I actually got a job even with being unbonded." She puffs up with a little pride at that, and it makes my chest ache. "I clean at our church when no one's there. The pastor is a beta and helped me find a few other houses to clean while the kids are at school. My mother will watch them when I'm in heat, and I'll use the clinic. I'm not in a rush to meet an alpha again. My kids are my priority. I'm a good mom, Ava, I swear. I'd never do anything to hurt them."

I reach out and grab her hand. "Maya, I believe you."

She looks so small in the chair, trembling but refusing to fall apart. The sight of her tightens something in my chest. She might be older than me, but she reminds me of myself when I was younger. Terrified but determined not to be seen as weak. It makes me wonder how different my life would have been if my parents hadn't whisked us away in the dead of night after I presented and helped me hide what I am. I'd probably be in the same position as her.

I inhale slowly, reining in my emotions. She doesn't need me lost in what-ifs; she needs me in control and vicious. "Can the same be said about your ex?" I question, leaning back in my chair and crossing my legs. "Is he a good father?"

She fidgets, shredding a tissue and twisting the pieces between her fingers and doesn't meet my eyes.

"I can't help you if you aren't honest with me."

Maya bites her lip, and I can tell she's trying to think of how to word her thoughts. I wait patiently, though her silence has already told me what I need to know.

"He isn't an abusive father. More of an uninterested one," she finally answers. "In his family, raising kids is an omega's only job, so he never took part. I don't think he could even tell you what grade they're in or who their teachers are."

I notice the slight inflection on the abusive *father*. "And with you? Was he a good alpha? Bonds are extremely painful to break. Not really something one endures just for a partner that doesn't help with raising the kids."

"No." Her voice is small. "He wasn't a good alpha."

My heart breaks for her, though I'm not surprised. I reach across the table and lay my hand on top of hers, giving it a gentle squeeze.

"He was abusive," she whispers. "Not the obvious kind, though. He'd punch the wall near my head or pinch my leg under the table if he didn't like something I said."

"I'm so sorry. You should never have had to deal with that. Was there anything else that people witnessed? Maybe verbal abuse?"

She takes a shuddering breath. "He screamed at me a lot. The neighbors called the cops a few times, but since I didn't have any visible injuries," she pauses, taking a shuddering breath before releasing a short, bitter chuckle, "they took his word and didn't file charges. Probably not much of a help for you."

A small, wicked smile flashes across my face. "You let me worry about that. You'd be amazed at what my team can dig up. If there are 911 calls, we'll get them."

Her lips part, hope flickering in her eyes. "Do you really think you can help me?"

"I don't think so," I say firmly, "I know. You're not a danger, and you're an involved, good mother. I will make the court see that. I've won some of these kinds of cases already. Precedent is on our side."

Tears spill down her cheeks, despite her effort to hold them back. She ducks her head, hiding her face behind her hands.

I circle the desk and crouch beside her chair, balancing with ease on my heels. Thank years of ballet class for small favors. Normally, I don't blur the lines with clients, but with omegas, I'm different. They're touch-starved in a way most people can't imagine. But I can. Vividly. I grip her hands with mine.

"You aren't alone in this fight, Maya. Not anymore."

She exhales a choked laugh and squeezes my fingers before throwing herself into a hug and wrapping her arms around me.

"Thank you. I never dreamed you'd actually help me. A lady at my church saw you on NYTV, then saw in the paper about you helping omegas, and she told me to email your office."

"You'd be surprised how often that happens," I say, laughing. "I really should send the mayor a thank-you basket. Best publicity I could have asked for, even if he hates me." I straighten and smooth my skirt. "This is why I do what I do. Criminal cases pay the bills so I can take on pro bono work for omegas and fight to improve your rights. The system is stacked against you, and I want to change that."

When she leaves, Shelby leans against my office doorframe, arms crossed, a knowing smile tugging at the corner of her mouth.

When I first started at the firm, she was the paralegal assigned to one of my cases. It only took about a week for me to realize I needed her permanently. Her official title is executive assistant, but in practice, she runs half my life. There would be no viper without Shelby quietly keeping everything on track so I can focus on doing my job. I pay her a small fortune in gratitude and out of a keen sense of self-preservation.

Her dark hair is pulled back in a neat ponytail, thick curtain bangs framing her oversized, white-rimmed glasses. Shelby's work wardrobe falls into what I have lovingly labeled as librarian chic, but my expensive tastes have rubbed off on her in the way of luxury shoes. Much to her husband Ron's eternal irritation, she now owns nearly as many designer heels as I do, and that's saying something.

Today is no exception. A kelly green pair of Manolos peeks out from beneath her wide-leg pants, white crisscross straps with delicate green leaves lacing over her foot.

"Ooh, those are new. I like," I say, pointing.

"Thanks. You should. They were your birthday present to me," she replies, grinning.

I shoot her an unimpressed look. "I can buy you gifts without your direct guidance, you know."

"Oh, I know. But you were very clear last week, when I took over combing through all those phone records for the Smith case, that I could buy myself whatever I wanted as a thank you," she says with a laugh.

I scrunch my nose. "Oh. Right. Well, happy birthday. I have fabulous taste, so you're welcome. What was with the smile when you walked in?"

"Only that you're such a softie with the omegas."

"Shelby," I remind her dryly, "*we* are omegas."

Besides running my calendar, my caseload, and most of my sanity, Shelby is also one of only seven people in the world who knows my secret.

"Yes," she says, rolling her eyes, "but no one else is aware of that. And your reputation is certainly not one that anyone would describe as *soft.*"

"I'm well-known for defending omegas," I reply flippantly, slightly uncomfortable.

"Yes, but not for hugging them and drying their tears," she counters. "I'm just saying it might be nice if the world got to see more of that side of Ava Kendrick. Perhaps a certain eligible district attorney…" She trails off, widening her eyes and pointedly pursing her lips.

I glare at her. "Be serious. I can list at least five reasons off the top of my head why that is a terrible idea. The first being that I hate him."

Shelby snorts. "Well, that's a lie, so try again."

"One, it's not. But two," I say ticking reasons off on my fingers, "how about the New York Bar Association having a meltdown over the massive conflict of interest? And three, I can't be with an alpha. You know that."

"That's three, not five." She waves a hand dismissively and comes to collect Maya's file off my desk. "I started working on a dossier of judges we're likely to see in her family court circuit. I'll have it for you tomorrow. Do you want me to have Tony dig into the husband?"

Tony isn't only my driver. Thanks to his less-than-squeaky-clean past, he has contacts throughout the city. The dirt he digs up on people, I'm not even sure they're aware of.

"Yes, please. And remind him I need to be picked up tonight by 7:00 for the gala. Did the jeweler drop off the earrings? I hate borrowing pieces; I'm always terrified something will happen to them."

"Yes," she says. "And they were thrilled at the chance to have one of their custom pieces photographed on you. They even sent some reinforced backs. I'm not convinced we won't need tools to get the damn things off you. Have you eaten?"

"Not lunch yet, but I had a decent breakfast," I say, rubbing my temples. "I could go for egg drop soup from the place on the corner, though. And more caffeine."

"You need some *water*," she stresses as she heads back toward the door.

I make a very childish mocking face to her back, and she flips me off over her shoulder.

"I could fire you for that, you know!" I yell.

"And I could change all the locks to your apartment before you get home," she sing-songs, sauntering out the door in her fancy new birthday heels.

The Montgomery Family Foundation Gala is held every spring at the New York Public Library, benefiting civic programs like education access and legal aid. It draws politicians, judges, donors, and enough press to keep *The New York Times* society section busy for weeks. As far as charity events go, it ranks in my top three, right alongside the Library Lions in the fall and the Met Gala.

We stop along Fifth Avenue, and Tony comes around to open the car door for me. Immediately, flashbulbs begin popping. Reporters and paparazzi crowd the library steps, calling names and angling for photos of celebrities and New York City elite for the papers and online tabloids. The stone lions loom on either side, dramatically backlit against the night sky.

I step out and straighten, pasting on the version of my smile meant for the cameras rather than my clients. Many people would feel nervous in this environment, but it's never bothered me. I've always believed in making an entrance. If you control people's perception of you, there is no limit to what you can do.

It doesn't hurt that I know I look good. My gown is a statement in itself—a long, flowing, custom piece that hugs every curve. The corset top has delicate emerald-green boning in the same shade as the skirt, which spills into a dramatic train behind me, over a nude lining. The high slit runs to my hip where the skirt is gathered, revealing my toned legs in a way that makes me feel sexy *and* shows off my shoes, so it's a win-win. Tony, God love him, shakes out my train behind me before he gets back in the car to drive off.

I've opted to leave off any additional jewelry, letting my hair and the borrowed earrings do the attention grabbing for me. They're large, Art Deco-inspired diamond pieces that hang heavy from my ears with emerald teardrops at the bottom, and my stylist had painstakingly curled and brushed my hair into Old Hollywood waves that fall over one shoulder.

"Ms. Kendrick, over here!"

"Ava, look this way!"

"Who are you wearing tonight?"

"Tamara Ralph," I answer before pausing at the bottom of the steps, giving them a practiced angle. Chin lifted, slightly over my shoulder, straight posture, and a flirty smile. Every bit of media attention brings me more clients and more eyeballs on my work for omega rights, so I use it to my advantage.

Inside, the marble floors of Astor Hall gleam beneath my heels as guests cluster with champagne flutes in hand, murmuring and mingling in low voices. The air smells faintly of citrus, perfume, and books. Thankfully, they have the air purifiers running, or else the combined scents of all the alphas and omegas in this room would be quickly overpowering.

Beyond the stone arches, the Rose Main Reading Room has been completely transformed. Soft purple uplighting washes the perimeter, casting a romantic glow against the carved walls and arched windows, while the long oak study tables have been replaced with round dining tables draped in linen and crowned with towering floral installations. Candles flicker between crystal glassware, throwing warm light across the people seated around them.

Above it all, the painted sky ceiling stretches overhead, clouds drifting across a vaulted expanse of blue and gold. No matter how many times I see it, a small thrill curls through my chest at the sheer beauty of the space. I love the library. After we moved to New York when I presented, it was the one place I felt like I could truly seek refuge to deal with all the rapid changes.

Then I see *him*, leaning against a marble pillar, drink in hand and surveying the crowd. Of course Mark's here. He's been everywhere lately. His classic black tux is well-fitted, and though it's a bit boring for my taste, I have to admit he looks devastatingly handsome in it.

The bastard.

I sharply remind myself that he needs to be avoided at all costs. The incident in the coffee shop the other day proved that. I move, hoping to avoid his notice, but his deep brown eyes lift and find mine, and a slow, cocky grin encompasses his face. Shit.

I don't want to look like I'm running away from him, so I school a bored expression on my face and glance away, looking over the room and hoping he'll leave me alone. Out of my peripheral vision, I see Mark push off the pillar and head my way, and it takes effort to suppress the whine in my throat. Why can't this man just leave me alone?

"Ms. Kendrick," he says smoothly, a hint of gravel in his voice. I surmise that he's not on his first whiskey of the evening, though he's far from intoxicated. Not that I blame him—I was fashionably late, and who can resist an open bar? "Suppose I should have expected to see you here. You aren't known for missing a photo op."

"Well," I say with a small smirk, "it would be a crime to let a dress this pretty go unappreciated. I have to give the people what they want."

"Indeed." His eyes sweep over me, darkening with something that looks an awful lot like desire, and my mouth goes dry. A server walks by with flutes of champagne on a tray, and I snag one, sipping it quickly.

"So, what brings the illustrious district attorney out tonight?" I question smoothly, shoving anything other than bored indifference deep inside myself.

"I support what the Montgomery Foundation does," he says. "Education initiatives. Legal aid funding. Plus, I hold an elected office. I'd be an idiot not to take advantage of a few photo ops myself."

"Legal aid, huh?" I lift a brow. "I thought you considered us defense attorneys the bad guys?"

He lets out a quiet laugh. "Nah, only the incompetent ones."

"I know you aren't lumping me into that pool."

"Trust me," he says, moving a step closer, and I have to keep myself from swallowing as his dark, rich smell envelops me. "You have never once struck me as incompetent."

"I'd hope not," I reply lightly, handing off my now-empty flute to a passing server and using it as an excuse to step away from him. My pulse races through my veins, and my inner omega is furious that I'm not doing something far more reckless. Like scenting the hollow of his throat with my cheek. "I'm sure that pains you to admit."

"Constantly," he agrees. "You're a pain in my ass at the best of times."

"And yet," I say quietly, "you never seem all that eager to avoid me."

His mouth twitches as if he's fighting a reaction. "You make it sound like I seek you out."

"Don't you?"

"Don't flatter yourself, Kendrick. I barely think of you at all."

I laugh. "Likewise, counselor."

The words are as contrite as ever, but there's a warmth to them I think we both feel. And it terrifies me. I clear my throat. "Well, if you'll excuse me, I'm going to go spend my evening with someone who doesn't make me mildly nauseous."

I turn away before he can say anything else, telling myself it isn't a retreat so much as strategic self-preservation. I can feel the weight of my own lie.

For the rest of the night, we avoid each other with deliberate effort, which is somehow worse than our confrontations. It grates on my nerves, yet keeps me painfully aware of him. I wonder if he feels it too, because every so often, I glance up and catch him turning, as if he had already been looking at me.

He disappears shortly after dinner. I notice his absence immediately.

I refuse to name the feeling that settles in my chest when he's gone.

4

Mark

My team is looking at me like I've grown a second head.

"She's going to lose her shit and tear you apart for a discovery violation," my second chair, Brad—a nervous beta if there ever was one—says. "Are you sure you want to do this?"

I don't look up from the notes on my desk. "We disclosed the statement as soon as we had it. It was uploaded to the discovery portal late last night. We're allowed to call a new witness if the evidence is material and we didn't withhold it."

Last night, a building guard walked in with an eyewitness statement for the Simmons case that places Ava's defendant near the scene of the crime. It isn't enough to completely slam dunk the case, but it plugs the hole that Ava has been picking at all week.

He scoffs. "Yeah, at like midnight. It's 8:00 in the morning now, and we go into the courtroom in an hour. You know it's unlikely that she's reviewed it. I don't care how good her office is."

"And if she hasn't," I snap, "she can ask the judge for time to prepare. That is exactly what continuations are for."

"All I am saying," he replies evenly, "is that this is going to look like you are trying to catch her off-guard. Not to mention, we haven't even had time to fully vet and verify this guy yet. You and I both know she is not the kind of attorney you can slip things past. Just seems like asking for trouble when she's gonna get pissed and come at us harder."

"I didn't realize you were so frightened of the viper, Brad," I say.

"You're an idiot if you aren't." He jumps up from his seat and throws his hands up. "Whatever, man, your funeral."

He leaves my office, and I sigh, pinching my nose. I've been in a shit mood for the last couple of days since the gala. Ever since she pointed out how I can't stay away from her. And what's worse is, I can't stop thinking about her. I lean back in my chair, shove my hands in my hair, and sigh.

It's because of that damn green dress. How it highlighted the ethereal luminosity of her skin and the dusting of freckles down her throat and over the tops of her breasts. My mouth practically watered wanting to pull the cups down and see how far the freckles went. Is she covered in them? I almost guarantee she is, and why the hell does that do it for me so hard?

She's a distraction and a menace. If I didn't know better, I'd think she was an omega, by the way my alpha can't stop obsessing over her. Maybe it makes me an asshole, but I want to lash out because of it. Take her down a peg if I can.

The moment I say his name, I feel the fury roll from Ava at my back before she even stands. Her chair loudly scrapes the floor as she surges to her feet.

"Your Honor, this witness was never disclosed," she snaps. "The defense has had no opportunity to prepare—"

I keep my face neutral, but inside, satisfaction washes through me. I look over at her and immediately regret it. Ava is always beautiful. Angry Ava is breathtaking and lethal.

Her jaw is tight, and there's a flush to her skin that makes her eyes seem even brighter than normal. Her fists are clenched at her sides, and as if she realizes I'm looking, she flexes her fingers outward and forces her shoulders to relax. If my goal was to think of her less, maybe I should have thought this through a little more.

The judge calls us to sidebar. Ava immediately launches into her argument, but I already know everything she'll use.

"Your Honor," I say evenly, keeping my tone cool, completely at odds with the heat coiling under my skin. "The state received this witness' statement only last night. We turned it over immediately."

"If that is true," Ava hisses, "it must have been between 11:00 p.m. last night when I left for the day and before we came to court." Her gaze flicks towards me, accusatory, as if waiting to catch me in a lie.

She was at the office until 11:00? She keeps worse hours than I do, not that I'm surprised.

I lift a shoulder in a deliberate show of indifference. "Defense counsel is welcome to check the portal. The statement is there. We're obligated to disclose discovery, not to personally alert opposing counsel every time we upload a document."

The judge watches us both, eyes tired, fingers drumming once against the bench. The fluorescent lights overhead buzz faintly. The entire room feels as if everyone is waiting on the edge of their seats to see how this plays out.

Finally, he exhales. "He is technically correct, Ms. Kendrick," he says. "You will have fifteen minutes to review the statement before the testimony begins."

"Fifteen minutes?" Ava fires back, before schooling her features and changing her tone into something far more polite. "Your Honor, may I request a continuance until tomorrow to properly vet this witness and prepare for cross-examination?"

"Fifteen minutes, Ms. Kendrick, and if that's a problem, I can make it zero," he says flatly.

I feel a brief flare of guilt, but I squash it down. This is the name of the game. Ava plays to win, and I will as well.

She gives the judge a fake smile and promptly turns to flash me a look of pure malice before walking back to her table, spine rigid. I'd be lying if I said part of me wasn't looking forward to the fight.

The guard's testimony lands better than I'd hoped. He's direct and self-assured, exactly the kind of witness juries eat up.

Ava's cross is sharp, but she's working with scraps. Fifteen minutes with a statement didn't give her nearly enough time to build the traps she's famous for.

When she finally sits, I rise for redirect. I could probably leave it there, but it's like I'm watching from outside myself. She's under my skin in ways I don't know how to deal with, and it's making me act uncharacteristically. Maybe it's because we are on camera and the mayor's words about voters linger. Or maybe I'm just in a bad mood because I can't actually *do* anything with all the feelings I have.

So instead, I flash a disarming smile at the jury. "Ladies and gentlemen, the State has had no difficulty gathering the relevant facts in this case," I say. "Any suggestion otherwise would merely stem from Ms. Kendrick's personal feelings towards me. It's unfortunate the defense let pesky little things like emotions make them unprepared."

Ava's head snaps up. For a split second, her composure cracks. She presses her lips together until they pale, fingers tightening around her pen as though she might snap it in half.

The jury shifts uncomfortably, and I realize the minute I said it that I've taken it too far. Ava Kendrick is never unprepared, and they know that. Now, I just look like a grandstanding jackass. Which admittedly, I am. Worse, a chauvinistic one, even though I'm not. Which won't do me any favors with the women jurors.

"Mr. Taylor," Judge Reynolds cuts in sharply, "that is an argument, not a redirect. I don't care if we are on television; I won't have showboating in my courtroom. Save it for closing arguments. I'm imposing a two-hundred-dollar sanction for contempt, payable by the State. Keep your comments to evidence, or the fine will go up."

I wince and dip my head in contrition. "Yes, Your Honor. Apologies."

Across the aisle, Ava's glare could strip paint. She'll make me pay for that, I know it.

"Jesus Christ, Mark, are you trying to get us murdered? Her client is a fucking hit man, for Christ's sake," Brad hisses in my direction as I sit down.

I give him a look. "Quit being dramatic. She can file whatever motion she wants, and I got in trouble for it. It's fine."

It'll make for good headlines. *DA Taunts Defense in Courtroom Spar on NYTV.* It's the action that the old alpha donors will love. I remind myself that you have to win the game to get the office. This is what I'm here to do.

So why do I feel a little dirty?

We break for the day, and the courthouse empties. Reporters hover near the exits like sharks circling, cameras raised and phones poised to capture sound bites. I weave between them, nodding at one of the security guards holding the masses back.

I glance around for Ava, hoping for a chance to talk, though I'm unsure what I would say. I catch a flash of her fiery red hair as she ducks in her car and pulls away. Disappointment churns in my gut. I'm not even sure what I hoped for, and that uncertainty pisses me off all over again.

Back in my office, I finish up some paperwork I've been avoiding. Jane, my assistant, leans against my doorframe. "Heard you pulled a hell of a move today. Any tips on how you want me to spin the optics? Requests are already flooding in. It's not often the district attorney gets fined for contempt of court."

I sigh. "Tell them to watch the playback from court, and we can't comment on ongoing cases. Though make sure it's noted that I'm paying the fine myself, not using taxpayer funds."

She nods and leaves me to my thoughts.

Sometimes I miss the days when the law was just the law, when I didn't have to worry about the optics or politics of it all. Once upon a time, I had wanted to work in defense like Ava. But once I set my mind to holding office, prosecution made more sense. The general public likes the idea of someone at the helm that 'puts the bad guys away.'

By the time I slide into my cab, the sun has long since set, leaving just the streetlights to reflect on the puddles. My phone won't quit buzzing. I pull it out—texts from staff, a note from the mayor congratulating me on a great day in court, and of course, Adam sending me a social media clip of my barb at the bench.

Ava's face flickers across my screen, zoomed in on that perfect, furious expression, and I have the strongest urge to screenshot it. Her beautiful face makes an ache form in my chest that I don't know what to do with. I scrub my hands over my face, but it doesn't help. The image sticks anyway.

I swipe up to clear the notifications and pull up my contacts. There's only one person I actually feel like talking to right now. She answers on the second ring.

"What's wrong?"

A grin spreads across my face, and I already feel ten times lighter. "Why does something have to be wrong? Can't I just call my big sister to chat?"

"You never call me this late," she answers, though her voice is more fond than annoyed. "You know I usually turn into a pumpkin after I grade papers, and you don't want to risk waking up your nephew and giving me a reason to plot your death."

"Shit," I mutter, glancing at the clock on the cab's dashboard. "Did I? I wasn't even thinking about the time." It is a little after ten here, which means just past nine in Missouri. Jess usually has him down by seven. Guilt settles heavy in my chest.

"No, you got lucky," she laughs. "He's out cold. T-ball wore him out. It's a lot for a tiny human."

I chuckle. "I can imagine. What the hell does T-ball even look like for four-year-olds?"

"Pure chaos. Kids abandoning their bases, chasing the ball in packs, occasionally forgetting they are supposed to play baseball at all. But they are adorable in their uniforms, so it evens out. What is going on with you?"

I sigh. "I pushed a little too far in court today. If you want to see it, the clips are already floating around online. NYTV filmed the whole thing."

"Isn't that, like, half of your job?"

"Usually," I admit. "But this time feels different. I am not talking about the surprise witness so much as... something I said. It got more personal than it should have."

"That doesn't sound like you," she says, voice growing concerned.

I rub the back of my neck with the hand not holding my phone, face suddenly hot. "You remember that defense attorney I told you about? That I go up against all the time?"

"The hot redhead?"

I snort. "No. Well, yes. But... anyways. I think I just let her get under my skin a little too much, and I acted out of character."

Jess laughs softly. "Mark, for someone who prides himself on staying in control, you are really spiraling here." Her voice turns teasing. "Do you have a thing for her?"

I frown. "Ava Kendrick? Don't be ridiculous. She's hot, yeah, but she's a vicious trust fund baby who lives solely to drive me insane." Even as the words fall from my lips, I feel a small voice inside of me singing *liar, liar, pants on fire.*

"Kinda sounds like the gentleman doth protest too much," she says lightly. "But fine. Whatever you say. Is she an omega?"

"An omega high-profile defense attorney?" I scoff. "Be serious."

"Right, I wasn't thinking," Jess admits. "They're not allowed to do that, are they?"

"Well, it isn't that they aren't *allowed*."

"Unbonded omegas can't go to school outside of the omega schools, though, right?"

"Well, yeah, for safety reasons. But once they are bonded, they could go to law school. It's just that the timeline doesn't really allow for someone to rise in ranks like Ava has." It sounds and feels like I'm making excuses, and I'm not sure why. "Anyway, no, she's not an omega. Just a beta." As if anything about her could ever be described with the word *just*.

"Mm-hmm," Jess hums. "And yet you are calling me at ten at night to unpack your feelings about her."

"I'm not calling about *her*," I say, rubbing a hand over my jaw. "It's just... the mayor was pleased with how I handled things today. Said it made me look strong. The kind of alpha voters like to see."

"And how did it make you feel?" Jess asks quietly.

I hesitate. "I don't know. Kind of dirty, I guess?"

"Mark," she says gently but firmly, "you did not claw your way out of Missouri and into that office so you could start acting like every power-hungry politician in Manhattan."

"I know. It's just that they expect it," I admit, "and I need the donors."

"Do you? You want to run for office because you want to change the status quo," she reminds me. "You can be ambitious and still be ethical. You can be powerful without being cruel."

I stare out the cab window, neon smearing across the glass. "Sometimes that doesn't feel true."

"Well, it is," she says. "You're at your best when you actually believe in what you are doing. Not when you are trying to impress men you don't even like."

A breath slips out of me, slow and tired. "You always call me out for being a dick."

"That's what big sisters do," she replies fondly. "You're allowed to be competitive, Mark. Just don't let it turn you into someone your nephew wouldn't recognize."

That lands harder than anything else she has said tonight.

"I know," I murmur. "That's why I called."

"All right, it's pumpkin time for me. Ayden will be up at five like clockwork. Come home and visit soon, okay? You can watch the awe-inspiring chaos of four-year-old T-ball."

"I will. Love you."

We hang up just as my cab stops in front of my apartment building. I pay the man and head inside and towards the row of mailboxes. I'm hoping the new collection of '80s rock vinyls I ordered has been delivered. It's a nice building, but we don't have a doorman—something I've never minded. Only fifteen units, so the management figured residents could handle their own packages. Usually, it's fine. We've set up a little system—oversized boxes get wedged behind the mail area, smaller ones tucked inside the cabinets by the stairs. It's not glamorous, but it works, and all the neighbors sort of keep an eye out.

I think it reminds me of my childhood home in that regard. It's easy not to get to know your neighbors or the people around you in New York City. But here in the small building, I know everyone's name and regularly pet their dogs when I see them.

I snag my albums with a grin and take the elevator upstairs to my apartment. It takes a bit of juggling to punch in my code on the keypad with the vinyls and my briefcase, but I manage and kick the door closed behind me.

I like my apartment, sleek lines and muted colors with a decent view out the large windows. It even has a balcony. The rent makes me nauseous every single time I pay it, but that's just the reality of New York.

Something about it just doesn't quite feel like my forever home. For now, though, it works. It's a short ride to my office and the courthouse. There's a decent gym downstairs, and it's only a couple of blocks to a subway station.

I set my briefcase down and carefully tear open the wrapping on the vinyls. The auction listing was truthful, and they're in excellent condition, which makes me grin. I take one out of the sleeve and place it on the turntable, gently dropping the needle on it until music fills the room. It's late, and I do have neighbors, so I keep the volume at a reasonable level.

I snag a beer out of the fridge, cracking it open. Leaning against the counter, I stare out the window, watching the city move below. For a moment, I'm blissfully alone. No reporters or opposing counsel, no politics breathing down my neck. And I can finally relax.

Still, though, it is lonely. Perhaps I should start dating. I haven't really tried in a while. Not seriously. Casual hookups here and there to scratch the itch. Not many people can deal with the hours I work or all the functions I have to attend in order to keep my name relevant.

I sigh. The thought has no genuine appeal to it. Instead, my traitorous brain keeps thinking about Ava. The flash of anger in her eyes. I wonder if she knows she flushes with a subtle shade of pink when she's flustered.

The thought wakes me up a bit. Shit. Maybe Jess is right, maybe I am developing a thing for Ava Kendrick. If that's the case, I definitely need to date some more.

It isn't like I'm about to let myself get tangled up with the goddamn viper.

5

Ava

I can feel a headache building at the base of my skull when I exit the courthouse. They've been happening more and more lately, and I can't figure out why. I probably just need food, water, and to punch something until my hand bleeds. I hurry toward my town car.

Sliding inside, half of me keeps waiting for Mark to reach out and grab my arm, ready to continue sparring. If he tries, I swear, I might stab him in the throat with my stiletto.

Tony glances at me in the rearview mirror. "Office?" he grunts in his deep Brooklyn accent.

I press my fingertips to my head. "Maybe. Definitely need to eat first." Guilt churns in my gut as I try to remember if I had breakfast. Shit. Then I remember, yes, I did. A protein shake, a boiled egg, and fruit. I'm good. Still in control. I breathe deeply through my nose and out my mouth.

Through the tinted glass, I glimpse Mark as we pull away from the curb. For a moment, I swear he's staring right at me.

Asshole.

I love my office; I really do. But on days like today, I envy Mark's setup. He's right across the street from the courthouse with no traffic or delays to worry about. Meanwhile, I've got to get across town, I'm starving, and I have a million briefs waiting for me back at the office.

Tony clears his throat, and I look away from the window to find a sandwich wrapped in white butcher paper being waved at me through the partition. "Eat. Traffic will take forever. Chopped cheese from the bodega."

I give him a grateful smile and unwrap it, the scent of the sauteed onions and beef making my mouth water. I force all the negative thoughts about the food out of my mind and think about how proud Jack will be when I tell him. He's a sucker for a good bodega sandwich.

I chew quietly as I watch the buildings and other cars slowly move past us. The blaring horns, the shouts, and the sound of the never-ending road construction all just sound like home to me. Normally, they'd help put me at ease. But I can't shake Mark's stunt in court. The ambush with the witness? Okay, fair game. I'd been pissed, but that's just how it goes. Honestly, I was more pissed at the judge for the bullshit fifteen minutes. Reynolds has had it out for me for a while.

Calling me unprepared in front of the jury, though? And worse, suggesting it was because of my pesky *emotions*? That was too far. My hands tremble slightly, and my chest is tight. Omegas are sensitive by nature, and I can usually control it better than this. I just feel… hurt.

Which confuses me and pisses me off further.

I don't understand. We always snipe and spar, but that felt oddly personal. Was it the fundraiser gala the other night? My comment about him always seeking me out? I didn't think anyone overheard, and I honestly didn't even think it was that mean. He gave as good as he got with the "I barely think of you" line.

A low, frustrated whine slips out unbidden between my teeth.

Finally, the car stops. I wrap the rest of my sandwich up and thank Tony, offering it to him. He grunts, takes it, and goes back to scrolling on his phone. His people skills aren't exactly top-notch, but you would be hard-pressed to find anyone in this city as loyal as him. Much like Shelby, he could destroy me with the blink of an eye, but I trust him with my life.

The Foreman, Weller, and Kendrick building rises above me, dizzying in height. Seeing my name on the façade still gives me a flutter of disbelief. I earned this. Sacrificed everything to get here. Yet, my secret is that I'm constantly terrified and waiting for the other shoe to drop that will snatch it all away.

The biggest threat at the moment is this pull toward Mark Taylor. A goddamn alpha, when here I am, an omega hiding in plain sight. If I were smarter, I'd ask to be transferred out of his borough. Though I doubt the other partners would go for it. My showdowns with Mark are a fantastic publicity machine that brings us big-name clients on a regular basis. Without our fights and NYTV coverage, would I have made partner as quickly as I did? It's hard to say.

I ride the elevator up, smiling at everyone as I pass. Finally, I reach my level, and Shelby meets me at the door. She reaches for my briefcase and coat, and I let her take them without much of an argument. I'm exhausted.

"I had a salad delivered, plus Gatorade. You've been surviving on energy drinks, right?"

"Excuse you! I had a great breakfast, and I actually just had half of a chopped cheese in the car," I say dryly.

"Suppose I have Tony to thank for that. Well, the salad can go in the fridge for dinner then. I'm sure you'll be here far too late."

We head into my office, and she kicks the door closed behind us. I make a beeline for my desk and crack open the Gatorade, swallowing some white pills sitting beside it. It occurs to me I have no idea what I just took. I probably shouldn't just trust Shelby blindly like I do.

"Those were headache meds, right?" I ask.

"No, they were ecstasy tabs," she says seriously as she punches in a code on the back wall, stepping aside as the hidden door swings open.

I roll my eyes.

A major perk of being the highest-earning partner? You can do all sorts of construction in your office without interference. Another perk of being a partner who's also a defense attorney? Colleagues are excellent at never asking questions they don't want answers to. Plausible deniability in practice.

Shelby, as a fellow omega, understands the importance of a nest when you're stressed or upset. She motions with her hand for me to go inside but doesn't step in herself, knowing that I won't want her scent in there. Omegas are territorial by nature about their nests. The scents should only ever be mine or my alpha's.

Since I long ago made peace with the fact that I'd never have one of those, my nest only ever smells like my own orange and vanilla scent. Just like I made peace with giving up on my dreams of having children. To do so, I'd have to go off my suppressants and find an alpha willing to be a sperm donor during one of my heats. Not exactly something you can do at the clinic under the assumed name I use.

Sometimes when I think about all the lies I have to constantly juggle to keep everything in the air, I feel so tired I can barely put one foot in front of the other. Then I think about Maya, fighting to keep custody of her kids simply because of her designation. Or the omegas who want to be lawyers or surgeons.

We aren't technically banned from those professions. It's just that none of us have ever passed law school or the bar—except, of course, for me. And I suppose any other omegas that might hide as betas. But without the financial privilege my family had to pay for the best suppressants and a whole new identity, I don't see that being common.

Not that there are no omegas smarter than me. Of course there are. The problem is gatekeeping. The discrimination is nearly impossible to prove. Schools hide behind statistics, pointing out that many omegas attend private omega academies emphasizing domestic or vocational training over traditional academics. Then they shrug and blame limited seats and high demand.

It creates a system that looks fair on paper while quietly shutting doors.

Everyone, particularly alphas reaping all the benefits, pretends not to notice.

"I'm heading home for the night," Shelby says, already gathering her things. "Gracie has dance practice and the twins have karate, so Ron and I are dividing and conquering. Make sure you unwind in the nest for a bit before you dive into those briefs. The last thing I need is you burning yourself out."

"Yes, Mom," I deadpan. "I will. Go home. And tell Gracie I'll be there Saturday for the recital."

She snorts a laugh. "You better. It's your ass on the line if you don't. She's terrifying."

I grin. "As my goddaughter should be. Love you. Now get."

I kick off my shoes and slip into the nest, closing the door softly behind me.

The space is small, not much bigger than a supply closet, but it feels like stepping into a private sanctuary. A giant, oversized chenille chaise lounge sits at the center, more bed than chair, buried beneath a chaotic sprawl of pillows and blankets in every soft texture imaginable. Faux fur. Cotton spun so fine, it almost feels like silk. Plush fleece. A couple of old knit throws that have been loved nearly threadbare from my childhood.

A narrow bookcase stands across from it, crammed with dog-eared paperbacks and comfort reads I have revisited more times than I care to admit. The lighting is kept intentionally low, warm and muted, with strands of fairy lights crisscrossing the ceiling and casting a gentle glow over the walls.

The world feels quieter here. Softer.

I flop onto the chair, letting myself sink into all the fabrics. Normally, I'd already feel myself unwinding just from being wrapped in soft things saturated in my scent. Today seems different. I don't feel soothed, and my headache lingers.

Why are my feelings hurt? I don't care what anyone thinks of me, let alone Mark Taylor.

I lay there for a few more minutes before admitting defeat and realizing that my nest will be no comfort to me tonight. I sigh and rise, closing it back up tight, and settle at my desk to attempt to focus on the briefs.

I lose track of how much time I actually sit there trying to work. The words keep swimming before my eyes, and I've probably read the same line about thirty times. I keep thinking about the way he smirked before he called me unprepared and the way it made me flinch.

Who the hell is he to make me react like that?

I shove the papers aside and bury my face in my hands.

I try to breathe through the spike of anger and embarrassment twisting in my chest, but it doesn't fade. It's gnawing at me, and I guess it's just some weird omega thing, because it isn't rational at all.

As if summoned by thinking of her, my omega side stirs, rising forward in my mind. We have a complicated relationship, she and I. Likely because I've always viewed her as separate, like a stranger living under my skin. My therapist says it's because I've never been allowed to actually be an omega.

My heats are the closest thing I have to letting that side of myself free, and even those are clinical. Scheduled in advance, twice a year, always in another state under an assumed name. Faceless prescreened alphas, quick and impersonal, just long enough to get me through. My mother calls it "keeping up my hormonal health."

At least, it had been impersonal. Then one of those screened alphas ignored my omega side rejecting him. He had smelled horribly wrong. Enough to break through the mental fog of my heat. It hadn't gone as far as it could have, thank god. But it had gone far enough. I haven't been back to a clinic since, and I've been putting off my heat for as long as I can while I figure out what comes next. I haven't mentioned this to my mother.

I tell myself it's fine. My therapist disagrees, and she's annoyingly persistent about it.

On top of that, there's my body. My eating disorder has prevented me from developing the soft curves that omegas are known for, and the suppressants and neutralizers dull everything else to the point where sometimes I can barely even pick up on my own scent.

My omega is insistent that Mark needs to pay for making us feel this way. Or at least, I think that's what she's insisting. That he needs to be in proximity to take my anger out on, like that is the only thing that might make us feel better and able to focus to get some work done.

I sit back, tapping my fingernails on the desk. I'm restless, and nervous energy buzzes through me as if I've had way too much caffeine.

I snatch my laptop out of my bag and open it.

It doesn't take long. I was adept at finding out information on the internet long before I became a defense attorney. Now, I could probably run circles around the CIA.

Mark's address stares at me from the screen.

I have no idea what I'm going to do with it or why I looked it up. But I have it now.

I screenshot it and send the information to my phone, snapping the computer shut forcefully before standing to pace around my office. Logically, I know that calling it a night and letting it go is the mature and adult choice. If I'm unable to focus on work, I need to take my ass home, soak in a long, hot bath, and go to bed.

I just don't understand why I can't let it go. It isn't even that serious, but my omega side is clinging to it as if I was publicly rejected and humiliated by my alpha. I bite my lip, thinking. Could I be closing in on a heat?

I suppose it's possible, even with how I've been doubling up on pills. Mom said my recent bloodwork looked a little "suspect." Something about my estrogen levels dipping in a way that she isn't thrilled with. I'd only been halfway listening, which was stupid and naïve on my part. I glance at the clock and debate calling her, but then I remember that she and Dad are in Prague for some big medical summit.

She's a public health scientist, brilliant in ways I barely understand. She's been studying omega suppressants for years, and my bloodwork has been a large part of that. Anonymously, of course. She's perhaps the most vocal proponent for better research on omega heat cycles and suppressants in the entire world, and her life's mission is to someday unlock a real version of omega birth control that doesn't just shut off the rest of omega biology. No different from what's available to beta women.

I'll have to call her tomorrow. It's the middle of the night where she is.

I recognize that I'm making excuses. If I talk to her about it, then I have to admit it was real. Besides, I reassure myself that

I don't feel like I'm closing in on a heat. I don't feel overly hot, and my clothes don't feel restraining and itchy. I just feel… off.

Pushing off talking to her a little longer won't hurt.

I press my hands to the sides of my head, breathing through the spike of tension twisting my chest. Rationally, I know this is crazy. Emotionally, my omega isn't listening.

I grab my phone, hovering over Tony's contact.

No, I'm being ridiculous.

I toss it aside again and pick up a file folder, determined to work on my briefs. But the anger and humiliation refuse to let me go. Fine, anger is an old friend of mine. I can be angry.

Mark humiliated me in court today. Publicly, not only in front of the jury but the entire city of New York. What if the alphas I face in court for my omega rights cases were watching? Or judges?

He needs a piece of my mind because he dared cross that line and took a swipe at my reputation. I have a moral obligation to confront the alpha who thinks he can push me around.

Satisfied with my line of reasoning, I open my phone and paste the screenshot of Mark's address into my chat with Tony. He won't ask questions; he never does. He also never shares his opinions. Well, except about me letting anyone but him drive me. He has very strong opinions about that.

"Pick me up as soon as possible. Please."

The ping back is nearly instant.

"Ten minutes."

I often wonder where he goes—ten minutes isn't time to get much of anywhere in New York—but I stopped asking long ago. He won't tell me. And considering that I met Tony after I got his cousin, a Russian bratva member, off on an attempted murder charge, it's probably for the best.

I pace while I wait, rehearsing what I want to say. I'll show Mark he messed with the wrong damn viper.

Somewhere beneath the anger, a quieter part of me shivers at the thought of being near him in his space, how heavy his scent will be there—I shove the thought aside. No, I'm pissed. That is all I am focusing on.

After a few minutes, I lock up my office and take the elevator back downstairs to the lobby. I smile and nod at our night security guard and wait until I see Tony pull up outside the massive window. I slip on my coat, bracing for the chilly night air. Spring is just settling in around the city, and it is still cool in the evenings.

Tony opens the rear door without comment. Once I'm inside, he returns to his seat and hands me a bottle of water through the partition. He looks pointedly at my seatbelt until I click it in place. "You good?" he asks once the car is moving, accent thick.

"Fine," I say quickly. "Just drive."

He nods and eases into traffic. The city rushes by in strips of neon now that most of the traffic has cleared out. I keep my hands folded in my lap, fingers digging into my palms to keep me focused. I can't let my anger fizzle out, or I'll lose my nerve.

We pull up in front of Mark's apartment building, and Tony looks over his shoulder. "You need a gun?"

The question makes me blink. I suppose I should have expected that he would think I was going to confront Mark with violence in mind. "Um, no. I'm just going to yell at him."

He shrugs. "Gun's faster."

"I'm not shooting the District Attorney of Manhattan in his own apartment just because he insulted me, Tony."

"You want me to?"

The question should horrify me, yet strangely, it makes me smile. It's sweet, in its own way. "No. Just... wait for me, if you don't mind. Or I can get a cab."

He grunts in annoyance and scrolls on his phone, dismissing me and my idea of a different driver. I laugh and step out of the car.

I look up at the apartment building towards the tenth floor, where I know Mark's apartment will be. A thought occurs to me, and I grimace. I didn't consider that he might have a doorman. How awkward would that be? *"Ms. Ava Kendrick is here to give you a piece of her mind, sir. Should I send her up?"*

It's almost enough to make me get back in the car. Except I've never backed down from something I've made my mind up to do before, and I will not start now. This bastard called me unprepared in front of the entire city.

It's definitely not because my omega is pushing me harder than she's ever pushed for anything in my entire life.

I clench my jaw and stalk to the front door, heels clicking on the pavement. The lobby smells faintly of lemon floor polish. There is thankfully *not* a doorman, so I'm able to walk straight to the elevator and push the round ten button. The doors close, and I face my reflection in the polished steel. I look pissed, which is good. I also look a little unhinged, which is less so.

My omega, traitorous bitch that she is, is practically purring at the idea of being in his space with only his scent to bask in.

Wait.

Will it?

I actually have no idea whether Mark will even be home. Or worse, what if he isn't alone?

The thought fills me with a little panic, but also oddly makes me angrier. Both of us, actually. And I'm certainly not going to make time to examine *that*.

The elevator dings, and the doors slide open. I step out onto the thick, plush carpet and take a deep lungful of air. I close my eyes so I can really dissect what I'm smelling. Mark's leather and bourbon scent is lingering, so he must have gotten home fairly recently, and I don't smell anyone else.

He might be with a beta whose scent is so light, I can't pick it up without being right beside them. Or with someone wearing scent neutralizers. It doesn't feel like the case, though. No, it feels more likely that he's home alone, and I can catch him off guard and really tell him what I think about him crossing a line.

My pulse thuds in my throat, hot and erratic, but I firmly and confidently knock on the door.

My omega, having calmed down from the idea of someone else being there beside Mark, is now back to quivering in anticipation in the back corner of my mind where I tend to keep her shoved. It's such an odd experience, feeling like you share your body with another person. She's excited, thinking I'll cave and admit this isn't about anger at all.

I bare my teeth, no one around to see it. No, he doesn't get to have that kind of power over me. No one does.

I can faintly hear music playing inside, and nervousness once again takes hold. Maybe I should go back downstairs, tell myself I tried, and drown this whole reckless impulse beneath a bottle of expensive wine.

Unfortunately, that's when the lock clicks, and before I have time to bolt back for the elevator, he's there.

His hair is damp, and he must have just gotten out of the shower when I knocked, because the t-shirt he tossed on is clinging to him with wet spots in a couple of places, like he hadn't had time to fully dry off. It's fitted tight across the chest and shoulders, and my mouth practically goes dry at the sight.

Fucking focus, Ava.

"What the hell are you doing here?"

I cross my arms firmly, letting my anger stiffen my spine and wearing it like armor. "We need to talk."

He blinks at me, then glances down the hall like he's hallucinating. Or maybe he's waiting for a camera crew to jump out and tell him he's being pranked. When his eyes come back to mine, they're mostly curious. Which... I didn't expect. I thought there'd be a lot more anger. "It's after eleven. You planning on serving me a subpoena in my pajamas?"

The smugness in his tone is like gasoline to my fire. "No, more so wondering if you're only capable of throwing your little punches in front of an audience. If the bravado holds up when it's just you and me."

That gets him. The smirk slips, his expression cooling. He pushes the door open wider and makes a mocking sweeping motion with his arm to invite me in. "Well, come on then, viper. Let's see if your bite is as vicious as your hiss."

My omega all but purrs at the low timbre of his voice, and it doesn't help my blood pressure one bit. I square my shoulders and walk past him, determined to prove to him and to myself that this is just about my anger.

6

Mark

She walks past me like she owns the place, even though she is in *my* apartment. At almost midnight. When she shouldn't even know where I live. Clearly, she had to do some investigating to find out. I should tell her to leave, but I find myself unable to. I'm too damn curious how this is going to play out. She's coiled tightly, like a spring that is going to snap back at any moment.

As she moves, I catch the slightest hint of her scent. I've never smelled it before. A light citrus scent of some kind. Oranges, maybe? It's so muted that it's hard to tell, but it does something to my alpha. I want to get a better read on it, which is something I've never felt before. Normally, I find most people's scents somewhat overbearing.

Unfortunately, when I feel uncomfortable, I tend to run my mouth. "So, are you here to critique my furniture, or does this little stalker visit have a purpose? I'd like to go to bed soon," I say dryly.

Her head snaps towards me, eyes sparking. "You know damn good and well why I'm here. You crossed the fucking line today."

"Come on, Ava. Like you've never gone for the jugular in front of the jury," I say with a roll of my eyes. "I got my ass publicly chewed by the judge, and the media is having a field day. Why are you actually here?"

Her jaw works, as if she's biting back words, and she doesn't answer right away. Interesting. She tips her chin back. "I'm sick of your shit. That's why I'm here. A chance for us to take the gloves off and just really get it all out in the open."

I shake my head and push off the door, taking a few steps closer, slow and deliberate, and watch her take a step backwards before she realizes what she's doing and forces herself to stop. It triggers something in me, almost a predator instinct, and I prowl closer. "No, I don't think so. Doesn't add up. You could have told me off at the courthouse. Or used your investigative prowess to get my phone number and call. Instead, you show up here to tell me in person."

She scoffs. "Awfully full of yourself, counselor. I came to tell you in person because I want to see your face. And I couldn't risk causing a bigger scene than you already had at the courthouse."

I agree with an exaggerated nod and purse of my lips. "Right. That must be it."

"Oh, fuck you, Mark."

I laugh. "You're such a brat. No, you're here because I landed a hit and you can't let it go."

"Bullshit. You've landed plenty of hits when we go toe to toe. This was personal. A dirty tactic that I'd expect from one of the bitchass alphas down at City Hall. I guess I thought you were better than that, though I don't know *why*."

That lands closer than I'd like. "Ava, not a damn person in that courtroom actually thought you were unprepared or emotional," I growl. "If anything, it made me look like an asshole."

"You *are* an asshole," she hisses.

I grin, feeling more alive than I can remember in a very long time. I don't know what it is about fighting with this woman, but it is addicting. "And yet, you're here. In the middle of the night."

She opens her mouth, then shuts it again, eyes narrowing like she's trying to decide the best place to strike.

I tilt my head and lower my voice. "Did you come here to yell at me, Ava... or to prove to yourself you could?"

She rolls her eyes. "What the hell does that even mean? I think the fact that I'm here proves that I can. I told you, let's take the gloves off. Say what you need to say to me so it's out of your system and we can get some damn work done."

I stalk forward another step. "And what do you think I'm holding back? That I think you're an ice queen who lives to grind people to dust under her Louboutins? Because I do." Even as I say the words, while they are true, I know it isn't all I think about her.

Her lips twitch, just shy of a smile. "Finally, some honesty. Took you long enough to admit it."

I laugh. "I never hid those opinions. Just couldn't say it out loud so directly in the settings we typically find ourselves in. You aren't special. Bit predictable, really."

"Predictable? Please. As if you aren't. Do you know you linger and follow me out of the courtroom every single day? You can't stand not having the last word."

I hate the truth in that. "Probably because you never shut up long enough to let anyone else have it."

She lifts her chin, smug. "Maybe because you don't say anything worth hearing."

I'm right in front of her now, close enough I can see how deeply green her eyes are, and the tiny flecks of gold within them.

Like the woods back home at the height of summer, with sunlight dappling between their leaves. The thought catches me off guard with its poignancy.

My voice drops, rough. "Careful, Ava."

Her eyes spark and narrow. "Or what? You'll hit me with another second-rate insult?"

I feel the last thread of my restraint snap. With a growl, I grab her by the back of the neck and crush my mouth to hers.

She freezes for half a second, caught off-guard, then grabs the front of my t-shirt and pulls me to her. The kiss is more like a collision than some passionate embrace. There's no romance, only heat. Her nails dig into my chest, and I shove my hand upwards to grip her hair and tilt her head back so I can get better access to her mouth.

I back us up so that she's pressed to the wall, plunging my tongue past her full, plump lips. That muted scent of oranges strengthens slightly, until I swear I can taste it. So fucking sweet.

I want more. My alpha *needs* more.

I release her hair and reach down to cup her ass with both my hands, hauling her upward so that she's forced to wrap those impossibly long legs around my hips as I hold her. The position forces her skirt upwards on her thighs, and I feel the heat of her pussy against the front of my pajama pants.

It makes me nearly feral. I've never really understood when they describe an alpha rut before, but I think I do a little more now. I want to tear the fabric between us away. How *dare* something separate me from what's mine?

That thought sobers me some, the possessiveness in it confusing. I almost pull away, but she makes a needy whine in the back of her throat as her tongue slides along mine, her fingers twirling into my hair and tugging.

And I'm lost again.

I carry her to my bedroom, never breaking from the kiss. I toss her onto my bed, rougher than I usually would. "Take off your fucking clothes, Ava," I demand.

I expect her to fight me. To tell me I'm insane.

Instead, she captures her bottom lip with her teeth, and a beautiful flush stains across her cheeks. Oh, she enjoys being bossed around, at least a little. Noted.

She quickly scrambles out of her jacket, tossing it off the side of the bed, and unbuttons her shirt as she pulls it up and out of her skirt. This reveals a pale, icy blue bra that looks like it's made up of very expensive lace and the twinkle of a tiny diamond in her belly button.

It pulls another growl from my mouth. Ava has a penchant for pushing the boundaries of fashion, and I've actually seen a fair amount of her body in various gowns. But here in the seclusion of my bedroom, with only my eyes feasting on her, it feels different. Special. More intimate.

I pull my shirt over my head and toss it aside before quickly pushing my pajamas off my hips so they pool on the floor. Her eyes widen as she looks over me, and it makes me smirk.

I work out as a stress reliever, and I enjoy playing sports. I know I have a good body, and I've been told by a decent amount of women that I have an impressive cock. Something about Ava responding to me, though, makes my alpha preen.

I press a knee to the mattress and grip her skirt with my hands, tugging it off. The thong matches the bra, because of course it does, and the straps look like they are made of a ribbon-like material.

I want to fucking wreck her.

I lift my eyes to hers, and I know they have to be completely dark with desire. "Yes or no, Ava? You don't get to claim you didn't want this."

Her eyes flash at the challenge, her chest rising rapidly as she breathes. For a second she doesn't answer, and I think she's changing her mind. Then, she hooks her thumbs into the waistband of that delicate thong and drags it slowly down her thighs, never breaking eye contact.

"Yes," she says at last. It doesn't sound as needy as I'd like. Almost a challenge. It rolls through me like gasoline on a fire. My jaw clenches. She's giving me permission, but still fighting me in a way.

I crawl over her, bracing my hands on either side of her head. Her eyes flick briefly to the flex of my arms before her lids flutter shut, and her scent sharpens just a fraction.

"Say it again," I growl, testing her.

Her nails rake down my chest, sharp enough to sting. "You heard me," she breathes. "I won't repeat myself. Either fuck me or get off."

I slam my mouth back to hers, kissing her like I want to devour her—because I do. She bites my lower lip, hard enough to draw a grunt from me, and I shove my hips forward, my cock nudging against the slick heat waiting for me.

It's still a fight, even now. And I'm losing.

I don't break the kiss as I fumble blindly for the nightstand drawer, fingers closing around a condom at last. My alpha snarls at the thought of anything between us, but I ignore it. I may have snapped, but I'm not a monster. Bareback requires a conversation neither of us will ever have. Hell, this can't even happen again.

I roll the condom on quickly, then drag my fingers down to her slick folds. She's so hot and wet. A needy groan slips from my throat, betraying me. I don't want her to know how much power she has over me.

She's wet enough to take me, soaked honestly, but I want her undone first. Because once I'm inside her, I doubt I'll last long. I slide down her body, hook one of her legs over my shoulder, and drag my tongue along her slit.

She moans hotly, arching her hips so her pussy grinds against my mouth, forcing me deeper. Suddenly her taste, her scent, the very essence of her fills me.

Fuck. This was a mistake. Because now I don't want to stop. I think I could spend the rest of my life right here, my mouth between her thighs. I've never really done drugs, but this? This could easily be my first addiction.

What started as a way to make sure she got off before me turns into something else entirely. I wrench three orgasms from her, and something happens to her scent that I can't fully explain. It intensifies to where I'd describe it as an orange dreamsicle. Like I'd expect from an omega. Which I know she isn't, but it's the closest thing I can compare it to.

My alpha loses his mind, and what's left of my frayed control snaps. I don't give her a chance to come down. She's practically crawling her way up the headboard, making the neediest sounds

I've ever heard, when I seize her hips and drag her down the mattress.

One hard thrust buries me inside her.

We both moan loudly.

She's so tight. So perfect.

Rut. Knot. Bite. My alpha roars in my skull, and my teeth ache with the strain of holding him back.

I drive into her, not with frantic, sloppy thrusts, but hard, measured strokes that bottom out, pressing my knot against her entrance with every snap of my hips. God, I wish I could knot her. I've never truly wanted to do it since a disastrous experiment in college, but I do now. I want to tie her to my body and force her to hold me.

I fist her hair and drag her mouth back to mine, not caring that my face is soaked with her juices. I kiss her hard, deep, never breaking rhythm, never letting up.

Ava comes for me again, her nails raking down my back hard enough to break skin. I hiss, feeling the sting and the wet warmth of blood, then suck in a breath of the intoxicating scent I still can't decipher.

I'm so caught up in it, I don't react fast enough when she shoves at my shoulder. For a split second, I panic. If she's changed her mind, I'll stop, no question. But the thought of being left this close to the edge almost kills me.

Instead, she uses the momentum to roll me onto my back and straddle me. Relief crashes into desire, my chest heaving as she plants her feet on the mattress and sinks down on me.

I tug down her bra, desperate for the view of her breasts bouncing as she rides me. She gives me an indulgent, wicked smile and reaches behind her to unhook it, letting it fall away.

Her breasts are full for her slender frame, freckles lightly scattered across their tops and petal-pink nipples that are begging for my teeth and tongue.

She tips her chin upward, her fiery red hair cascading down her back as she moves.

Maybe I died earlier tonight, and I'm in heaven. Because this has to be the most beautiful goddamn sight I've ever seen.

She rides me like she's determined to break me, her nails gripping my chest, leaving little half-moons in their wake. Every thrust drives me deeper inside her, and I groan.

"Fuck," I grit out, grabbing her hips, trying to guide her pace, but she swats my hands away.

"Don't," she pants, strands of sweat-dampened hair clinging to her cheeks. "I'm not done with you yet."

If I didn't die earlier, she might kill me now. She grinds down, rolling her hips until my vision whites out. My alpha howls inside me, demanding I flip her, pin her, *claim* her. But the vision of her on top, using me like this, has me wound so tight I can barely breathe.

She leans forward suddenly, bracing her hands on either side of my head in a mirror of how I did her earlier. Her breasts brush against my chest as she slams herself down on me again and again. Her scent thickens, coating the back of my throat, and it's all I can do not to bite her.

"Ava—" I choke out, warning, plea, threat. I don't even know.

"Shut up," she snaps, but her voice breaks on a moan as she clenches around me.

That's it. My hands clamp down on her ass, dragging her harder against me as I thrust up to meet her, each stroke deeper, rougher, my knot swelling and pressing hard at her entrance. She cries out, back arching, and then she's coming apart above me, spasming so tight around my cock I lose it completely.

I roar her name, bucking hard and spilling into the condom as my vision goes black. The world narrows to the sounds of her cries, the feel of her body writhing on me, and the scorching heat of my release.

We collapse together, her chest heaving against mine, sweat slick between us. My alpha is still snarling for more, for the knot, for the bite, but I force him down.

For now, this is enough. It has to be enough.

Ava

I stare at myself in the mirror. I just finished my shower and need to get dressed to head to the courthouse, but for the first time, I'm dreading it. My body is littered with fingertip-sized bruises and hickeys. Luckily, none of them will show when I'm dressed. Right now, though, I can see every one.

Mark and I fucked twice more before I left last night—or, I suppose, this morning. Knowing I was going to see him in court in just a few short hours had filled me with more anxiety than I knew what to do with. So the moment he'd fallen asleep, I'd made my escape. Poor Tony had been asleep in the front seat when I took my walk of shame back to the car. He hadn't said a word, God love him, just looked me over and grunted before driving me home.

I flex my shoulders experimentally and wince. Every movement reminds me of him. I'm sore in ways I have only ever felt when leaving a heat clinic.

I have *never* had sex like that. I don't let men take control during the rare times I actually sleep with someone for fun and not just because I'm in heat. Given what happened at the clinic, I thought I would be completely sex-repulsed. I haven't been with anyone since. But with Mark, when he threw me on the bed and told me to take off my clothes, the urge to roll over and present to him was so intense that I was helpless not to submit.

What now?

We obviously can't do it again. I still can't stand him, and at the very least, he associates himself with people that would prefer to lock omegas away unless we are needed for cleaning, child-rearing, or breeding.

What if he wants to have a serious talk? Or worse, want to become an "item"?

I had wanted so desperately this morning to curl into his side and go to sleep. I don't sleep anywhere outside of the safety of my apartment or my office the two places I have nests.

That terrified me.

I towel off the last damp strands of hair and pull on a blouse and skirt that hide everything, but make me feel like a competent adult again. Competent and sore. Mostly sore.

My omega whines that his scent is barely lingering on me after the shower, and when I spray my scent neutralizer on myself, she really complains.

God, she's pathetic. We're pathetic. I'm pathetic. I don't know. Being an omega is weird.

I sling my briefcase over my shoulder and step out of the elevator into the lobby downstairs. My penthouse sits on the upper levels of one of the few remaining Gilded Age buildings that survived demolitions and renovations in the '60s and became a co-op of luxury apartments. The lobby feels like the heart of it all. It's grand and imposing, with soaring ceilings and painstakingly preserved original features. A few big-brand stores occupy the ground floor, their modern displays almost jarring against the building's old-world elegance, though they have attempted to adapt their branding to match the overall aesthetic.

Sunlight streams through tall, arched windows, catching the dust motes in the air, and for a moment, I pause to take it in. The brass fixtures gleam, the carved wood radiates warmth, and every detail—from the intricate crown molding to the sweeping staircase in the corner—reminds me why I bought my penthouse. How could I not want to live in this kind of history and beauty? It had really hit my trust fund hard, but real estate anywhere, especially New York City, is never a bad investment. They aren't making more land.

Besides, I have no intention of ever leaving. This is my forever home.

The crisp morning air hits me as I step outside and find Tony dutifully waiting. I shake my head. I had told him to take the morning off after working so late. This man never listens. He acts like driving me around is his sole life's mission. I pay him a ridiculous amount for it in return. I hope it's enough.

Many New Yorkers don't drive, but I never even got my license. I tried to learn, but getting behind the wheel gave me panic attacks so severe that my parents finally gave up. My therapist calls it a control thing—I'm at the mercy of other drivers. Technically, I still am as a passenger, but at least I'm not responsible for navigating while dealing with that.

Traffic hums around us as we make our way through the crowded city blocks between my penthouse and the Central Manhattan Courthouse. Snagging a protein bar and a manila folder from my bag, I try to focus on preparing for today's proceedings as I eat. Recovering from yesterday's surprise witness is going to be difficult. I probably won't be able to. I'm making peace with the fact that Mark will likely win this one, despite my best efforts.

Still, my mind drifts to last night. The way my body trembled beneath him, the hard, chiseled heat of his body, how I'd come apart again and again.

I shove those thoughts down. I can't let this consume me. I can't go there again. My omega will just have to get over it.

I exit the car and head up the steps, the courthouse looming in front of me. 100 Centre Street is an imposing monolith of a building, with fluted granite columns and subtle metalwork that catches the morning light. I walk inside, waving to the guards by the metal detectors as I put my briefcase on the conveyor belt. They nod back with easy, friendly smiles. As they wave the wand over my body, I glance up at the massive clock that hangs above the entrance, ticking away the hours.

I'm such a nerd for old architecture.

Clearing security, I head toward the courtroom, my pulse skipping despite my best efforts. Will he already be here? I bite my lip, anticipation curling low in my belly. Somehow, my traitorous, greedy body still aches for him. And that's not even touching on my omega's whining to be near him again. Jesus. Were the eleventy-billion orgasms not enough?

I push open the door and pause, scanning the room. Most of the seats are filling up, the voices fading to a low hum under the high ceilings. I'm arriving a little later than I normally do, thanks to my contemplations in front of the mirror.

Then I see him, leaning casually against his table, chatting with his second chair. Mark's jacket is perfectly creased, and other than just the faintest puffiness at the corner of his eyes and a darker five o'clock shadow than normal, you'd never know he was running on only a couple hours of sleep. Meanwhile, I'd spent nearly fifteen minutes having to color-correct to be satisfied I didn't look like a zombie.

Men.

I bite back a sigh and force a smile to my face, straightening my posture. I refuse to look flustered. My professional court mask is firmly in place.

I am the viper. Not the needy omega whining in the back of my mind.

As if sensing me, Mark turns and catches my gaze. For a fraction of a second, his smile falters, and hungry recognition darkens his eyes just long enough to make my heart skip. Then, just as quickly, it's gone, and his game face takes over.

"Counselor," I say with a terse nod as I walk past him to my table.

"Ms. Kendrick," he drawls. "Almost fashionably late. Drawing out the moment before you lose this case?"

I roll my eyes, though internally, I feel a small bit of comfort in the familiar exchange of barbs. I turn and smile reassuringly at my client, who is looking sullen and angry ever since the witness yesterday. I lean closer and whisper in his ear, "If you want the jury to believe that man is lying, you need to look a little less like you're planning bodily harm against the DA, as tempting as it is."

He gives me a dirty look, and I remind myself that this man is definitely a murderer, so not exactly someone I want to be antagonizing for the fun of it.

The gavel slams, echoing through the courtroom, and with it, my case is over. I pack up my briefcase and sigh as Mr. Simmons is led out by the bailiff in handcuffs. I'm not overly sad that he's facing the justice he deserves, but I do hate losing. Not to mention, the mob won't be thrilled with the outcome.

Hopefully I've kept enough of them out of jail that they'll understand. Can't win them all.

Mark had been his typical infuriating self, though on far better behavior today, which caused the reporters to look increasingly bored. They had apparently hoped for a round two.

I head out the door, bracing for the inevitable. He'll linger and corner me somewhere, like he always does. And he'll want to talk.

Sure enough, when I step into the corridor, he's there.

He walks a few steps behind me, giving me space, matching my pace instead of taking control. It confuses me and makes me feel a little off-kilter. I glance back at him, and his face is carefully neutral.

Is he letting me take the lead on this? Decide how we will play it out?

If so, he's going to realize that I have no desire to talk about it.

We exit the courthouse together, the city noise washing over us. Reporters linger outside, and he's pulled over to make a comment on winning the case. Coward that I am sometimes, I take the chance to make an escape back to my car.

I see him glance at me, a look of annoyance flashing across his face, and I give a small wave. I ask Tony to take me to the Queens County Family Court, where I have the opening for Maya's custody case this afternoon. Since I'm now hiding from the district attorney, I have a few hours to prep, and I intend to make every second count.

Tony unearthed quite a bit of information on Daniel, and Shelby filled in the blanks with a little bit of mildly illegal internet hacking. I claim an empty conference room at the courthouse and spread the files across the table, organizing them into piles that match the way my mind tends to lay things out. Work history. Financial records. Neighbor's statements. Etc.

Maya was right that there wasn't anything criminal on paper, but we'd recovered some of the 911 calls. There were also old pictures of bruises that she'd been smart enough to take and send to a friend for safekeeping. I also had the therapist's notes, which paint an ugly picture of the children's anxiety and the history of abuse in the home.

Family court is tricky. I have a duty to point out patterns of abuse, but I have to do so in a way that doesn't come across like I'm just trying to block Daniel from his children. That would anger the judge. So there's less wiggle room than I have in the criminal courtroom. I can only stick to evidence and not leave breadcrumbs of insinuation for a jury to pick up on.

First, I need to focus on showing Maya to be the anchor of the family, the reliable parent. This, thankfully, is incredibly easy to do. I have an abundance of documentation showing her at every doctor's visit, class party, PTA meeting, etc. I have a written statement from the school secretary and the children's teachers that they have never so much as spoken to Daniel and wouldn't know who he was if he came to pick up the children.

I'll need to brace for their attacks on her character, but luckily, I already know exactly what they'll try to do. It's the same old worn-out song and dance routine. They'll come after her hormones and heat cycles, claiming emotional instability. That should give me the opportunity to bring up her getting the kids into therapy and a chance to present the therapist's notes. They are pretty damning, if I can bring them up organically. The oldest boy has growing resentment and anger toward his mother and sister, and has acted out in school toward other girls as well. In play therapy, the youngest daughter frequently shows the daddy doll yelling at the mommy doll, who then falls down and cries.

Every time I read over that line, I debate if it would just be easier to have Tony kill the man and be done with it.

I shake my head to clear the thought and practice my opening statement. In my head, I picture how the judge might react to each phrase. I picture opposing counsel's posture, the quiet smirks, the smug certainty they will have about Maya until I walk in. That look is one of my favorites. The panic on the lawyer's face and the confusion on the alpha's.

I mentally walk through any potential objections or weak spots. Every piece of evidence is checked and double-checked until I'm satisfied I know this case inside and out. I pride myself on being thorough. Hence why I'd been so infuriated yesterday at Mark's comment.

Soon, though, there's nothing left to go through, and I still have time to kill. It becomes harder to ignore the elephant in the room. I tap my pen against the folder. It's impossible to completely disentangle this case from what happened between me and Mark.

Maya is a perfect example of how the system stacks the decks against omegas. The judge we drew wasn't the one I'd hoped for, but he also isn't the worst. He has a reputation for being mostly neutral on omega rights, but unfortunately, that can also just mean quietly biased because there hasn't been a chance to show how he really felt.

Just like Mark.

Most of Mark's actions would suggest that he disagrees with the foundations of the more conservative laws aimed at omegas, but he doesn't openly champion against them either. And he sure had a tendency to rub elbows with the types of alphas I loathe. Hell, just last week he was in the paper, shoulder to shoulder with Harold Fucking Harvey, our illustrious mayor who once publicly called omegas a "necessary burden." That kind of proximity says more than words ever could.

What's the saying? *If you are neutral in situations of injustice, you have chosen the side of the oppressor.*

I shake my head. Irritation and shame simmer beneath my skin. How could I be so stupid? I know better than to blur the lines, to let myself get drawn into the orbit of a sexy alpha. It doesn't matter how many glimpses of softness I catch when the cameras aren't around. Like it or not, Mark is a man who plays politics in a world where my kind get crushed under the weight of "it's always been this way."

If he figures out my secret? I go from a fun lover to a liability overnight. Or worse, he tries to bond with me and make me his dutiful little omega. Gets me deemed unfit to work like so many other omegas have been by alphas "just looking out for their safety," stripping my ability to fight for people like Maya.

The thought makes my throat tighten. She is heading to the courtroom right now, terrified and fighting for her children because men like Daniel exploit the biases against omegas. And here my dumb ass is, playing with fire and sleeping with the enemy.

Could Mark be a good guy? Sure, maybe. But I don't know him, not really.

Last night can never happen again.

8

Mark

I'd actually forgotten about the wedding entirely until Trinity texts to confirm our plans. Which really says everything about how the last week and a half has gone, because initially, I'd been looking forward to this blind date. Ever since a certain tall, leggy redhead shoved her way into my apartment, turned my entire life upside down, and then decided to act like none of it had happened—my mind has been a shitshow.

I know with certainty it was the best damn sex of my life, and I'd be willing to wager a sizable amount of money that was true for Ava too. Yet she's avoided me where she can, and where she can't, she's pulled back on sparring, which somehow is worse. This careful, deliberate nothing is its own kind of answer. Damn her for having the self-control to do what's in our best interest. I don't have a single good argument against it. That might be what irritates me the most.

I'm especially annoyed that I have no interest in sitting through this wedding and reception with a gorgeous woman. A casual hookup after an open bar might be just the ticket to forgetting all about my ill-fated one-night stand. However, I'm not actually naïve enough to believe that is possible. Fairly certain I'd need a sci-fi-level memory wipe to forget Ava on top of me.

I'm a man of my word, so I pick Trinity up on time and spend the cab ride doing my level best to be charming and present. We cover the standard first date territory without much trouble. Her work, my work, how neither of us knows the couple particularly well and isn't it funny how these invitations find you anyway. Greg had prosecuted out of my office for a few months, and we'd been friendly enough in the way proximity encourages. Then a federal offer came through and he left, and as work friendships often do, it had been quietly fizzling ever since. But I'd already RSVP'd. Plus, it's a decent networking opportunity.

Trinity is lovely. That's an honest assessment, and it makes my mood even worse. She's smart, asks good questions, and laughs at the right moments. Under other circumstances, I'd have been here for it. Instead, I keep catching myself wishing she'd say something that makes my pulse spike. Or that her eyes were a different shade, instead of the blue that now looks bland to me. Green, maybe.

Get a fucking grip. The sex wasn't that good, I chide myself.

Liar. My alpha side grumbles.

There's a moment of confusion at the door when the usher, a teenage kid who is almost certainly a younger brother of Greg's, realizes that I know the groom and Trinity knows the bride. The poor boy looks genuinely stricken, like this particular scenario hadn't been covered in whatever ten-minute usher briefing he received. I take pity on him.

"It's fine," I say, glancing at Trinity. "We'll sit on the bride's side. Figure you might know someone over there, and I genuinely don't care where we end up." She shrugs and smiles. I don't know what I was hoping for from her, but whatever it was, I didn't get it.

We find our seats and make another run at conversation. It soon becomes clear that neither of us is really feeling it, and eventually I stop forcing it and let the silence settle. Maybe it will be better once we have some snacks and drinks. I scan the room instead, spotting a few familiar faces from the legal circuit and give a small wave. At least I'll have someone to talk to at the reception if Trinity decides to ditch me.

The music starts and the pastor appears, followed by Greg, who looks equally happy and nervous. Mandatory for every groom I've ever seen. There's a pause, then the doors open again, and the bridal processional starts. I'm not really paying close attention. Mostly I'm doing the mental math of how long until we can move to the golf club, whether the open bar will be worth staying for and exactly how many glasses of whiskey it might take to shake me out of my Ava-induced mood and have some fun.

Then I stop counting.

Because three bridesmaids deep, looking straight ahead with the relaxed composure of someone who had absolutely not yet spotted me, is the viper herself.

You have got to be shitting me. Is this some kind of karmic payment for sins I'm unaware of?

She's resplendent in a pale pink satin dress that really should clash against her hair and skin, but somehow doesn't. Her hair is mostly down and curled, with one side pulled back and held in place with a jeweled comb. She has one arm linked through the arm of a groomsman, a small bouquet of white, long-stemmed flowers clutched in her hands. There is an unguarded softness on her face that I've never seen before. It makes her look younger. Not that she looks old—lord knows she probably has a skincare routine that would bankrupt a small country—but this is different somehow.

My heart skips a little in my chest, and I have the strangest urge to growl and rip her away from the man daring to touch her skin. It's so unexpected and unsettling that I can feel my skin pale, even as I focus with a laser intensity on where they meet. I force myself to lift my gaze back to her face, and it's then that our eyes meet. Hers widen in surprise, giving her an almost comically adorable, doll-like expression. She nearly misses a step, but manages to catch herself, and the look is gone as quickly as it came. The cool and detached face I'm more familiar with reappears, and it makes my chest ache.

I manage to get through the rest of the ceremony on autopilot. Vows, rings, the kiss, applause. I clap at the appropriate moments and smile when Trinity looks over at me, and I absolutely do not spend the entire time acutely aware of exactly where Ava is standing on that altar.

That would be pathetic.

The receiving line takes forever, as they always do. It's a practice I loathe. If I ever get married, I hope to hell my wife will let me nix the tradition. By the time we make it through and Trinity has air-kissed and hugged the bride while I shake Greg's hand, it's been nearly forty minutes since I first spotted Ava. More than enough time to reinforce the mental pep talk I've been giving myself to stay the hell away from her at the reception.

The golf club is exactly what I'd expected. Floor-to-ceiling windows overlooking the course, large, tasteful floral pieces, satin draping, and a combined monogram of the couple's initials illuminated on the dance floor. Pretty, but exactly like every other wedding I've been to over the last couple of years. I hope they've managed to showcase something about their actual personalities and relationship in this reception. I head to the bar, get Trinity a gin and tonic and myself a glass of Bulleit, and return to her at the table with our names on it.

She thanks me, and we make a few more passes at small talk, but it's just not taking. As expected, she excuses herself to go mingle with people she knows. I don't blame her. When it isn't there, it isn't there. I do the same, and the cocktail hour keeps me busy enough that I almost forget who is busy taking pictures outside.

The lights dim and the DJ's voice fills the room, telling us to find our seats and put our hands together for the new Mr. and Mrs. Hawthorne. A high-energy pop song kicks in with a bass line that vibrates down into my sternum, and the doors swing open.

The wedding party comes through first, and the crowd reacts immediately. The bridesmaids have changed into short, sequined versions of their ceremony gowns in the same pale pink. Only now, it's cut high on the thigh and falls outward from the bust line, something between a 1960s Bond Girl and a babydoll lingerie set you'd find in an old Frederick's of Hollywood. It somehow works.

The men have all ditched their jackets and ties, sleeves rolled to the elbows, and they look considerably more comfortable and relaxed than they had a couple of hours ago. I spy Ava amongst them, and my mouth goes a little dry. The cut of the dress and the way it flounces around her only accentuates her legs that go on for miles. The sequins catch the light every time she moves, which she's doing a lot of, as the entire bridal party is dancing and encouraging the crowd to do the same as the newlyweds enter.

"You two face off against each other in court, don't you?" Trinity asks, from somewhere to my left.

I turn to look at her. She's watching me with the same pleasant, unreadable expression she's had all night, and I wonder how obvious it was that I was staring. "Who? Ms. Kendrick?"

She snorts out a laugh through her nose. "Uh, yeah," she says, as if I'm being deliberately obtuse. I guess I am.

I feel my cheeks heat. Has she noticed how closely I've been watching Ava? "Yeah, we do." I clear my throat. "I'm actually kind of wondering how she fits in here. I'd have thought Greg would have mentioned knowing her when he worked in my office," I respond, keeping my voice mostly neutral if a little bored.

"Her and Samantha went to college together. They were in the same sorority. Maybe he never mentioned it because everyone knows you two hate each other. You were Greg's boss, right?"

I nod. "Yeah, I guess that would be kind of weird."

The reception settles into the expected routine. Waiters bring around our plated dinners. I see Trinity glance toward someone she'd been speaking to earlier that has an empty spot beside her. "You won't hurt my feelings if you want to go sit with her," I finally say gently.

She looks over at me, and I smile. "You seem lovely, but I think we both aren't really what the other is looking for. There's no harm in it."

"You sure? I don't want to be a bitch. You seem like a good guy, just... preoccupied." There's no bitterness in her tone, just honesty.

"Yeah. And I am. Sorry about that. Work has been nuts, and I've had some personal stuff happening. Long as you don't go telling everyone I was the worst date you ever had, we're good."

She grins at me. "Deal. Though I hope you'll keep the same promise. I look hot in this dress."

I nod. "You do. Go find you a groomsman or something so it doesn't go to waste."

She gathers up her plate and walks over to the other table, and I bite back a sigh. I probably should make a hasty exit as soon as it's polite to do so.

Ava is at the head table with the rest of the bridal party. She leans in close to the bride, whispering something that makes her laugh hard enough to cover her mouth. A second later, Ava grins, wide and unguarded, and bumps her shoulder lightly into the bride's. I can't seem to keep my eyes off her.

The groomsman beside her is trying to get Ava's attention, trying to draw her into a conversation. She gives him a soft smile, and the surge of jealousy inside me makes me almost choke on the bite of grilled salmon and lemon risotto I've placed in my mouth. Surely she isn't going to entertain this asshole? He looks like a thumb.

When the speeches start, I try to ignore her and focus on what is being said, but I'm hyperaware of all things Ava in my peripheral vision. She listens attentively during the speeches, her chin propped lightly on her hand. She tears up during the maid of honor's toast, swiping discreetly at the corner of her eye before anyone can make a big deal of it. When the best man makes a joke that lands particularly well, she tosses her head back laughing in a way I've never seen her do.

By the time the DJ calls everyone to the dance floor, I'm restless. I know I should leave, but instead I find myself at the bar, getting another drink. I sip at it, leaning against the rail as all the predictable first dances take place before the DJ shifts gears. I try to mingle some more with the people I know.

Older family members of the newlyweds begin to make their exits as an upbeat, familiar song fills the room. Like a switch has been flipped, the dance floor floods. The bridal party leads the charge, pulling reluctant guests in their wake. I find myself edging closer and closer, drawn like a magnet to the woman I should be doing everything in my power to stay away from. She's in the thick of it, because of course she is, her body rolling in perfect harmony with the beat.

Soon, Mr. Thumb reappears, and I have to school my features before anything slips. From the outside, I'm neutral, detached. Inside, not even close. His hand settles at the small of her back and he turns her, and she goes with it, ending up with her back to his chest as the music shifts, their bodies lining up in a way that's less dancing and more grinding.

My alpha snarls within my chest. Abso-fucking-lutely not.

I make my way through the throng of bodies until I'm standing in front of her. There's no real surprise on her face, so I have to wonder if she's been as hyperaware of me as I have been of her.

"Evan, can I introduce you to Mark Taylor, youngest district attorney of Manhattan?" Her voice is cool, but there's a fire in her eyes that I can't decipher. I barely manage to drag my gaze from hers to look up at Mr. Thumb.

"Hey, man," he says with a smile, extending his hand. "I'm Evan. I don't really follow politics. What does the district attorney do exactly?"

I glance back at Ava just in time to catch the faint wince she can't quite hide. "It's an elected position," I say, managing just barely to suppress a laugh. "I oversee the prosecutors. We're the ones who put away the bad guys." I pause just long enough, unable to keep a hint of a grin pulling at my mouth. "When Ava isn't busy getting them off on technicalities."

There's no real bite to it, just enough edge to sound like the way I always talk about her. Evan laughs like I've said something genuinely funny, and I don't miss Ava's upper lip curling a little in disgust. If he had a shot of getting into her panties, I'm fairly confident he just fumbled it. One thing Ava doesn't have patience for is stupidity.

"Evan, I'm getting kind of hot with all these people out here. Could you go grab me some water?" she asks.

He nods, like a puppy eager to make her happy, and heads away.

"He seems... nice. Gonna head home with him later?"

"Oh, shut up," she snaps, and starts to spin away from me, but I reach out and grab her wrist, pulling her body flush against mine.

"I'll shut up, but you're going to dance with me. You were clearly having fun, that doesn't have to change," I growl into her ear. It's a calculated risk—she could tell me to go fuck myself. But just like at my apartment, her body language seems to relax a fraction at my command.

"Dance, Ava."

Ava

I should tell him to go fuck himself. I've felt his eyes on me all night, and I couldn't breathe with the way he was watching me, even though he was trying so hard to pretend he wasn't. I try to run through all my thoughts from the other day about silence in the name of oppression, only the champagne has been flowing since mimosas this morning and everything is a little bit fuzzy, and his body feels so good against mine. His scent envelops me, and it's like it short-circuits my brain.

So even as I'm trying to remember all of my very solid reasons to not interact with and definitely *not* sleep with Mark Taylor, I find myself moving to the rhythm again. In my heels, my ass is lined up perfectly with his hardening cock, and a small sound escapes me as I feel it.

I know he heard it, because I feel his grip tighten on my hips. Damn him. His fingertips sit in the same spot that had bruises all week from a similar position, and my omega responds in kind. She surges to the front of my mind, fighting for dominance. The urge to pull him away from the brunette beta bitch he came with claws at my insides. I want to coat him in my scent, make sure any other woman knows he's *taken*.

I shake my head to dislodge the thought. He isn't ours, and she needs to understand that.

It's a bizarre sensation, feeling like another sentient being is fighting you within your own mind. But that's exactly how I feel at the moment. The fact that Mark is actually a good dancer and his hips roll in time with mine is adding fuel to the fire. My omega snarls inside me, and I feel my arms rise almost on their own volition and weave around his neck.

I'd worry about people watching, but the dance floor is too crowded and the liquor is flowing too freely. Any attention is solidly on the bride and groom, where it should be.

"You're quite the dancer," he says hotly in my ear.

I don't respond, because I'm still busy battling for control against my omega. I'm afraid if I say anything just yet, the only words I'll be able to get out will involve begging him to fuck me.

The DJ seamlessly blends the end of the song with the beginning of the next one so the energy doesn't drop. I see Evan starting to push his way through the crowd, and Mark must see him as well, because he spins us so that his body blocks Evan's view of me.

"Jealous?" I manage to gasp out.

"Shut up," he answers in a mirror of my words from earlier. There's an edge to his voice that makes my nipples harden. I'd smirk in triumph if I didn't feel like I was literally drowning in horniness.

The reaction this man elicits in my body should be studied.

I arch my ass firmly back into him.

"Christ, Ava," he growls. The way his hands flex on my hip, I think we might be about a half-second from dry humping on the floor.

Thankfully, at that moment, Samantha appears and grabs my hand. "Ava! There you are! Come dance with us!" She tugs me away from Mark and towards the other bridesmaids. I smile at her, hiding my disappointment. It's her wedding, and she just saved me from making a scene.

"Lead the way, Mrs. Hawthorne!" I say, forcing excitement into my voice.

Unable to help myself, I glance back over my shoulder towards Mark, who is still standing where we were, eyes dark and predatory. My omega whines within me, but without his scent enveloping us, I'm able to push her back down.

The next time I look back, he's nowhere to be seen, and there's an ache somewhere deep within my body that tells me he must have left. That's for the best.

Right?

I thank Tony as I slide out of the car. He grunts his normal response, and I grin. It doesn't matter how out of sorts I am or how chaotic my life feels, Tony is one thing that never changes.

I head upstairs to my penthouse, taking deep, calming breaths once I'm alone in the elevator. My blood has felt like it was on fire ever since I danced with Mark. I need a cool shower, stat.

Valentino, my fluffy, white ragdoll, chirps at me in greeting once I'm inside. I stroke my hand along her back and up her tail, savoring the softness of her fur. She really should be named Valentina, but I had thought she was a boy when I first got her, and named her after one of my favorite designer houses.

A sudden cramp nearly doubles me over in pain, and I suck in a breath between clenched teeth. My brow furrows in confusion. I'm not in heat, but that definitely felt like the cramps I get when I am. A deep, pulsing need washes through me, and I realize what's happening. My omega is throwing a tantrum, demanding the release I denied her on the dance floor.

I don't exactly know how, but I get the distinct feeling that this is a threat of sorts. Give in to this obsession she has with Mark, or she'll fight me harder than she ever has. A shiver of fear crawls down my spine. Is my omega side strong enough to break through the suppressants if she was really determined?

Flashes of my night at his apartment fill my mind, and the look he gave me as I walked away from the dance floor. If it's possible for a vagina to ache from being empty, mine is definitely doing it now.

"Oh my god, fine! But he might not even come over!" I say out loud to my empty apartment.

Great. Now I'm talking to myself, like a crazy person. I grab my phone, punching in my address and instructions on where and how to utilize the service elevator. I press send before I can second-guess myself or my omega can punish me with another cramp.

I know, despite my words, that he will definitely come over. Everything that I feel, Mark seems to as well. Something about that certainty tries to catch my attention, but I purposefully ignore it.

Instead, I unlock the front door and make my way to the bathroom. It takes some effort to maneuver out of my reception dress. Thank god I'd opted against an updo and I didn't have to fight ninety-seven bobby pins to get my hair down. I quickly take off my makeup while the water heats up, and I step beneath the spray.

Anticipation, desire, and anxiety are all at battle in my mind as I wash away the sweat from the dance floor. This is very different from the night at his apartment. That was an error in judgement, our tempers getting the best of us. If he shows up here now, it is a deliberate step forward into something that I'm terrified to name.

I've almost convinced myself to text him that I've changed my mind when I hear the bathroom door open. I turn and find Mark leaned against the frame. He's lost the tie and jacket, and now his collar is unbuttoned and his sleeves are rolled up. My mouth practically waters at how good he looks.

He watches me with the same look he had on the dance floor, and it makes goosebumps break out along my skin. The urge to present is strong, but I fight through it. Instead, in an effort to maintain some kind of control in this situation, I close my eyes and lean back into the water, letting it rinse my conditioner away.

I thought he'd join me, but when I finish and open my eyes, he's still standing in place, enjoying the show. He hasn't spoken, and I think a part of me understands. He put the moves on me when I showed up at his place. This time, he's going to make me come to him.

A flash of annoyance makes my skin flush. I texted him my address, isn't that enough? Yet even as I think it, there's a begrudging respect underneath too. Mark always gives as good as he gets. I will never be able to railroad this man into anything.

I turn the water off and grab my towel. His eyes trace a slow path along my entire body, and it's possible that I'm a little more sultry and suggestive as I dry off. Maybe. Allegedly.

I move to my vanity, spraying in my leave-in conditioner and quickly braiding my hair into a single long rope. With anyone else, I think the mundane action would have tempered the desire smoldering between us, yet with Mark and the way he's watching me, it seems like it only increases it. He makes no effort to rush me, and by the time I'm done, I'm so wet it might as well be slick. I need this man inside of me like yesterday.

I walk toward him, slowly. His eyes are hooded, and the normal brown of his irises are practically black with how blown his pupils are. Once I'm within arm's reach, I have a better understanding of his nickname, because what he does is best described as a pounce. He's on me so quickly, I squeak in surprise. His large hands grip my ass and lift me up so that I'm forced to wrap my legs around his hips.

"Tell me where your bedroom is right now, or I'm fucking you here against this wall," he grinds out between clenched teeth.

Unable to speak, I just point across the hall at the open door. Thankfully, the door to my nest is safely closed, namely because I don't like Valentino to get in there when I'm gone.

He carries me to the room, his mouth meeting mine in a kiss so desperate, it's like he's drowning and I'm the only source of oxygen around. He kicks the door closed behind him and tosses me onto the mattress.

"On your hands and knees, Ava," he demands.

My omega is happy to oblige to this request. I move into position, and I expect him to push himself inside me. Instead, I feel his tongue drag upward from my clit and dip inside of me. Something about being eaten from the back like this always feels so much more explicit, and I moan his name in a needy display that I should be more embarrassed about than I am.

He nibbles, sucks, licks, and fingers me until I've forgotten everything in the entire world outside of this bedroom. If cunnilingus was an Olympic sport, Mark would win the gold, hands down. He takes me over the edge to where I'm not sure if it's multiple orgasms or a single, never-ending one.

I'm practically sobbing with overstimulation and need when he finally pulls away from me. "Tell me you have a condom," he says against the curve of my ass, breathing hard.

I desperately want to lie and tell him I don't, because my omega hates the idea of anything between us. But that will require a bit of conversation, so I point to the end table beside the bed. I'm fairly certain there's a couple in there. It's been a while since I've had anyone over.

"Don't fucking move," he growls, and I hear the drawer open and the ripping of the wrapper. Then he returns, his hands sliding into place on my hips mirroring how they were on the dance floor. He grips them and pulls me forcefully back, burying his cock within me. He's still standing at the edge of the bed, and he moves one hand around to my stomach, tugging me so that my back is to his chest.

The pace he sets is relentless, almost as if he's punishing me for making him feel this way, and I think in a way, he probably is. But fuck, if it doesn't feel incredible.

Mark moves his other hand forward until he finds my clit, stroking and rolling it between his fingers gently, in direct contrast to the pounding of his cock inside me. The mismatched sensations tip me over again, and my entire body tenses and shakes as I come.

His teeth graze the juncture where my shoulder meets my neck, and I think for the briefest moment he's going to bite me for real. I inhale sharply, and he pulls back with an audible snap of his mouth. I know he thinks I responded out of fear of a bond mark, but what's more frightening is that I'm not scared at all. In fact, the desire for it takes my breath away.

I pull myself off him, and I see the brief flash of hurt and disappointment before he shutters it. He thinks I'm rejecting him because of how close he came.

I should.

Instead, I turn and cup his cheeks between my palm to kiss him greedily, not caring that my wetness is on his lips. I tug him toward me, and he grips my ass once more, lifting me easily and seating himself back inside of me.

"You're gonna be the death of me, Ava," he moans.

"Shut up and make me come again, Mark," I answer, and I feel all my logical and righteous reasons to not pursue this float away like a feather on the wind as my omega and I find some sort of compromise.

I won't let him bond me and I won't tell him my secret. But this—this I can do.

10

Mark

One Month Later

Per usual, my stomach is twisted into equal parts dread and eager anticipation at the thought of facing Ava in court. We wrapped up jury selection last week, and today marks opening statements in a high-profile case involving a wealthy omega heiress. She was caught purchasing illegal heat suppressants, and the media has been swarming since day one.

I tried to get out of prosecuting it. Everything about this case screams *headache.* The defendant's family has the kind of money that makes enemies, and if I plan to campaign next year, antagonizing potential donors is not exactly strategic. On top of that, I hate the suppressant ban. If the government would properly fund research into omega heat cycles, we could have safe, legal suppressants and avoid this entire circus.

But Harvey is on my ass. As the DA, he isn't technically my boss, because I hold an elected office. But you know what the mayor has power over? My office's budget. He's already made vague threats that if I don't fall in line, he'll halve it, and I'll be forced to lay people off.

Lately, his behavior has escalated. Not just toward me, but toward Ava as well. His fixation on her has crossed into something that feels unhealthy. He has even threatened to scrap his NYTV project, though I think he'd have a riot on his hands if he tried to cancel it now. It's obvious he resents the growing attention Ava and I attract. At this point, we are practically New York celebrities. The press has labeled us the city's "golden enemies," and audiences love watching us tear into each other in court.

And despite our total inability to stay away from each other outside the courtroom, we fight harder there than ever.

We are playing a dangerous game. If I were a better man, I would end it or disclose the conflict to the bar and force Ava to stop taking cases in my jurisdiction. But that loops straight back to the NYTV problem. I cannot buy this level of publicity, and it makes me less dependent on wealthy donors.

It eases my conscience in some ways. In others, it makes it far worse.

I shift in my chair, rotating my shoulder and neck to get a crick out from how I've been leaning over the documents I was reading. The gouges on my skin pull and protest. I know the cops have dubbed her the viper, but honestly, she should be the one to be called the tiger. Or at least some kind of feline, the way she's constantly scratching or biting me when she's in the throes of a really good orgasm—not to be confused with the orgasms I chase like Captain Ahab after his prey. No, those are rarer, but something happens to her scent when she comes like that, and my inner alpha craves it like a drug. I can usually coax those out of her if I can get about four or five regular ones first.

I shift for an entirely different reason now, my cock hardening at even the briefest thought of that scent or the way she looks when she comes undone. I never mind the bites or scratches, because I'd probably sell my soul to keep having access to her.

Hell, I'm not entirely certain I haven't already. I've deleted her number more times than I can count. It never sticks. One late-night text is all it takes, and we fold like we always do.

Somewhere along the way, I stopped fighting it. Lately, I've been finding myself wishing for a way to bridge the gap between us. Maybe we could be more like friends with benefits than enemies that fuck.

Sometimes, I'll spot her talking to someone else, less guarded than normal and laughing. The jealousy that rips through me is so fierce that I have to count backward from ten to keep myself from ripping whoever it is apart. She never laughs like that with me.

Or even worse, when she falls asleep after a particularly enthusiastic romp. It's only happened a handful of times, but I always just end up lying there watching her sleep, like some kind of creeper. She just looks so... serene. Her beautiful, freckled face relaxed, long ginger lashes fanned across her cheeks, lips plumped from my kisses, hair a mess from my fingers.

It's those moments when I worry I'm so far over my head that I'm doomed and probably more than a little in love with her.

Course, then the minute she wakes up, she opens that fucking mouth and bolts, and all those thoughts go out the window because I'm ready to strangle her again.

I glance at the clock and realize I need to get across the street if I want to beat her to the courtroom. Another one of our silent competitions. I think I'll probably win today; she looked exhausted earlier, and I saw her get in her car, so I figure she either ran home or to her office for a nap.

Part of me wants to preen that I wore her out, while another part worries over her. There's an equal chance she went and did something stupid between cases, because she never takes care of herself. Her fridge is always practically empty, and I can probably count on one hand how many times I've seen her with water instead of an energy drink.

I push open the door to the courtroom and grin when I see I've arrived first. I know it's stupid, but I don't care.

I hear the click of her heels on the floor behind me. I barely managed to beat her. I glance at her and am immediately annoyed by the way my heart skips a beat. The sunlight is streaming in from the high windows, and it hits her hair just right, which she has taken down out of the chic bun it was in earlier. Now it's loose and flowing over her shoulders, the reds and golds shining in the light like a beautiful sunset.

I hate when she wears it loose in court. It's next to impossible to not think about how she looks when she's riding me and it flows over her breasts and bounces with my thrusts. My cock will be half-hard all afternoon, and it makes me scowl.

Sometimes I think she does it on purpose.

I'd thought about trying to crack a small joke with her today. Work on bridging that gap. But now I'm pissed off and horny. So instead, I say, "Nice of you to join us, counselor," in a voice snarky enough that it nearly makes *me* wince.

Her eyes narrow, and her chin tilts upward. Shit. She'll be a brat now for sure.

"Sorry, I was on a lunch date with this hot alpha, and I guess I lost track of time," she purrs.

It's a lie. I'm almost certain of it, but I can't guarantee it, and it only adds fuel to my anger. We've never officially talked about being exclusive, though we haven't been using protection for a couple of weeks now. One night, she silently handed me paperwork showing her STI results and information about her IUD. The next time I saw her, I handed her mine, and that was that.

"Oh, good. Well, let him know that if he needs any pointers, he can contact me. I can fill him in about that thing you like where I finger you with one hand and grip your throat with the other," I deadpan.

Her eyes widen and her mouth falls open. Honestly, I'm also a little shocked. We've never directly talked about it before, and certainly not in the courthouse. I can't get the idea of someone else getting to experience whatever that scent is out of my head, and my alpha side wants to throw her over the table and claim her right there.

That's not a possibility, though, so I'll just remind her. No one fucks her like I do. No one can, and no one ever will again.

I turn away from her, trying to get myself back under control. That last thought was far too possessive.

I must have really taken her by surprise, because she doesn't snap a retort at me. As she takes her seat, I steal a glance, and it almost makes me smirk. A blush is staining the pale skin beneath her freckles, and the way she has her full bottom lip between her teeth tells me that there's a part of her that enjoys being reminded in public.

Too soon, we are no longer alone. Her client joins us, and the rows behind us fill. We rise as Judge Carter enters, and I swallow a sigh. I'm going to lose this case. Ava is going to push the birth control angle, and it'll land. Carter's a woman and old enough to remember when betas also didn't have access to it. Not to mention that the jury has a majority of women. I'd burned through my peremptory challenges, and sometimes the random draw just tilts the scales.

I knew this case was hopeless from the get-go. Harvey is a damn fool. He'll probably end up slashing my budget regardless, so I ought to just plea it out.

I'm getting a headache.

I give my opening statement. It's short and drives home the point that I won't have any issue meeting the burden of proof. On paper, this should be an open-and-shut case—the defendant was caught red-handed with illegal suppressants. But nothing is open and shut when there's a sympathetic defendant and a defense attorney like Ava.

Ava squeezes her client's hand before standing. Normally, I'd roll my eyes at the performance, ice queen that she is. However, I've seen her with other omegas enough to know it's genuine. With them she is warm, friendly, and open.

Surprisingly, that is the opposite of how I feel when I'm around an omega, which makes no sense, since I'm supposed to be biologically predisposed to want to care for and nurture them. Truth be told, I think I'm a broken alpha. Omega scents are too cloying, and they leave me feeling more choked than turned on.

"The state," Ava starts her opening, "is going to try and convince you that my client, a young woman with no criminal history, was caught with contraband. What they will fail to do is prove that those pills were anything illegal at all."

What the fuck is she talking about? A pit forms in my stomach as I ponder her words. There's no way they didn't actually test the pills, right? Ava isn't known for saying anything she can't back up with evidence. I am going to have someone's head on a spike if she's right.

"And beyond the flaws of mishandled evidence," she continues, giving me the briefest glance, eyes alight with barely concealed enjoyment, "what this case really represents is stripping my client of her dignity." She takes a step toward the jury box, hands open wide, playing on their emotions as easily as a concert violinist at the symphony.

I have a love/hate relationship with watching her work.

"Suppressants for omegas are medicine. Illegal medicine, yes, an unfortunate reality of a legal system that has not caught up with scientific advancements. Yet this was once also true for beta birth control. It was seen as dangerous and immoral."

She pauses and lets the words hang before pressing a hand to her chest. "I'm standing here as a lawyer because of the freedom that became possible when it was legalized. Judge Carter sits on the bench for the same reason, and I'm sure many of you have similar stories of what that freedom has allowed in your life."

Her voice sharpens, snapping the room back to the case, and she looks directly into the camera when she speaks instead of at the jury. "They cannot prove she had suppressants in her hand. But even the mere idea that she might have is enough for the mayor to send his highest prosecutor after a nineteen-year-old girl with no criminal record."

One juror cuts me a side-eye.

I'm definitely losing this case.

It's been forty-five minutes since I texted Ava to come over, and my phone remains stubbornly silent.

Maybe it's too early. Normally, our messages happen late, but I couldn't wait any longer. I've been going out of my mind thinking about her all damn day.

I rake a hand through my hair, annoyed with myself for caring this much. Honestly, it would be better if she left me on read. Best if she ignored me entirely. We need to end this before it detonates in spectacular, career-ending fashion.

I know that.

So why does the idea of never touching her again feel like being trapped in a nest of fire ants?

You know why, my inner alpha growls in my head.

I glance at my phone again, tempted to send another message. Something casual and flippant. "If we are finally done, let me know at least so I'm not worried you're drowning in the Hudson or something." Is that too desperate?

Jesus. I'm such an embarrassment.

I push up from my chair and start pacing the living room, restless energy crawling up my spine. Emotions rise in my chest like high tide, threatening to choke me. Anger. Want. Jealousy. Sadness.

Then I hear it. A soft knock at the door.

Relief floods me so quickly, it almost hurts. I cross the room and swing the door open wide. Ava stands on the other side, her face a mask of cool disinterest. Oversized sweatpants hang low on her hips, swallowing her frame. A cropped black top shows a wide swath of skin from just under her breasts to her waist. Wait, are those sneakers? I wouldn't have guessed she owned any.

I blink in surprise, and my eyes travel upward. Her hair is pulled into a high ponytail, loose strands escaping, damp at the temples like she's been moving hard and sweating.

Jealousy flares instantly, sharp and irrational.

"Where have you been?" I growl, opening the door further to let her slip inside.

She arches a perfectly shaped brow. Talking is not generally something we do. "Not that it's any of your business," she says coolly, slipping past me, "but I was at dance class." She kicks the door shut behind her, and then tugs her top over her head and lets it fall to the floor without looking at me.

"If you want this," she adds lightly, glancing back at me over her shoulder, "we're doing it in the shower. I'm not sitting around in sweat."

Heat fills my veins, and I follow her to the bathroom. We've both been to each other's apartments enough that we know our way around them. I grab the end of her ponytail, wrapping it around my hand and pulling her back to me. I inhale along her throat, filling my lungs with her. There's sweat there, yes, but underneath it is the orange creamsicle scent I'm obsessed with. Fuck. It's closer to the surface than it's ever been before.

"Maybe I want you sweaty," I rasp in her ear, cupping one of her breasts in my other hand. I gently tug and roll her nipple between my fingers, and she gasps, melting back into my touch briefly before shaking her head like she's trying to make herself focus. She wiggles out of my arms and shimmies out of her shoes and sweats, leaving her in the simplest black thong I've ever seen her in.

Ava in fancy, high-end lingerie always sets my blood aflame, but for some reason, seeing her in sweats and cotton underwear has me half-feral.

I tug my clothes off as she turns on the shower and steps inside. She barely has a chance to get under the spray of hot water before I have her pressed to the wall. My alpha is livid that her scent is already being washed away.

I press my mouth to hers, devouring the taste of her. She makes a tiny, needy sound low in her throat, sweeping her tongue against mine.

This woman does things to me I cannot describe.

I grip the round globes of her ass with both hands, giving them a firm squeeze before sliding my palms to her thighs and picking her up. I press her back to the wall of the shower, smirking at the hiss she makes when her skin hits the cold tile. She quickly forgets it though, as I slam myself inside her with one thrust.

"Fuck, Mark," she moans against my mouth.

My hips set a deep, brutal rhythm as I take out all the emotions I've been feeling on her body.

“I’m going to fuck you until I’ve had my fill,” I growl into her ear. “Then I’ll clean you up and take you to my bed, where I’m going to devour you until you beg me for mercy because you can’t take another orgasm. And then I’m going to keep going.”

I can’t let go of her ass to work her clit like I want to without risking injury to us both, so instead, I hike one of her thighs higher. “Put your fucking leg on my shoulder, Ava,” I say, knowing she’s flexible enough. One rare occasion when she’d been feeling mildly chatty, she’d told me about her ballet and dance background.

She whimpers, but does as she’s told, and the change in angle puts me deeper while rubbing her clit against my pelvic bone. She half-sobs in pleasure as I keep up my relentless pace. I feel her flutter around my cock, and I can tell she’s close.

“Come for me, baby, I’ve got you,” I whisper hotly against her mouth. Orange and cream floods my nose, and the dangerous fog of a rut closes in at the edges of my consciousness. I manage to stay in control and focus on nothing but the woman in my arms.

11

Ava

The fact that I have spent the last several minutes scanning this ballroom for a glimpse of Mark feels like the worst kind of betrayal. Et tu, brain?

My pulse stutters every time I spot a broad-shouldered, dark-haired alpha in a tux, only for him to turn, or for me to catch a trace of his scent and realize he's not the one I want him to be. I am officially suffering from the most advanced case of dumb-bitchitis in recorded history.

My date drones on about load-bearing walls and tensile stress, his nasally voice grating along my nerves. I nod mechanically, making a half-hearted sound of interest that I hope doesn't show my boredom.

I'm not even sure why I agreed to go on this date. Not that he isn't attractive. He is. He's tall and lean, with a chiseled jaw and dimples that would probably make most girls melt. Just like his looks, his smell is fine, a muted scent of sandalwood mixed with bergamot. It's just... wrong, and it annoys me.

Every man I've tried to go on a date with for the last year has smelled wrong, even before Mark and I started sleeping together, and it's becoming harder and harder to pretend I don't know why.

My fingers curl around the flute of champagne as I take the last sip. The bubbles pop on my tongue, making my mouth practically tingle. I flag down a waiter and swap out my glass with a new one. I don't particularly want more alcohol; I just need something to keep my hands occupied.

Samuel, my date, frowns at my new glass. "You know, it's kind of a turn-off when women drink too much."

I cock my head to the side, eyes narrowing as anger rises within me. This is only my second glass, and I haven't even started drinking it yet. Meanwhile, he's easily on his fourth. Did he really just say that to me?

"Good fucking thing I'm not trying to turn you on then," I say coldly.

He blinks his eyes in surprise, clearly not used to pushback from the women in his life. Apparently, he wasn't aware of who I am. It isn't like I got the viper moniker because of my propensity for snakeskin.

I tip my glass back and swallow the champagne in one gulp, keeping my eyes locked on his before turning away from him.

"Ava—"

I brush past him without another glance, head held high and my heels clicking loudly on the marble floor. This date is officially over.

The night has been a complete waste from the very start. The only redeeming factor is how good I look in this Armani Privé dress, and the one person I actually care about seeing it doesn't appear to be showing up.

I frown at my thought. I don't care if Mark sees me in this dress. What a stupid thing to think.

"Ms. Kendrick." A hand touches my arm lightly, distracting me from the chaos in my head. I turn to find Senator Whitaker, his wife beside him in a floor-length black gown with an obscenely large diamond necklace at her throat. "We were just talking about the McKenna trial. Brutal cross-examination. I believe you and Mr. Taylor are better than any pay-per-view fight."

I flash a smooth, practiced smile. "The evidence just wasn't strong enough to convict. It doesn't matter how good the district attorney is, he can't out-lawyer poor police work."

"Oh, don't be modest," Mrs. Whitaker purrs. "We watched every night on NYTV. You had that jury eating out of the palm of your hand."

"Oh, I assure you, modesty is not something I'm known for," I laugh. "Mr. Taylor is one of the few attorneys that actually stand a chance against me. Now, that isn't to say that I *like* the man, but I respect a good adversary."

An image of Mark's head between my thighs flashes through my mind, making my cheeks flush. *Liar*, my omega whispers.

"You know," the senator says, drawing out the last syllable, "you have enough star power to make a run for office yourself. Especially with your family's connections."

"I have never seriously considered it," I admit. "My priority is improving omega rights."

"You should reconsider," he says smoothly. "If you want to make real, lasting change, sometimes you have to work from inside the house." He reaches into his tuxedo jacket and offers me a business card. "If you ever have questions, give me a call. I support what you are trying to do, Ms. Kendrick."

He turns, smiling fondly at his wife. "Some of us recognize that omegas are actually the most important people in our society."

I smile, a genuine one, as the couple walks away from me.

A waiter walks by with a tray of hors d'oeuvres balanced on mother-of-pearl spoons, and my stomach grumbles. I chew on my lip, debating. They look heavy, and I'm already drinking empty calories, so I decide against it, even though that decision makes an internal alarm bell go off in my mind. I'm aware that I'm not making healthy choices, but I can't seem to stop myself.

I snag another glass of champagne off a tray from a different waiter and swallow a healthy mouthful. My mood requires more alcohol than I'd normally indulge in. Crabby, restless, and, if I'm being honest, more than a little lonely.

I'm tired of dates that go nowhere and not being able to let anyone in. I'm tired of the only relationship in my life that feels real being with someone I hate and can't be with. I've tried so many times to stop this thing with Mark. A corner alcove near a large window overlooking the river is calling my name, and I head that direction with my glass and thoughts.

At our last session, my therapist told me that at some point, I had to accept that my omega will not let me walk away from him, and to make peace with it. She's of the opinion that I tell him the truth, or at least, I think she is. She has that infuriating habit therapists have of never coming right out and telling you what they think, instead just making you circle it on your own.

Drinking on an empty stomach is a recipe for disaster, but I've been whipping up a lot of those lately, haven't I?

Maybe I just want to float outside of reality for a little while. It isn't as though I'll be driving home. I can let loose a little. Right?

Three glasses become four. Faces blur one another—bankers, real estate moguls, socialites. They ask about my caseload, my family, whether I plan to join my father's firm or keep "slumming it" in defense work—never mind that I make more than my father does in tax law. I keep my replies short and to the point, or dismissive when they need to be. But every exchange is just another layer of noise over the dull throb beginning at my temples.

The smells in the ballroom are either growing more oppressive, or I'm becoming more sensitive as I get more intoxicated. Either way, my nose is in overdrive. Chilled champagne mixes with the sharp sweat of a newly bonded omega server. I'm honestly shocked his alpha let him out of the house already. The earthy musk of an alpha couple near the piano who are holding hands and getting progressively more turned on by each other. Over it all, the metallic tang of the scent neutralizers we all try to wear in the name of polite society.

I hate wearing mine. The only time I truly catch my scent anymore is when I'm in bed with Mark. My omega can almost break through with him sometimes. It's terrifying, but maybe that's why I can't stay away.

Thoughts of Mark's hands on my body and the way he pulls orgasm after orgasm out of me have my belly clenching in desire. If I could currently make slick, which thankfully, the high-powered suppressant I'm on prevents, it would be running down my thighs.

I shake my head, trying to rid myself of the images, which makes the room spin at the edges. I don't get to be a needy omega. Not in this world. Not ever.

"Ms. Kendrick!" Another voice calls me, and I school my expression before turning. It's a banking executive I recognize from other galas, Alastar Greene—a tall, silver-haired alpha who always reeks faintly of cigar smoke.

He grasps my hand, tugging on me in a way that sets my teeth on edge, as if he somehow has the right to lead me where he wants me to go. "We were just discussing some of your more controversial opinions on omega rights, and I thought, why not get it directly from the horse's mouth?"

I pull my hand out of his with a glower, barely keeping my lip from curling in disgust. "Controversial? Basic human decency is controversial now?"

He chuckles, low and condescending, and looks over at two nearby alphas, one of whom is openly leering at me. "See, boys, I told you she's a firecracker."

I laugh, matching his energy. "Does that usually work with impressing women? This whole," I gesture lazily, "negging thing you have happening right now?"

The leering alpha scoffs. "Relax. We're just having a little fun."

I look around dramatically. "Who is *we*? I'm not having fun, and it certainly doesn't appear that you three have the faintest idea how to make a woman have fun."

A few nearby guests go still, watching us with interest.

Greene forces a chuckle, though I can tell he's embarrassed. "Now, Ava, there's no need to get hostile."

"First of all, I did not give you permission to call me Ava," I say, tilting my head and giving him a wide, sickly sweet smile. "And if we want to talk about hostile, I think you inviting me over to mock my beliefs and leer at me like a piece of meat is far closer to the definition. I haven't even begun to get hostile; you'll know it when I do."

The leering alpha bristles. "You think you're better than us?"

I laugh so hard, I nearly cry. "Yes."

I spin on my heel and walk away, leaving him red-faced and angry, muttering "fucking bitch" loudly enough that I can still hear him. It's a risk, turning my back to an angry alpha, but we had enough attention on us that he won't do anything publicly. Still, it's probably my cue to leave the party so he doesn't have a chance to corner me alone.

I slip my phone from my clutch, and before I know it, I have my text conversation with Mark open. I haven't deleted it in a while, so the string of "come over" and "my place, 20 minutes" messages is a little embarrassing. My pulse skips, and my thumb hovers over the letters, trying to think of what I'd even say.

"I'm bored and just pissed off an alpha. Come get me"?

"I miss you"?

No. Absolutely not. With a decisive motion, I power the phone down and slide it back into my bag. Out of sight, out of temptation. I can have the front desk call Tony. The hotel's valets are used to drunk patrons stumbling out in designer heels.

I snag another glass of champagne and make my way toward the lobby.

I'm not going to text him.

I repeat it to myself over and over as everything around me gets blurry at the edges.

12

Mark

I rub the towel over my hair before hanging it up on the shower bar. I resist the urge to go into my bedroom and check my phone for the hundredth time. I'd gotten pissed at my lack of self-control earlier, so I'd thrown it on the charger and gone down to the gym on the lower floor of my apartment building to work out my frustration.

It's after midnight now. Ava clearly won't be reaching out, and I'm not prepared to be the one that breaks the silence. I've done so the last two times. My ego can't handle a third.

When I open the fridge, the cans of her favorite energy drink that I stashed in there a few days ago mock me, silently calling me a fucking loser. Jesus. It's no wonder she doesn't want me.

I'm not typically one to struggle with these kinds of feelings, and they make me angry all over again. I'm smart, handsome, well-off, and popular. So why does this one damn woman make me feel like something she found on the bottom of her heels because she doesn't want to do anything more than fuck me? Is it because she's part of New York City's upper crust and I'm just some hick from Missouri?

I slam the fridge door closed, making the items inside and on top of it rattle. I blow a breath out, shaking my head. I need to take my ass to bed. It's too late for a self-deprecating thought spiral over my situationship.

I'll just switch off the lights, lock the door, and then head to my room.

I pull the sheets back and slide beneath them, not bothering to put on any pajamas. I rarely do. One perk to living alone. Like most alphas, I run pretty hot. Settled in bed, I finally give in and grab my phone off the charger, the glow illuminating the dark room. Unsurprisingly, I have no new texts.

I click through a few different apps, mindlessly scrolling, before finally opening the dating app I keep deleting and reactivating. I scroll through a few profiles, mostly swiping left on ones I'm not interested in. There are some that I swipe right on, but I feel my stomach drop when I get the alert that one of them is a match.

Probably not the response you should have when matching with a beautiful woman on a dating app.

Her name is Marnie, and she's a 27-year-old omega. Which I wish I had noticed before I swiped on her. I don't typically date omegas.

Her message pops up before I can even back out of the match.

"Hi Mark "

That stupid little face makes something feel funny in my chest. Friendly. Harmless. Which it should be. Just two people flirting on a dating app. An omega and an alpha, as natural as it gets. Only it's never felt that way to me. I don't like their scents. They always seem almost... sticky.

I shut my eyes, the ghost of Ava's scent sliding into my memory without permission. God, if I could find an omega that made me respond the way that Ava's elusive creamsicle scent does, I'd bond with her in an instant.

Maybe I should give Marnie a shot. What if her scent is finally one I like?

I type back.

"Hi Marnie. I'm about to head to bed, but would love to chat tomorrow?"

And then, just to match her, I send a second message of a smiley face. Like an idiot.

I groan and back out of the chat window, setting the phone face-down on my nightstand. My chest rises and falls like I just finished another round at the gym. It's just a stupid message on a dating app. Ava and I are not exclusive, and we need to end this thing.

So why do I feel like I'm cheating?

I should be thinking about my upcoming cases. I have another round with Ava in the heiress case, and then opening arguments against a different defense attorney. I'll rip that person to shreds, so I'm honestly not overly concerned about it, but that's not the point.

My phone dings, and even though I know it's almost certainly a response from Marnie, I still snatch it up quickly.

"Sweet dreams!"

I shove both hands into my hair and sit up, restless.

Just then, I hear the telltale sound of the front door keypad beeping quietly from someone entering the code, followed by the sound of the lock turning. Only three people know the code to my front door: my sister, my housecleaner, and Ava.

Given the time of night, I know which one is most likely. Sure enough, I hear the sound of heels on my hardwood, then a soft *oomph* as if she ran into the hallway table. She giggles softly, and a wolfish grin splits my face.

Is Ava Kendrick a little tipsy?

My door opens, and she's there, backlit by the light above the stove in the kitchen like some kind of angel. I reach over and flip on the lamp, taking her in. Her dress, if you can call it that, looks like she has nothing but gems pasted to her body. The underlining matches her skin tone perfectly, and it's so sheer, I can see the tiny scrap of jeweled thong that barely covers the mound of her pussy.

My mouth practically waters, even as possessive jealousy tears through me. The idea that other men got to see her in that outfit makes my fists clench. "Ava, what the hell?"

She giggles again and grips the skirt of the dress at her hips, shimmying it up until she can pull it over her head and toss it to the floor. She kicks out of her heels, sending each one flying in a different direction across my bedroom. One crashes into my dresser, sending one of my watches toppling to the floor.

"Oopsie," Ava says, her mouth pouting outward and her eyes widening. "Don't be mad. I'll buy you a new watch if it's broken. I'll buy you whatever you want." Her words are slurred, and I'm quickly realizing she passed *tipsy* quite a while back.

She crawls on the bed, straddling my hips. Her scent is the pleasant, muted orange it normally is, but it's closer to the smell of a mimosa now. Oranges layered with the sharp sweetness of champagne.

"You get a little wasted at whatever fancy party you were at tonight?" I ask, allowing myself the liberty of sliding my hands onto her hips. I already know I won't let it go further; she can't consent in this state. Her skin is silky smooth beneath my palm, contrasted by the sharp bite of the gems lining her thong.

This is going to be hard. I certainly am.

"It was boooooring. My date said it was a turn-off to see a woman drinking. So I drank more." She giggles and runs her fingers down my chest.

I snort. That definitely sounds like my cereus.

The word slips into my mind before I can stop it, and I sigh. I'd coined the nickname in my head for her weeks ago, though I'll never speak it aloud. It's a genus of cactus, one of those random facts from a long-ago biology class that somehow stuck with me. They bloom at night. Rarely seen but breathtaking, if one is fortunate enough to view it, and there couldn't be a better metaphor for the woman on my lap.

She grasps my hands and pulls them so they are cupping her breasts before she reaches up and tugs her hair free from the sleek bun, forcing me to swallow and remind myself that I'm a gentleman. If she were sober, I'd already be inside her.

As it stands, I'm grateful the blanket is still trapped between us, keeping my cock from its preferred location, though she seems determined to rectify that.

"Maaaark. Gimme," she whines. With any other person in the world, I'd have called that an omega whine. My alpha responds like it is. The urge to give her whatever she wants, particularly if it includes my bite, fills me so quickly, it makes my teeth ache.

"No can do, little viper. I make it a point to only take consenting women to my bed, and you are not in any shape to do that right now." I release her breasts and wrap my arms around her back, tugging her down beside me.

Ava pouts and strokes her fingernails over my bare chest and my abs. "I know you want me. I can feel how hard you are."

I catch her wrist before she can slide it under the blanket and touch my cock. "I always want you, Ava," I say earnestly.

"You're like a fucking drug. But right now, I think we're just gonna cuddle for a bit. Let you sober up some, maybe then we can play, yeah?"

I know she'll pass out long before that happens, but it seems to appease her, and she curls into my side. She tosses one long, lean leg over my hips.

"I was sad you weren't there. And then I was mad I was sad," she whispers, her voice getting husky and sleepy as she starts to relax.

I smirk. "I'm sad I wasn't there too. That dress was wasted on anyone but me, and maybe I could have stopped you a few glasses of champagne earlier."

"Mmmmm... pulled me into a closet like we do at the courthouse sometimes." Her eyes start to drift closed, and I let myself press a gentle kiss to her temple.

"I would have. You're beautiful and I can't seem to resist you," I respond quietly.

She doesn't say anything, and a brief moment of listening confirms my suspicion. Her breathing has slowed and become regular. My little cereus is sound asleep.

I sigh, turning on my side so I can face her. I shift her leg enough to pull the blankets up over her body. I'll move her to the guest room soon. I could lie to myself and say that I want the extra time to make sure she's well and truly asleep, but I know it's because I want to soak this up as much as I can. She'll put her walls higher than ever in the morning, ashamed of letting me see her this vulnerable, and she'll bolt. So for now, I'm going to pretend a little longer.

13

Ava

It feels like someone has wedged a jackhammer between my temples. I grimace and attempt to sit up, immediately regretting that choice as a sour wave of nausea rolls through me as the room tilts and spins.

"Oh, fuck," I whine, squeezing my eyes shut and turning to bury my face into my pillow.

Only, it isn't my pillow. The bedding is soft, but not my silk blend, and the mattress is smaller and firmer than mine at home. I inhale quickly, realizing that the room smells a little dusty, like it isn't frequently used.

Panic claws the inside of my ribs, making it feel as though my lungs are in a vise. My breath comes in short bursts as I push myself upright too fast, vertigo knocking the air from me. My heart thunders as I try to make my brain put the pieces together.

I don't know where I am.

I don't know *what happened*.

The uncertainty drags me into a flashback, and suddenly I'm back in the clinic during my last heat. The sharp, metallic burn of the synthetic spray in my nostrils that made my eyes water as it kicked in. Normally, it tricks your omega into compliance to ensure that the assigned alpha is a compatible match.

Except this time, it didn't. The man in the room with me reeked of cloves and the chemical suppressant, and my omega had responded in kind. He'd smelled *wrong*.

The memory of his scent floods my nose as my present situation blends in my head with the memories from that day. I'd been lucid enough to tell him no, a rarity during a heat, but he hadn't stopped. And the guards that were supposed to be paying attention to ensure that sort of thing didn't happen had taken far too long to intervene. Bile licks up my throat as I remember the feel of his hands on my skin.

I squeeze my eyes shut, nails biting into my palms as I fight to separate then from now. *It's not the clinic. It's not the same. You're not there. You're not there.*

My body doesn't believe me. My omega is shrieking inside me that I need to run. Find the alpha whose scent reminds me of the old leather-bound law books in my father's study.

My throat is tight, lungs refusing to pull in enough air. I go through the steps my therapist taught me to calm a panic attack.

Five things I can see, four things I can touch, etc. It's only when I get to the things I can smell that my omega calms, because I *can* smell him. Leather and bourbon surrounds me.

Mark.

Relief floods me so hard, it's almost painful. A glance down makes me realize that I'm wearing an old UCLA sweatshirt that is comically oversized on me. If the panic hadn't gripped me so quickly, I would have realized exactly where I was.

Shame quickly replaces the relief. Because if I'm here in his apartment, then I didn't resist the urge to see him. Which is its own sort of panic. How had I gotten here? Tony wouldn't have left me anywhere if I was that wasted. Oh god, and what kind of things had I said?

I frown as I look around the room and swing my legs over the edge of the bed. There's no familiar twinge between my thighs to indicate that we had sex. He'd obviously put me in here to sleep it off, but why?

As soon as I ponder the question, I already know the answer. He wouldn't have. Not when I was drunk. Gratitude makes tears fill my eyes, and I rub angrily at them with my palm. Goddamn him for being such a good man. It makes it so hard to keep up the hate that I'm trying to cling to.

I spy my purse on the dresser across from me, and beside it, my phone. He even put it on a charger for me.

I groan, throwing myself back on the pillows and covering my face with my arm.

I'm not ready to face him. He's already been so sweet with how he's handled this, and I'm feeling incredibly vulnerable and uncomfortable. Mainly because I want to give in to it and him so badly. I can see it in my head—how easy it would be to find him wherever he is in the apartment and wrap my arms around his middle, lean my head against his back. How I could whine about feeling like shit and he'd take care of me.

He'd tease me mercilessly, but he'd still do it.

I stay like that for a while, letting my heart and breathing settle as I try to think of what to say to him. I wonder if I'm lucky enough that he's still asleep.

Eventually, my bladder forces my hand, and I slip from the bed, trying to silently ease open the door of the guest room I'm in. Of course, being in an old building in New York, it groans on its hinges, making me wince. I dash for the bathroom.

I think I hear a suppressed chuckle from the area of the kitchen, and my cheeks flame. So much for my hopes that he would still be asleep.

As I'm washing my hands, I notice the new toothbrush and tube of toothpaste sitting on the small shelf. They're the small sample kind you get from the dentist in the little baggie after a cleaning, but the fact that he thought to set them out for me makes tears well in my eyes. Jesus Christ. This man cannot be real.

I brush my teeth quickly, look in the mirror, and take a deep breath. I look like a hot mess, of course. One thing he hadn't done was take off my makeup. I appear to have lost one of my strip lashes, and dark rings of smudged mascara sit beneath both eyes. I grimace and remove the other lash so at least I match, and I glance around the bathroom until I find a small bottle of face wash. It's some kind of foaming action for oily skin, and it's going to dry me out something fierce, but at least I won't look so awful. I quickly double-cleanse my face, patting dry with a hand towel. Thankfully, Mark has dark ones that won't stain.

Out of things to do to stall, I throw back my shoulders and prepare myself to exit the bathroom. "Come on, Ava. You can do this," I whisper to myself. I've never backed down from a challenge before; I'm not going to start now.

I open the bathroom door and walk into the kitchen. Mark has his back to me, pushing around what smells like eggs in a skillet with a spatula. He's wearing a pair of loose pajama pants, and they are slung low on his hips.

I tell myself that my mouth is only watering because I haven't eaten in way too long.

"Morning, Ava," he says over his shoulder. Did he hear me coming, or did he scent me?

Shit. I don't think I have any neutralizer with me. Or my suppressants.

The clawing urge to bolt is nearly overwhelming, to get out before he can figure out my secret. But he's been so kind. I can't do that to him.

"Good morning," I say quietly. "Did I make too much of an ass of myself?" I ask, figuring it's better to rip the Band-Aid off and address the elephant in the room. Besides, this will test how he plans to respond. Is he going to continue to be nice, or start a fight because we don't know how else to interact with each other?

"Nah," he answers. He turns the burner off and slides the eggs out onto two plates. "You made it fairly clear what you wanted, but it's not really my style. Once I distracted you from my overwhelming masculine charms, you fell asleep pretty quickly."

I swallow, a little unsure of how to respond. I think I'd been mentally prepared to fight, so now I'm frozen. As I take my plate from him, our fingers brush, and it's like I can feel all the awareness of my body pinpoint on the contact. It makes me jerk back slightly, and I nearly drop the eggs.

Smooth, Ava. Real smooth. Acting like a skittish virgin when I've been actively having sex with this man for nearly two months. Hell, I've fucked him on this very island.

We've never shared breakfast, though, so this feels like a whole new world.

We move over to the table, and I sink into the chair opposite him, acutely aware of how his sweatshirt smells like him every time I breathe in. My stomach is still queasy, but his scent and the smell of food make it more tolerable.

"You didn't have to cook," I mutter, stabbing at my food. I frown, not liking how small my voice sounds, and I clear my throat. "I could have just grabbed something on the way home."

Mark shrugs one broad shoulder, completely unbothered. "I was hungry, and I figured you would be too. You probably didn't eat much at whatever fancy party you were at."

I freeze, fork halfway to my mouth. "Why would you think that?" For a split second, I wonder if he knows about my issues with food, but that doesn't make any sense. And besides, it's not something I'm ashamed of. I worked damn hard for my recovery. No, I'm just on edge.

He smirks, tearing a piece of toast in half. "In my experience, people don't typically get quite *that* wasted unless they don't have much in their stomachs."

Oh. Right.

I snag my own piece of toast, nibbling on the edges of it after slathering it with the strawberry jelly he has on the table. I might have issues with food that I'll likely fight in some form or another for the rest of my life, but I'm still an omega. We adore sweets.

I glance at his cup of coffee and realize I'm fairly thirsty. "Is it okay if I get something to drink?"

"Shit, sorry. I meant to tell you that before you sat down. There are some energy drinks in the fridge." He starts to stand, and I put a hand up to stop him. He's already done enough; I don't think I can handle much more.

I walk to the fridge and pull the door open. Neatly lined up along one side are several cans of my favorite peach-melon energy drink. My pulse speeds up. Surely it's a coincidence, right? Maybe he also just happens to like them.

Except I've never seen Mark with anything but coffee, water, or whiskey.

My cheeks burn, and I snag one before returning to my chair. I can't bring myself to look at him. I feel exposed at the same time as my omega is practically preening that he's paid enough attention to know what we like. Like we matter to him outside the bedroom.

We eat in silence for a few minutes, the clink of silverware against the plates loud in the small space. Sunlight streams through the windows, catching the dancing dust motes in the air. It feels blissfully comfortable. Like I could see myself doing this for the rest of my life.

I have to dig my nails into my thigh with the hand not holding my fork to try and drown out my omega's screams.

Just. Tell. Him.

I clear my throat. "Thank you for being so kind. It was... unexpected."

"I'm actually a pretty nice guy, Ava," he says quietly. "You'd know that if you'd actually talk to me every now and again. We could be friends."

I can practically feel the tension rolling off his frame. His scent has gone slightly bitter at the edges. I know he's trying very hard not to spook me.

I hate that he recognizes how easily that could be done. If only he understood why.

"Friends usually like each other," I say. It could be taken as me trying to start a fight, but my voice is smaller than I had intended, and I just sound sad. I dare to sneak a glance at his face from beneath my lashes.

He pauses, obviously chewing on my words as he sips his coffee. "I think there's a chance we could like each other a lot if we'd try."

I squeeze my eyes shut, feeling as if the air is being sucked from the room. "Mark, don't. Please," I practically beg. Because if he keeps pushing it, I'm going to break. I'm going to crawl across this table and press my face into his throat and beg him to take care of me.

He sighs, leaning back in his chair. "Okay. It's far enough for now. But we need to have this conversation eventually, Ava. We've put it off for too long."

I nod. "Okay. I promise." I know he's right. He's been letting me take the lead this whole time, no matter how I've buried my head in the sand. I can't keep doing that. Even if the talk is just me telling him that I can't be the woman he wants me to be. That I can't *do* this. No matter how badly I want to.

Not now, though. I'm hungover, off-kilter, and on his turf. Everything feels raw and exposed, not at all helped by my earlier panic attack.

He seems content with my agreement, and we finish breakfast.

I help him clean up silently. I should be getting out of here as quickly as possible, but I can't seem to bring myself to do so. If this is the last time we'll be around each other before we have our big situationship-ending discussion, I want to enjoy it while I can.

"Can I keep the shirt?" I ask suddenly, surprising myself. "I mean... just to wear out of here. I don't really want to do the walk of shame in a designer gown," I clarify quickly. Though, if I'm honest, I'm going to conveniently forget to return it. It's definitely going into my nest.

"Of course. You looked stunning in that dress, by the way," he says. His scent shifts to how it is when he's feeling jealous—something I'm quite familiar with, since it's my favorite way to annoy him. It's occasionally backfired on me quite spectacularly, like the time he interrupted one of my dates after I'd pushed a little too far.

I catch my bottom lip with my teeth, my pussy suddenly aching as I remember it, gluttonous traitor that she is. He'd made up some bullshit excuse about needing to speak with me about a time-sensitive plea deal, and once I'd stepped away from my date, he'd tugged me into the alley and fucked me hard and fast against the brick wall. "Enjoy the rest of your date," he'd growled. Then he'd just left me there... panting and shocked after he'd pulled my panties back up, his release still dripping out of me.

Mark's head snaps up, pupils blown, and I am reminded that I do not have suppressants or my scent neutralizer. Shit. My scent must be intensifying. If I'm not careful, I'm going to start producing slick.

Stupid. I am a stupid, stupid omega. I need to get out of here.

"I know that look, but I have to go soon," I tease lightly, moving to put distance between us. "Tony is probably going to murder me for not having him drive me here last night."

"He's already downstairs," Mark says, his voice huskier than normal. "He buzzed up earlier to tell me he'd be ready whenever you are. So it doesn't seem like there's much of a rush." He prowls toward me, a predator stalking his prey.

I take another step back. If he touches me, I'm done for. I'll climb him like a fucking tree, consequences be damned.

"Even more reason I should go. He doesn't need to be sitting out there in the daytime. Someone could recognize him as my driver, and we don't need the press catching wind that I'm in your apartment," I say with my hands up. It's a flimsy, bullshit excuse, and I'm perfectly aware that he knows it as well as I do.

Mark purses his lips and looks like he's about to argue, but I bolt for the spare room before he gets a chance. I quickly gather my things. When I emerge, he's standing in the same spot.

I start to turn the handle on the front door, but turn back to thank him one more time for being so kind and chivalrous. Except he grabs my arm and spins me into him. His mouth captures mine, and I melt against him. It's the same level of passion we always have, but it somehow feels different. There's no anger or fighting for dominance. It's thorough and filled with the promise of more later on.

He pulls back finally, leaning his forehead against mine, both of us breathing hard. "Best get home, little viper. We'll finish this conversation later."

Dazed, I nod and head out of his apartment, fingers pressed against my lips.

What the hell just happened?

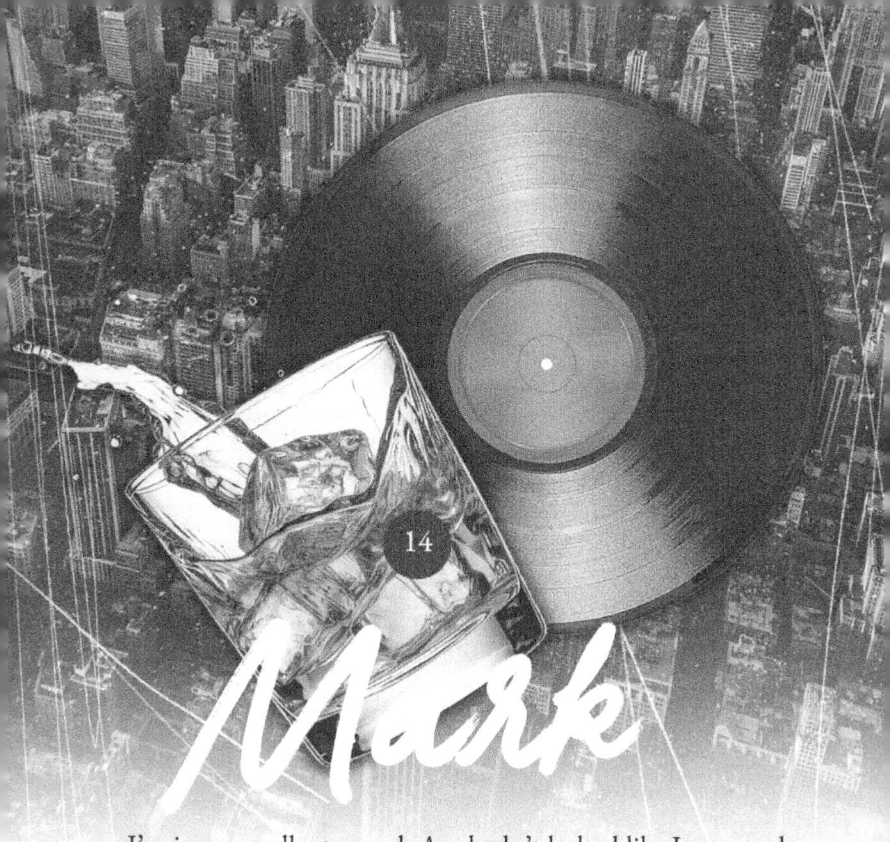

14

Mark

I'm in an excellent mood. Ava hadn't bolted like I expected her to. She'd clearly wanted to; I could see it in the coiled tension in her body. Yet she'd stayed and eaten breakfast with me, like we were two normal adults. I'd even seen some cracks in her armor.

And god, that kiss before she'd left. My pulse skips just thinking about it. I can practically still taste her on my lips. She'd melted into me, and it had taken every ounce of self-control I possessed to push away.

For the first time in too damn long, I feel hopeful. So, I don't want to push her too hard. Overplay my hand, if you will. I'm going to give her some space, not text her today, and possibly not tomorrow. I'll talk to her on Monday at court. Maybe I can take her to lunch.

Satisfied with my plan, I open my phone intending to text Adam, my best friend. He's a reporter that works on a lot of criminal cases, and we'd become close when I first moved to the city and started in the DA's office.

Notifications from the dating app pop up first, and I sigh. Right. Marnie. I should tell her I'm not going to pursue anything with her. Whatever this thing with Ava is, it's too complicated to drag anyone else into.

Before I get a chance, my phone rings, and Adam's contact picture—an obscene close-up of his nostrils—flashes across my screen as if I'd summoned him.

"How did you know I was thinking of you?" I ask with a grin.

"Bro, I hate to break it to you this way, but I don't think of you like that," he quips dryly.

I roll my eyes. "What do you want?"

"I'm bored as hell," he says, "and since you don't have a life, I figured you are too."

"Excuse you. I have a life," I say, balancing my phone between my jaw and shoulder as I let myself into the guest room and lie on the bed. Ava's scent, stronger than normal, surrounds me, and I have the strongest urge to roll around in it. "I just... don't have anything going on at the moment," I add.

He snorts. "When's the last time you got laid? I never see you out with anyone."

"First of all, you can have a life without copious amounts of random sex. Secondly, you don't have to go out to get laid. I promise, I do just fine," I say smugly. "So did you just call to talk shit, or did you actually want something?"

"There's an ice hockey pick-up league this afternoon at Chelsea Piers Sky Rink. It's a no-commitment thing. Thought it might be fun."

I chew on the inside of my cheek, debating. "I don't have any gear."

"They rent gear. Quit being a crybaby. What the hell else are you doing?"

I hesitate, which is basically admitting he's right. Ava almost certainly won't reach out today, and I promised myself I wouldn't either. Which leaves a whole lot of nothing other than work. "All right, fine, I'm in. What time?"

He makes an excited whoop. "Hell yeah. 4:00 p.m. But don't embarrass me out there, tiger."

I scoff. "Of the two of us, methinks the guy with the bum knee should probably watch his fucking mouth."

Adam just laughs and, in his typical fashion, hangs up without saying goodbye.

The lobby of the rink is decorated in so much Americana theming, it almost hurts to look at. The walls are covered in horizontal pinstripes of red and white, while the floors and ceilings are done in a deep blue. I spot Adam near the concession stand, studying the glass case of pastries, candies, and bottled drinks. Grinning, I slide up beside him.

"I feel like stuffing your mouth full of carbs before ice skating is not the vibe," I say. "What if you barf?"

He laughs and elbows me in the side. "Shut up. I'm getting water."

We head to the rental window, where a bored teenager leans against the counter, barely lifting his eyes from his phone. I ask where we need to go for the ice hockey league.

"West Rink," he says, "but it's rented for another fifteen minutes for private use. You can go inside, just stay on the chairs outside the rink until the lady is done."

I glance at Adam. "One lady rented the entire rink for herself?"

He shrugs. "New York, man. Some people have too much damn money."

We push through the door, the chill hitting me harder than I expected. Inside, a handful of what I assume are players from the league are already gathered in the bleachers. Some are chatting, some are lacing skates, and a few are quietly watching the ice. I start toward a guy holding a clipboard, figuring he is the one we need to talk to about the actual hockey equipment.

"Holy shit," Adam says, leaning on the railing. "Is that the viper?"

The distraction pulls me off course. I turn to follow his gaze, my stomach dropping and my heart stuttering.

Sure enough, cutting across the ice is Ava. Her hair is slicked back and pulled into a tight bun. She's wearing some kind of skintight black unitard. She looks completely at ease on the ice, the lines of her body graceful as she moves, which I suppose makes sense. I know she used to do ballet a lot as a kid; I'd gotten that much out of her in the past. Ice skating seems like a natural sort of progression.

"Certainly appears that way," I say quietly, moving closer to the edge of the rink, unable to tear my eyes away from her.

The song over the loudspeakers switches, and it is popular enough that even an '80s rock guy like me recognizes it. It blew up on social media after the blonde pop princess who sings it dropped her latest album. The track is slow and emotional, built around lyrics about wanting to rewrite fate, wishing for a different outcome, and asking the universe for a chance to be loved.

Adam whistles low. "Guess she's got more hobbies than making people cry on the witness stand."

I ignore him, watching as she starts to gather speed. I can feel his eyes on my face, and I know I'm probably giving far too much away, but I can't seem to break the spell. How many times have I wished for a chance to crack her shell open and see what she's feeling? And now it's laid out in front of me, her heart laid bare on the ice.

She spins once, twice, her body held so tightly that it's like she's flying. When she stops, her chest heaves almost like she's holding back a scream. She skates backwards, and even from a distance, I can see that her eyes are closed. I understand why she wanted the rink to herself now. A chance to work out her emotions through the music without risking running into anyone.

She launches into the air again, twisting once before she lands, her knees bending to catch herself. I don't know what it's called, but the image it brings to my mind is of someone throwing their whole body into trying to break free.

The music builds, and so does she. Her strides are longer, cutting across the rink in bold, sweeping arcs. She skids to a stop in the middle, dropping to her knees, head bowed. She twists and moves her body, the ballet background clearly on display. Her back arches and her fingers extend, every motion graceful and controlled.

Yet, it also *isn't* controlled. Not really. I get the feeling she's fighting herself. The movements are sharp one moment, melting in the next. She rises and skates backward again, fast enough that I'm sure she's going to crash into the boards, but she skids to a stop only an inch away from them. She throws her head back, hands clutched to her chest.

As the music builds to its crescendo, she pushes off again, faster this time, carving sharp lines across the ice before catching the blade of one skate, leg lifting high as her body spins like a tornado. When she finally releases, the spin spits her forward, and she lands hard, the slap of steel on ice echoing through the empty arena. She staggers a half step before finding herself again.

The fight inside her is so obvious. Maybe not to everyone else. But I know this woman's body like the back of my hand. The way her jaw clenches and her fingers curl and uncurl into fists. What is she fighting exactly? Herself? Me?

My mouth is dry and my knuckles are white as I grip the handrail along the wall of the rink. This feels important, like she's coming to terms with something that will affect us, whatever *us* there is.

By the time the last note fades, she's in the center of the rink again, bent forward with one hand pressed to the ice and the other curled tight against her chest. Her shoulders tremble as she stays like that, motionless, long after the song has ended.

And then, slowly, she straightens. Her eyes sweep the rink as though she's pulling herself back together, but she's more relaxed than she usually looks in public. Until they land on me.

It feels like getting caught with my hand in the damn cookie jar. Like I've intruded on something sacred, something not meant for my eyes.

Her lips part slightly, surprise flickering across her face, but the corners of her mouth tip upward in the beginnings of a soft smile. For one dizzy second, I think she's going to let me in.

And then Adam laughs. "Damn, I thought vipers were supposed to be cold-blooded. Since when does New York's scariest defense attorney spin around like a wannabe ballerina?"

The dismissive way he says *ballerina* lands wrong. Ava's expression shutters instantly, the softness vanishing like it never existed. By the time she skates toward us, her face is carved from marble.

"Enjoy the show, boys?" she asks, her voice edged with disdain.

Adam smirks, oblivious to the shift he caused. Or maybe he isn't. Is he doing this on purpose? "Definitely unexpected. Never would have pictured you in sequins. Guess the viper's got layers."

Her gaze slides to me, and it feels like staring at a stranger. Not the woman who sat across from me just a few hours ago in my old college sweatshirt.

"Enjoy hockey, counselor," she says lightly. "Try not to injure yourself. I would hate to win on a technicality if you cannot make it to court." Her smile is colder than the ice she stands on. And just like that, I know she's gone. Whatever fragile progress I made this morning shattered the second Adam opened his mouth.

She turns and walks away, and without sparing Adam a glance, I follow her.

I reach for her arm. "Ava, wait—"

"For what?" She yanks it away from me. "Go back to your friend. I'll see you in court."

I drop my hand away, and she glances at it. For the briefest moment, I think I see a flash of regret and sadness. It's gone so quickly that I think I might have imagined it. At this point, I probably did.

Anger at her and at myself wells within me. "Right. See you in court, Ms. Kendrick," I hiss.

The low thrum of conversation mixes with the clink of pint glasses and the faint smell of fried food. My muscles ache pleasantly from the skate, but I can't think of anything but Ava. To say I'm distracted would be an understatement.

Adam takes a long drink of his beer before side-eyeing me. "All right, spill it. You've been in your head since before we hit the ice. And don't give me some bullshit 'I'm just tired' excuse. What's going on?"

I hesitate, my thumb tracing my glass. I know I shouldn't talk about it. But goddamn, I'm tired of holding onto this secret. And whatever we had is probably already over anyway. "It's... complicated," I say at last, keeping my eyes on the table.

"Yeah, no shit," he says with a dry snort. "I picked up on that."

"I have been sort of seeing someone for a while," I say quietly, "and it's messy. I want more than I think she can give me."

Adam lets out a long breath and scrubs a hand over his jaw. "I've got a bad feeling you're about to say it's the viper. And surely—*surely*—that's not what you're about to say, right?"

I don't answer, just sit there tearing my napkin into shreds.

"Shit." He leans back in his chair, flagging the waitress down with two fingers. "We're gonna need something stronger over here. Bourbon and triple sec for him, whiskey neat for me."

After she walks away, I finally lift my head to meet his eyes. "I've got it really goddamn bad for the viper," I admit.

He stares at me, then shakes his head in disbelief. "But... why? I mean, yeah, she's a smokeshow, but you two do nothing but fight. I've seen you at each other in court and at fundraisers. Hell, didn't you two almost come to blows over a sandwich at that deli by your office?"

I sigh. "What you haven't seen," I say, "are the decidedly non-fighting things we've been doing for the last six weeks or so when we're alone."

"*Six weeks*?!" Adam hisses, pitching forward. "You've been sleeping with Ava fucking Kendrick for months, and this is the first I'm hearing about it? I'd be impressed if I wasn't kind of hurt."

"Keep your goddamn voice down," I snap. He raises his hands in apology. "It's been exhausting keeping it quiet," I continue, "constantly worrying someone will find out and we'll end up in hot water with the bar. Or with Harvey. You know how he feels about her."

Adam grimaces. "I didn't even think about the bar. That'd be a big deal, right? Since you've tried so many cases against each other?"

"Yeah," I say with a nod. "Lose our licenses big. Especially if it looks like we hid it instead of recusing ourselves."

"So why not come clean?" he asks. "She could move to a different borough easily."

I blow out a slow breath. "Goddamn NYTV. I cannot pay for that kind of publicity if I want a real shot at Harvey's job."

He gives me a look. "Then why not just stop?"

I laugh humorlessly. "Don't you think I've tried?"

We sit quietly for a minute, staring into our drinks.

Finally, he clears his throat. "You gotta tell me. Like, it's gotta be top-shelf sex, right? With the way you two go at it in the courtroom? She looks like the type to fuck like she fights." He overdramatically waggles his eyebrows, successfully breaking the tension.

I shake my head, though a smile tugs at my lips. "You don't have a clue, brother. Liquid heroin straight to the heart is less of a high and less addictive than she is."

"Goddamn," he mutters. "No wonder you're twisted up."

"It's not just that, though," I say, swirling the liquid in my glass, watching the light reflect on the amber. "She challenges me. Every day. I'm never bored with Ava. She's infuriating and brilliant, sometimes in the same breath. I've never met a woman like her. Some nights she falls asleep beside me and I just... watch her. Like if I blink, I'll miss how that big, beautiful brain of hers works."

He studies me like he's never seen me before. "Jesus. You weren't kidding. You do have it bad. You sound like you're in love with her. Does she feel the same way?"

"Sometimes I think so. But she won't let me in. Every time I get close, she bolts. This morning, I thought we'd made a lot of progress, but then after you opened your big dumb mouth at the rink—" I shake my head. "What the hell was that about anyways? I expect some of the cops to give her shit like that, but you've never acted like that about her."

He grimaces and has the decency to look sheepish. "I don't know. I think I must have known on some level. You were looking at her like she hung the damn moon. And she's the viper. I was just reminding you how she can be, I think."

My jaw tightens and I give him a dirty look. "I didn't need that. I know who she is better than anyone. What she needed at that moment was for someone to see her for the woman underneath the mask."

"I'm sorry. It was kind of dickish." He scratches at his chin, lips pursed in thought. "So the question is, why is she running from you? She's single. You're a good guy. She keeps coming back, so she's clearly into you. She could take cases anywhere in the city, so what the hell is the problem?"

I rake a hand through my hair. "Hell if I know. Maybe somebody broke her heart. All I know is she keeps me out."

"Look," he says, pausing to take another sip from his drink, "maybe you need to give her a reason to figure it out. Or maybe you need to give yourself a reason to walk away. Start dating again."

"I don't know. It seems unfair to drag someone else into this shitshow."

"I'm not saying go out and propose to the first woman you meet. Get a couple good dinners. Maybe a nice makeout session. Just think about it."

I shrug. "Maybe."

We change the subject and keep drinking till we have a nice buzz going. The ride back to my apartment is quiet, the city flickering past the cab window in streaks of neon and headlights. By the time I unlock my door, I'm exhausted. But I can't get my mind to settle. All my thoughts are on Ava. Her on the ice. Her at my table, barefaced, and wearing my sweatshirt. Ava snapping at me like I was a stranger when Adam was watching.

I strip down, toss my clothes in the hamper, and head to the shower to wash off the day. I try to ignore the toothbrush and toothpaste I'd left sitting out for her on the sink. After I dry off, I drop onto the couch instead of heading to bed. My phone glows on the coffee table, and for a long moment, I just stare at it.

Adam's voice echoes in my head: *Give yourself a reason to walk away.*

With a curse, I grab it and swipe it open. The dating app is still there, a red notification dot on my inbox next to Marnie's name. I open her profile and look at her picture again. She's bright and smiling, with a sweet heart-shaped face and bouncy blonde curls. She looks like someone who probably bakes banana bread on Sundays and remembers everyone's birthday. Someone who is probably the exact opposite of Ava.

My thumb hovers over the screen, hesitating. Every instinct screams that this is unfair—I'll be comparing her to someone she can't possibly compete with. But Adam's right. If I don't at least try, I'll just be stuck in Ava's orbit forever.

So I type.

"Hey, sorry for passing out on you last night and just now responding. Let me make it up to you when you're free. How about meeting up for a coffee or drink sometime soon and getting to know each other?"

It's not long at all before my phone dings.

"That sounds great. What are you doing tomorrow?"

I have to think about how I want to respond. Is this really what I want? I think it is. Besides, she seems like a nice girl, and I've already set the wheels in motion. I can at least meet up with her for coffee.

"I don't have any plans. Would you wanna meet at Grindhouse around 5? Coffee and donuts? Or we can get something harder if that's your thing. Maybe go walking around after and take in the city some? I think it might be a good 'get to know you' atmosphere."

She responds quickly again. It's nice to have someone that seems like they might actually want to talk to me.

"Sounds great! I can be there earlier if you want. Just message me here when you get done with your day, and I'll be there ASAP. Can't wait!" with more emojis.

I hate how guilty I feel, like I've done something wrong. But sometimes the only way out is through.

15

Ava

I can't seem to get warm, no matter how hard I try. It's like the cold from the rink settled into my bones and refuses to let me go. I tried a hot shower, and now I'm bundled up in Mark's sweatshirt, which I thought would help, but it isn't. His scent is already fading because I wore it most of the morning. Now it mostly just smells like me.

I sigh, burrowing further under my heavy throw blanket. I hear a soft "mrp" sound, and Valentino jumps onto my lap and starts a very serious biscuit order on my legs. I reach out and run my fingers through her soft fur, listening to the loud rumble of her purr.

"It's been kind of a shitty day, V," I whisper to her.

My body feels heavy, like it's weighed down by concrete. I've battled depression for most of my life—another glorious side effect of having to hide who you really are—and tonight is no exception. I want to lie here wrapped up like a burrito in my blanket and never move again.

When I left Mark's this morning, I'd been leaning towards letting him in. I'd been a mess, but I'd thought about all the times my therapist had suggested that I consider being open with him. But I'd been all twisted up in the logistics. How could I make him understand why it's so important to keep my secret? Would he see how wrong he's been to stay neutral against what happens to omegas every day?

So I went to the rink, the place I always go when I need to clear my head. The quiet there helps drown out the constant internal noise. Losing myself on the ice does more for me than therapy in a lot of ways, at least when it comes to actually sorting through what I am feeling.

When I saw him watching me from across the rink, it felt like for the first time in a long while—hell, possibly ever—someone finally saw *me*. Isn't that what we all want, deep down?

I'm not even sure what it was about his friend's comment that snapped everything back into place. Maybe it was the mocking way he said *ballerina*. Maybe it was the reminder of the viper nickname. All I know is it felt like a bucket of cold water dumped over me, and suddenly I remembered that no matter who we are when it's just the two of us, our roles are already written out in the real world. And they're not changing.

A buzz on the intercom pulls me from my spiral. "Ms. Kendrick, your brother is here. Shall I send him up?"

I push the button. "Yes, Alfred, thank you."

A few minutes later, I hear a soft knock at the door, and I swing it open to reveal Jack. I can't help the smile that splits my face, despite my awful mood. As the baby of the family, he's equally spoiled and adored by both my mother and myself.

"Hello, baby brother," I say.

"Hello, ancient sister," he replies, following back to my makeshift nest on the couch, dropping beside me. He scoops up Valentino and settles her in his lap, and her purrs get louder, if that's possible. Everyone loves Jack. It's impossible not to with his golden retriever energy.

He leans back after giving her chin a thorough scritch, resting one arm along the back of the couch. "You look like hell. What gives?"

I toss a throw pillow at him. "Fucking rude."

He shrugs. "It's true," he says unapologetically.

"Yeah, well, we can't all be walking supermodels like you, Jack."

"Excuse you, I prefer 'walking, talking sex god.' At least that's what Mateo calls me."

I snort a laugh. "I cannot see Mateo ever saying that to your face. He knows your ego would grow too large to be supported on planet Earth." Though I can admit that it's likely Mateo thinks it. Jack is tall, with a lean athlete's build. His copper hair is more auburn than mine, but his eyes are the same shade of green.

"Sadly, you're correct. My husband is far too reserved for my liking. But seriously, why do you look like something Valentino dragged in?"

Did I say that I adore him? I take it back.

"A couple of things, okay? For one, I'm more than a little hungover, and I've got a lot going on."

"Have you gotten off this couch at all?" he asks casually. Too casually.

I roll my eyes. "If that's a subtle way to ease into asking me if I've eaten or moved my body, the answer to both is yes. I had a real breakfast, got lunch delivered, and then went skating to clear my head."

He grins. "Good girl."

I fake a gag. "Ew," I say, wrinkling my nose. "Don't ever say that to me again."

Jack throws his head back with a laugh. "Well, I'm glad you aren't sitting here spiraling on an empty stomach at least. You wanna talk about it? Mateo swears I'm a good listener."

I sigh, curling my fists into the blanket. "I got drunk last night," I say slowly. He cocks his head, giving me his full attention. "I ended up at Mark's apartment. We had a really good morning, and I agreed we'd have a real conversation soon. I was thinking about telling him everything."

He makes a sympathetic face. I've been filling Jack in on some of what's been going on between me and Mark. Clearly not *all* the details, but about how my omega feels and my emotions. "I sense a *but* coming," he says.

"But then I ran into him and his friend at the rink. And I dunno, things went a bit sideways. And I shut down. It's just been a rough day." My voice falters, and I press my hands to my face.

He leans forward, elbows on his knees. "Are we talking like, need a whole pint of ice cream rough or torture yourself with sad breakup songs rough?"

"Both," I mutter, peeking through my fingers.

He nods solemnly. "The worst kind of day, then."

I laugh a little. "What do you know about a horrible day? I don't think you've ever had a bad day in your entire life," I tease. I know it's not true, of course, but Jack does seem to naturally move through life with a sunny optimism that seems to always work out for him. My dad likes to say that we are two sides of the same coin.

"That isn't true," he says with a lopsided grin. "One time, the gym was closed because of a water main break, and my favorite pair of shorts ripped right up the crotch. On top of it, Mateo was at work and I ended up bored."

I fake gasp. "The horror!"

"I know," he says. "I barely survived." After a moment, he reaches over and grabs my hand. "But in all seriousness, I'm here to listen if you need to cry or vent or whatever. I know I don't get all of the omega stuff, and I personally think you should tell Mark. But it's *your* life. I'll support you however I can."

"I know. I just... I've kept this secret for so long, Jack," I say quietly. "I don't even know how to let someone in anymore. Mom and Dad gave up so much so I could have the chance to write my own story."

He lets out a slow breath and leans back. "You know I love Mom and Dad. I get that they thought they were doing what was best for you. And from the outside, maybe they were. You've got a good life. A great one, even."

"Now *I* hear a *but* coming," I say.

His expression shifts, the grin replaced by something far more somber. It's such a rare look on him that it carries more weight than it probably would from anyone else.

"But you're fucking lonely," he says, "and miserable. And I've watched too many of my friends tear themselves apart because they felt like they had to hide who they really were. Pretending. Shrinking themselves to fit what everyone else expects. That's no way to live your life, sis."

I blink in surprise. Who knew my baby brother could be so insightful?

Just as quickly as it came, the seriousness is gone. "Now," he says, standing and grabbing my hand, pulling me to stand beside him. "There's only one thing that can truly cure a hangover and a case of the blues."

My lips twitch at the corners. "What's that?"

"Ice cream. Ice cream always helps. Come on, let's go get some. I'll even buy."

I whine at the idea of leaving the couch, but he drags me along by my arm.

"Come on, lazybones," he says. "I can hear mint chocolate chip calling my name."

I trail after him, shaking my head, smiling despite myself. In the elevator, he whistles while he presses the call button, rocking back on his heels like he has nowhere else he would rather be. For all his himbo energy, there is no one more loyal or protective than Jack.

The ice cream shop down the street smells like sugar and waffle cones the second we step inside. It has a very vintage soda shop vibe, with framed ads from the '50s scattered around the room and pale pink walls. The mint green ice cream case hosts over twenty flavors that rotate out monthly. A couple of kids at one of the tables are arguing about who got more sprinkles while their parents look on.

Jack studies the menu with the seriousness of a surgeon selecting the proper blade. I laugh, rolling my eyes. "Just choose something so the poor girl can get it scooped." I give her a smile.

"Um, excuse you," he says, wagging a finger at me. "One doesn't just rush these kinds of things."

I move closer to the case. "Well, while Mr. Indecisive here tries to come up with the perfect ice cream blend, I'll take a scoop of vanilla with crushed Reese's Cups and sliced bananas, please. Oh, and some hot fudge."

"See, you always get the same thing. Boring," Jack admonishes.

After he finally makes a choice—waffle cone with powdered jelly donut and honey sponge cake flavors—we find a small table near the window. He talks through the first few bites, launching into whatever new fitness kick he's on this week, something about cold plunges? It sounds like a form of medieval torture to me, and when he presses me to give it a shot, I give him a look that has sent many a witness into a panic.

"Fiiiiine. But you're missing out on the benefits," he says.

Mateo calls halfway through, managing to snag a break on his shift at the hospital. Jack answers immediately and flips the phone to the video chat, holding it up so I can wave.

"You whores! You got ice cream without me?" Mateo chides.

"You should be here! Jack said I looked like shit, and the only solution was ice cream," I say with a laugh.

"Well, some of us aren't trust fund babies, and the trauma nurse life waits for no one. You two behaving?"

"Define behaving," Jack demands with faux seriousness.

I can feel the tension slowly unwinding from my body. Things don't seem quite as heavy as they did an hour ago. I know how I feel about Mark when I'm honest with myself. But I don't know if I'm capable of letting him in, and it's not fair to keep stringing him along while I try to figure it out.

I still owe him that conversation, even if it's to finally end things. It's the right thing to do.

16

Mark

As expected, I don't hear anything from Ava. So I try to fill my day with running errands, working out, and laundry in an attempt to do anything besides look at my phone. Her walls are firmly back in place, and they'll stay that way unless we end up in bed together again.

Thanks, Adam.

Even as I think it, I know it isn't fair. Adam's cutting remark may have been the catalyst, but it wouldn't have made an impact if Ava wasn't already primed to push me away. The only person in this world that can make her do anything is herself.

It's up to me to decide if I want to keep playing.

My date with Marnie looms over me, feeling more like a chore than something worth being excited about. Which tells me it will only be the one date. My initial instinct was right, I can't drag someone else into this, but I'm not going to back out of plans at the last minute. Plus, I owe myself one attempt to at least see how it goes. Who knows, maybe she'll be my scent match, and Ava Kendrick will cease to matter.

I'm not hopeful. Since I woke up I've felt queasy, like I'm about to have an affair.

Finally, it's late enough in the day that I need to get dressed. I've sent her a few messages to confirm plans and say hi, and she really does seem sweet. I pull on a pair of faded, well-worn jeans and a soft cable-knit sweater layered over a plaid button-up. Casual enough for a coffee date, but still shows a little bit of effort.

The subway ride to Brooklyn, where Marnie lives, is my one shot at quieting my nerves. Headphones in, audiobook on. I let the narrator's voice fill the space in my head so my thoughts can't.

The car's packed today with the Sunday crowd, families and couples out enjoying a beautiful fall day. I give up my seat to an elderly couple and reach up to grip the pole with one hand, swaying as the train moves. More people press in at the next stop, and the person next to me smells strongly of coffee. I wonder if it's their biological scent or if they're just that big of a coffee drinker.

The subway is sort of an assault on the senses. It wouldn't be so bad if the Transit Authority would properly maintain the scent neutralizers, but they always seem to be broken. The train lurches forward, then stalls, and we all collectively groan. Hopefully it's only a brief delay. I should have just taken a cab.

I'm trying very hard to not take this as a sign.

Maybe I should have asked her to meet in Central Park instead. Open air and sunshine. The thought barely finishes forming before I shake it off. That would have been a lot to ask her for a first date. From her place, that would be a whole trek across the city—an hour if the trains behaved and longer if they didn't. No, I'm the one that asked her on the date, so I should be the one to travel. It seems like the gentlemanly thing to do.

I check my phone, even though I know the time hasn't changed much. Luckily, the train starts moving again, and I take a deep breath. Just a few more stops.

Once I arrive at the coffee shop, I spot Marnie almost right away. She waves at me, a friendly smile plastered on her face. She's wearing an oversized sweater over a short sundress, and there's an actual, honest-to-god ribbon tied neatly into her long, curly blonde ponytail.

Am I on a date with a Disney princess?

Not that I mind. She's beautiful. A year ago, her luscious curves and bright blue eyes would have snagged my attention and probably held it.

Now, though... my alpha side stirs with a low grumble, and I shut the thought down before it finishes forming.

I return her smile. "Hey. You beat me here."

"Not by much. It isn't like you're late or anything," she says warmly, stepping into me for a hug. I know what she's doing:

a quick scent check. I get it. I'm curious too, so I breathe in deeply.

Her scent is pleasant enough. Lemongrass and something warm and bright that reminds me of sunshine. Lighter than most omegas' scents. It doesn't hit me in the chest or fog my head, though. If anything, it's easy to take in. My alpha bristles at the attempt, more annoyed than interested.

This omega is not my mate.

Marnie pulls back, and I catch the quick flicker of disappointment that crosses her face. I'm pretty sure she felt the same lack of click. I offer her a soft, understanding smile and gesture toward the menu. We both know now, but I won't let it ruin the mood.

"Sorry, this was on such short notice," I say.

She recovers quickly, grin back in place. "Oh, it's totally fine. I love meeting new people. Let's get our drinks, and then we can chat."

"Have you been here before? I'm a sucker for their cortados."

She nods, then blushes. "Kind of. I've had their stuff delivered. This place is pretty close to my family's business."

We step up to the counter and order. Lavender oat milk latte for her, cortado with honey and cream for me. Then we find a small table by the window.

She wraps her hands around her cup. "So, tell me about yourself, Mark. What do you do?"

I clear my throat. This question always puts me in a weird spot. I'm proud of what I do, but it can change the vibe fast. "Uh. I'm the Manhattan District Attorney."

Her eyes go wide. "Oh my god. I knew you looked familiar. My grandma is obsessed with watching your cases on TV. That must be such a wild job."

The conversation flows easily from there. Marnie is incredibly easy to talk to. She tells me about helping her family run a crystal shop that's surprisingly successful. "There are a lot of witchy types in this city," she says with a laugh. "Mom and Dad are even talking about opening a second location. Ya know, when I can run it myself and I'm not stuck living with them."

I frown. "Why do you have to wait?"

Her brows knit together. "Well, I'm unbonded. I'm not allowed to have a retail job on my own. I can only work when my dad or brothers are around. The whole omega protection laws. You probably know all that stuff, right? Because of the lawyer thing?"

Heat creeps up my neck. "Uh, not really. I mostly prosecute criminal cases—murder, theft, whatnot. I don't interact with that side of the law too much."

"Well, except for that suppressant case. With the heiress," she says. "I think I saw you on the news for that one." There's no judgment in her voice. Somehow, that makes it worse.

"Yeah, the mayor sort of strong-armed me on that one," I admit. "For what it's worth, I think the suppressant laws are bullshit. We should be funding real research instead of punishing the people who need them."

Her eyes light up. "Oh my god, yes. I bet if we had real suppressants, we wouldn't have to plan our whole lives around heat cycles or panic about alphas losing control. The laws about where we can work or go to school would have to change, too." She sounds so hopeful, like she can already visualize a different world.

It makes me feel... gross.

I think about the donors I charm at fundraisers, the ones who smile and nod when people talk about 'protecting omegas' like it's some noble cause. Does it really go this far? Limiting where and when they can work? How did I not know this?

Saying it's not my area because it isn't criminal law feels like a cop-out. I probably did know, in some vague, abstract way. I just never stopped to think about what it looked like in someone's actual life. Because I didn't have to. I don't *know* any omegas.

Jesus. I'm such a stereotype. Typical white man, comfortable enough in my privilege that I don't have to think about what other people might face.

And then I think of Ava. She knows all of this. She fights it. Loudly. Constantly.

I say I love her, and yet I've never really sat with the thing she cares about most.

Marnie's voice breaks through. "You just suddenly got quiet. You okay?" Her voice is full of genuine concern, and she reaches across the table to place a hand on top of mine.

I nod, trying to refocus on the conversation. "Yeah, sorry. I guess I got lost in thought. I've never really considered how much oversight there is on the day-to-day for omegas. And I feel like an asshole."

Her smile is a little sad at the edges. "You probably don't know very many then, huh?" she says softly.

I grimace sheepishly. "No, I don't. I'm from a really small town, and there weren't even many alphas, let alone omegas. When I moved away for college, I was too busy to get to know anyone properly. Plus, um," I blush, rubbing the back of my neck. "If I'm being honest, most of omegas' scents are kind of a lot to me. So I tend to avoid them."

Her laugh is gentle and understanding, and I realize I've just admitted something I've never told anyone else. I smile at her. "You have a knack for getting people to open up to you, huh? I've never said that out loud before."

She lifts her shoulders in a shrug. "I've been told I have that effect on people."

She guides the conversation to a different topic, and I find myself relaxing and enjoying talking to her. There isn't anything romantic here, so I won't pursue another date. But there is something refreshing about her straightforward honesty and positive outlook. I hope she'll consider being my friend.

Marnie chats about her plans to eventually run the new shop, the quirks of her family, and the odd mix of their customers they see. I laugh, contribute my own anecdotes, and find myself genuinely sad to bring the evening to an end.

By the time we finish, the setting sun is spilling across the wooden floors, and the coffee shop is starting to wind down. I stand and offer her another hug.

She returns it warmly and sincerely. "Thanks for meeting me," she says. "I hope we can do it again sometime. I know we aren't mates or anything, but I enjoyed this."

I nod. "Yeah. I'd really like that. Maybe we could be friends? I admit, I don't have that many."

She grins. "Well, if you do have any alpha friends, send them my way. I'm not getting any younger. But yes, I'd like that very much."

I see her safely into a ride share and then take a deep breath of cool air. I need to clear my head. It's early enough; I think I'll just walk until I get tired. Catch a cab or the subway from wherever that may be.

My phone buzzes in my pocket, and I snatch it out quickly. I groan when I see that it's just Brad about an upcoming case. I knew it wouldn't be Ava, but I'd still been hopeful.

As I walk, I consider what Adam said yesterday. How he'd wondered what could be holding Ava back. With my conversation with Marnie fresh on my mind, I have to wonder—is it because she thinks our morals are misaligned? Does she believe the campaigning bullshit?

Have I ever given her a reason not to?

I blow out a frustrated breath. Even if that's the case, it doesn't make it any easier to be shut out. If she'd have just talked to me, maybe we both would have realized some things.

I want more from her than I've allowed myself to admit. I want the nights where we fall asleep in each other's arms and the relaxed mornings afterward. I want to fight over the *Times* crossword. I want to make love in the sunlight and then take a midday nap.

I don't know how much longer I can keep waiting around for scraps. Every time I get even a little too real, she bolts. And yeah, I'm starting to get a sense that I might have given her a reason for that. But does that change anything? She hasn't bothered to ask me, so would she believe me if I explained?

And what if that isn't it at all? What if she just genuinely doesn't want more from me? What if she genuinely can't open up to anyone? I don't know her past; there could be deeply rooted trauma there. She won't let me in enough to find out.

I growl in frustration.

I'm so tired of this.

I shove my hands in my pockets and just focus on moving my feet, heading toward the Brooklyn Bridge. All around me there are scenes of normalcy, reminding me that life continues whether Ava and I get our shit together or not. The smell of fresh bread from a shop on the corner. The echo of a saxophone spilling out an open apartment window.

I pause at a crosswalk. The light flashes green for me to walk, but I remain rooted in place, watching the wind whip a plastic bag down the street. My thoughts are full of her. How she looked yesterday in my shirt with her hair piled in a messy bun. The softness of her lips against mine, the warmth of her skin beneath my palms—and then the coldness at the rink later when she'd shut me out.

The blaring of a horn makes me jump back onto the curb and realize the light turned green. A yellow cab tears past, the driver leaning out just enough to flip me off and yell for me to fucking pay attention. Cold street water splashes up onto my jeans. I grimace and, out of habit, flip him off right back.

You'd almost think I was born here.

I turn down a quieter street lined with brownstones, some of the stoops dotted with giant bunnies and other Easter décor. Kids' chalk drawings scribble across the sidewalk: rainbows, crooked hearts, lopsided cats. The sight tugs at me, and it makes me think of Jess and Ayden. Maybe I need to go home for a visit. Get away from all of this for a bit.

I pull my phone out again, debating on calling Jess to chat, but I remember it's Sunday night and she's probably at church. We aren't a very religious family, but there aren't many other opportunities for community in a small town. My thumb hovers over Ava's name in my contact list, and for a second I imagine calling. Just telling her everything. All of the confusion, the wanting, and how she's been under my skin since the first time we met.

But I don't. Because what if she doesn't answer? Or worse, what if she does and she tells me to leave her the fuck alone?

I shove the phone back in my pocket and keep walking.

I end up at the river without realizing how far I've gone. The water's black in the fading light, dotted with glints of orange and yellow where the lights from surrounding buildings hit. I lean against the railing, the metal cool against my forearms, and stare out at the skyline. Manhattan rises across the water. There are some tourists lingering on the bridge, snapping pictures for their scrapbooks and social media.

I've always wanted to do touristy things, but felt silly doing them alone. Ava's a native. Would she be willing to do those things with me? I don't know the answer. In some ways, I can tell you everything about Ava Kendrick. Other times, I don't think I know her at all.

This should be easy. Two adults with off-the-charts chemistry taking the time to see if maybe, just maybe, they could fall in love. Because ultimately, I think that's what I want. Real communication, real access to her life, the real her. Not the ice queen or the viper. Not even my sweet cereus that only blooms for me at night. I want it all. I want to date her. Hell, I'd probably marry her if she gave me half a chance.

A decision is forming. No more half-measures; I'm done waiting. I've left this in her court long enough.

He has to be fucking kidding me.

Any triumph I felt at the email from Mark titled "Plea Offer" evaporated the minute I read the details. A felony? After three days of me running circles around him and poking holes in everything he had while getting nothing but radio silence at night? He's out of his mind. The mayor must really be leaning on him to make an example of Katie.

Rage bubbles up inside me, and it takes me a minute to realize I'm also sweating in my cool office, and my dress is starting to feel itchy. Did I take my suppressant today? I think back and grimace when I remember that I definitely did. I really have to figure out a way to have another heat soon. This is happening more and more, and I'm going to end up with an unplanned breakthrough soon. Or possibly an overdose on suppressants. Doubling or even tripling up occasionally, like I've started to do, can't be healthy.

Not that there's any real research on it other than what my mother does, and I'm sure as hell not admitting to her that I've been doing that. She'd flay me alive. People think *I'm* scary? I have nothing on the matriarch of the Kendrick family.

I push a button in my desk drawer, popping open a hidden compartment. I snag the emergency bottle I keep in my office and frown at the nearly empty rattle. I must have been doubling up more than I've realized. I have my bottle at home, but at this rate, I'm going to need to get more very soon. I wash them down with the drink on my desk and put the empty bottle back in the compartment.

I open a new browser on my laptop and fire up my VPN, navigating to a web-based SMS service to send a text to Vinny. I refuse to call him my dealer. He's just... my friend. That procures me illegal pharmaceuticals.

"What's the weather going to be like on Friday? Sunny?"

It only takes a minute to get a response.

"Clear skies in the early evening around 5."

A quick glance at my schedule confirms I can make that work.

"Perfect."

That settled, I close the window and return to Mark's email, reading over it again. It makes me just as angry the second time. I glance at the clock on the wall. I bet he's still at the office.

This late in the evening, there won't be much traffic, and I can probably be there in less than twenty minutes.

Half of me screams that it's a terrible idea. I know I'm already on edge, and with a potential breakthrough heat this close, being around him is the sort of bad idea that makes people into my clients. But my omega is closer to the surface than ever after the events of the weekend, so before I fully realize what I'm doing, I'm having Tony take me downtown.

The whole ride over, I think about how scared Katie is. How it's only been a matter of luck that I'm not in the exact same position. She just wanted to go to college and walk across campus without worrying about an alpha losing control around her, and to study something she can't find at the omega academy.

By the time I climb out of my car, I've moved past furious and into nuclear territory. And Mark is about to catch every bit of it, even the parts he doesn't deserve. I'd feel bad, but he brought it on himself with that ridiculous plea offer, and if I'm honest, because my feelings are hurt that he hasn't reached out to have our talk.

I stomp into the building, pausing briefly as I wonder which night guard is on duty. I hope it's Henry; I like him. He's an older, bonded alpha reaching retirement age, and looking forward to being at home every day with his omega and their slew of grandchildren.

Frank, on the other hand, is unbonded and makes me feel like he's watching me no matter how much scent neutralizer I have on. I can't tell if he just has an overly sensitive nose or if he's a little bit rapey. Either way, I avoid him whenever possible.

Luckily, I spot Henry's balding head leaned over a magazine. He lifts his eyes as I approach, and they crinkle around the edges as he smiles at me. "Well, well, Ms. Ava. To what do I owe the pleasure?"

I grin back. "Oh, you know—need to give the DA a piece of my mind. Is Mr. Taylor in?"

He sighs and leans back in his chair. "You know he is. You two are a pair of workaholics. It's not good to go nonstop like you do."

I duck my head and spread my hands, conceding his point. "I know, but that's just the name of the game, I'm afraid."

He hits the button to unlock the security door and waves me forward. "Now, listen," he says seriously, "I know you might get real tempted to kill him in whatever battle you're about to have, because there's no one else on the floor up there. But I'm really close to retirement, and I'm gonna ask you to refrain, as a favor."

I step through with a laugh and reach across the desk to pat his hand. "Tell you what, if I can't, I'll personally pay enough to make sure you and Grace can live out your days somewhere sunny instead of dealing with any headache from little ole me. But I promise to behave."

He smirks and motions for me to go upstairs.

I'm annoyed that Henry made me laugh and lost me some of my righteous anger, so I spend the elevator ride deliberately digging up thoughts that make me furious.

Immature? Definitely. Do I care? Not even a little. The need to see Mark is thrumming through me. If I walk in angry, I'm in control, and I won't risk doing something reckless, like climbing in his lap and asking if I can have his shirt.

This morning, I realized the UCLA sweatshirt has completely lost his scent. I had to throw it in the wash, and until I can sneak something else out of his laundry hamper, I've got nothing to wear that smells like him. The smaller forgotten items I've stolen over the last few months—forgotten ties, mainly—line my nest like trophies.

Being an omega is so strange sometimes, I swear.

A thought intrudes, a reminder that if we end up having the talk, I won't have access to him or his scent anymore. I shove it away because it makes my heart ache, and I'm focused on being angry right now.

My heels click on the tile floor, echoing down the empty hallway as I exit the elevator, and I frown at the sound. I'm not giving him a heads up that I'm coming so has time to prepare. Absolutely not. I slip them off and carry them as I pad silently down toward Mark's office, only putting them back on before I open the door. I need the extra height for the boost in confidence.

I swing the door open, relishing the look of surprise, desire, and annoyance that flashes across his face before he shuts it down.

He sighs, throwing down his pen. "The plea offer, I suppose," he deadpans.

"You're goddamned right, the plea offer. If you can even call it that," I say, closing the door behind me.

He leans back in his chair, steepling his fingers and looking at me with exasperation. His hair is rumpled, like he's been running his hands through it while he works. His sleeves are rolled up to his elbows, and his tie is tugged loose. It's so unfair how sexy I find him. My omega wants to pull that tie off the rest of the way and offer my wrists to be tied up with it. Or maybe tie him up with it. I'm flexible.

Shit. Focus, Ava. This isn't what we came here for.

Isn't it, though? I can practically hear her croon in my mind.

"You know that's a bullshit offer," I say. "I have this case in the bag. Class E felony with a year attached? Even if you won, which you won't, the judge isn't going to hand down that sentencing. She's a teenager with no record. Does the mayor have your balls in that tight of a vise?"

"Yeah, Ava, he does," he snaps. I nearly grin in triumph. Good, he's going to take the bait and fight with me. I need to let some pressure off. "Some of us aren't trust fund babies with cushy partner positions. We have to worry about things like budgets."

"Oh, don't you dare," I fire back. "Do not imply I didn't earn every inch of what I have. I work just as hard as you do. Harder, actually, since I do it in heels and with the," I clutch my chest dramatically, "*sheer audacity* to have a vagina in this profession."

"Ah, yes," he says dryly. "Definitely the vagina that pisses everyone off about you," he says. "It's definitely not," he makes a wide, sweeping gesture with his hands and rolls his eyes, "this. You get what you want because you bully the shit out of everyone and everything, then retreat to your penthouse to decide your next attack."

I scoff. "Right. I'm definitely the only bully in this room. You knew that deal was garbage, Mark. And you knew how I'd react."

He opens his mouth, ready to snap back, then stops. Takes a breath and closes his eyes. "You're right."

I blink. "Excuse me?"

"It's a shit deal because it isn't mine," he says. "Harvey had someone in my office send it over. I've been fighting with him for the last three hours because of it. I hadn't had a chance to talk to you yet. I'm in the middle of drafting a new plea."

"You are?"

He motions toward the paper on his desk. "Misdemeanor possession charge. No jail time. A hefty fine and community service working with you on omega rights cases."

My anger deflates, and I can almost feel tears pricking at my eyes, making them burn. "Why?"

He makes a motion with his hands and shakes his head. "Because I'm the District Attorney, not Harvey, and it's a bullshit law. I've been doing a lot of thinking about those lately."

I inch closer to him, leaning one of my hips on the edge of the desk. His scent wraps around me, and though it's a little bitter from being stressed and frustrated, it still soothes me. He eyes me warily, as if he's not entirely convinced I'm not going to grab the letter opener and stab him.

"What about them?" I ask quietly.

His eyes lift to mine, and his face is serious. I have the strongest urge to reach out and smooth the lines between his eyebrows with my fingers.

"It occurred to me the other day that I don't really know any omegas. And I'd never stopped to really think about what the omega protection laws actually look like in practice," he says earnestly.

"How do you think they look in practice?" I shift so that I'm fully sitting on the edge of his desk, one of my legs against his.

"Control," he says, "wrapped up in a pretty bow so no one has to look at it too closely." He wraps a hand around my calf, tugging on one of my legs until he's able to press his body between them. The tension in the room is thickening, and I can feel fire building beneath my skin.

"That isn't going to make you very popular with the big alphas that like to donate to campaigns," I whisper.

"Fuck 'em. There are other ways to raise campaign funds."

My mouth crashes into his, and I dig my fingers into his hair with a moan against his lips.

"Ava." He groans my name, grabbing my hips and pulling me firmly into his lap. I can feel him hard beneath me, and I grind against his length. I feel like I can't get enough contact.

I undo the buttons on his shirt, pushing the lapels wide so I can press my palms flat against the dusting of chest hair. It isn't enough. Tiny, needy mews escape from my mouth as I kiss along his jaw, his lips, his throat.

He moans roughly, more of a growl than anything. He stands, supporting my ass with his hands so I can wrap my legs around his waist. I know my heels are digging into him, but previous experience tells me that Mark likes that. He carries me to the small couch between two tall mahogany bookshelves along one wall.

He drops me unceremoniously onto it, and the look he gives me is direction enough. I untuck and unbutton my shirt before tugging up my skirt around my hips, revealing my sheer black underwear set and heels. Mark makes a sound of approval and pauses undressing to look down at me. His gaze is almost... reverent. Like I'm the most beautiful piece of art he's ever seen. It makes me feel sexy and cherished.

I reach for him, guiding his cock to my lips. His scent, his taste—it overwhelms my senses until I can't think of anything but him. My omega is fully in control, and my head is blissfully quiet.

18

Mark

Something is different about her. I can't quite put my finger on what, but I'm not naïve enough to think that a couple of offhanded sentences about my expanding views on omega rights just magically made her change. If I were a better man, I'd pull back and force her to talk to me. But just as I think that, she hollows out her cheeks around my cock, and I forget everything.

I bury my hands into her hair, working myself deeper. She feels so good that it takes effort to not completely lose myself to the rut and fuck her face. Which, don't get me wrong, has a time and place, and I'm certainly not above it. But I don't want her to leave my office with her makeup completely destroyed. That's more of a bedroom activity.

Finally, I tug her head away, and she makes the cutest little squeak of protest. "Don't worry, I'm not taking it away for good," I say with a chuckle.

I sit beside her on the couch, pulling her into my lap with her back to my chest. I love picking her up and just moving her where I want her. It pleases some part of my alpha side.

I snake a hand between her thighs, testing that she's wet enough for me. She's positively drenched, so much so that there's almost certainly a wet spot on my cushion. "Is all that for me, gorgeous?" I growl in her ear, letting my teeth graze along the outer rim.

Her whole body shivers. "Please, Mark, don't tease. I need you inside me," she says with a gasp.

Who am I to deny such a sweet request?

I lift one of her thighs, hooking my arm under her knee as my hand guides my cock to her entrance. I drag the head through her slick folds, absolutely feral for the sensation. Is this what it's like to play with an omega's slick?

I push the thought away, focusing on the woman in my arms. Who must be tired of having patience, because she wiggles until she can sink herself onto me. The groan that slips out of my mouth would probably embarrass me, but it's impossible not to respond when Ava's tight, wet heat engulfs me.

She begins to ride me as best she can with her leg still over my arm. It's more of a grind, really, and I can tell it must be doing the job nicely for her by the sounds she's making. I slip my fingers to where we are joined and begin rubbing gentle circles on her clit. "That's right, baby," I say, "use me to get yourself off. I want to make you feel so fucking good."

"Oh god, Mark, right there. Don't you dare fucking stop," she demands.

I grin against the back of her shoulder. "So fucking bossy."

I don't change anything, though, keeping my attention on her clit to the exact same pressure, pattern, and speed. She grinds for another couple of moments, and I can feel when it hits her. Her walls clamp down around me, and her thighs start shaking.

I don't give her a moment to come down. Instead, I grab her other leg and put it in the same position, thrusting up into her as hard as I can. I fuck her through the orgasm. I can't tell if she continues coming or if she comes again, but either way, I set a brutal pace. She's at my mercy the way I have her practically impaled on top of me, and I use every bit to my advantage until I can feel my own orgasm building.

"Knot. Knot. I need it. Gimme," Ava sobs, almost incoherent.

Poor thing must be really lost in the haze if she's begging for something I can't give her. But God, I wish betas were able to take one. To lock myself within her so she'd be forced to sit and talk to me, unable to get away? That might actually be what heaven is like.

The mental image of knotting Ava is enough to push me over the edge, and I bury as much of myself as I can get inside her with my knot full and hard outside her tight hole.

We both pant, trying to catch our breath as the afterglow from the endorphins settles in.

"That was incredible," I say gently. I'm feeling a little bold, so I press a light kiss to a very alluring freckle at the nape of her neck. We don't usually *do* those kinds of touches.

She shivers, then slowly relaxes back into me. I ease her legs down, my mind drifting to the decision I made on my walk home from Brooklyn the other night. I need to be more assertive with Ava and stop letting her run from me. Either she lets me in, or she ends this for good. I wrap my arms around her waist, keeping my grip loose so she doesn't feel trapped, but firm enough to make it clear that I want her close.

"What are you doing?" she asks. She doesn't sound angry, which I take as a win, but there's genuine confusion on her face.

"I want to hold you," I say. "I don't want you to fix your clothes and bolt out of this office. I want to talk. Hell, maybe even order some dinner and actually spend time together without having sex." I feel tension coil inside her, but she hasn't run yet. "And I think you want that too," I add quietly.

"Mark—"

I shake my head, cutting her off. "No. You agreed we'd talk. Maybe cuddling half-naked is too much too soon for you, but you can't run from this. Not this time."

She climbs off my lap, chewing on her lip as if she's weighing her next move. After a long breath, she seems to decide. "Fine, but I am fixing my clothes."

"Fair enough," I say. I pull my slacks back up and button them, but don't bother with my shirt, draping an arm along the back of the couch as I watch her. Once she's dressed again, she perches on the edge of the cushion, already rebuilding her shields.

"I agreed you could get dressed," I say. "I didn't agree to you sitting there like we're about to negotiate a contract." I reach for her and pull her back against me. "Relax, Ava, we have been sleeping together for nearly two months. I'm not a stranger," I whisper.

"I can't do this," she says, voice small.

"What? Cuddle?"

"This," she says more firmly, motioning with her hand between us. "I can't do relationship stuff."

"Can't? Or won't? Because that feels like an important distinction," I say.

"Is it, though? At the end of the day, aren't they one and the same?" She pulls back to look at me. There's a sheen to her eyes, almost as if she's holding back tears, and I can't even begin to conceptualize her crying. I'm pretty sure I'd end up offering my very soul to get her to stop.

"Are you scared? Is that it?" I reach out and cup her cheek, and the way she closes her eyes and leans into it makes my chest ache.

"More than you'd believe. But it doesn't change anything," she says sadly.

"Baby, let me in. I'm not going to hurt you. I *love* you." The words slip out before I can stop them, and I curse myself as I feel her whole body go rigid.

Fuck. Completely overplayed my hand.

"I need to go," she says quickly, pulling away from me and standing. "I just... I'm sorry, but I can't."

"Ava," I say, scrubbing a hand over my face and desperately trying to think of how to save this. "I can't keep doing this. Please, stay and talk to me. I don't expect you to say it back or anything. I didn't even mean to say it. But don't run."

She takes several steps backwards, her eyes wide and pupils blown. The bitter scent of burnt oranges is filling my office, stronger than any scent I've ever gotten from her before. "I'm sorry, I really am. But I can't. I wish I could."

She backs up until she reaches the door, and she turns to open it.

A bone-deep weariness crashes over me. How many times are we going to do this song and dance? At what point am I just being a masochist?

"If you walk out that door, this is done. For real. I can't do this anymore," I say quietly and even I can hear the pain in my voice.

I see her shoulders stiffen, and she pauses. I think for a moment she's going to come sit back down, but then she opens the door and steps out of my office, closing it behind her.

I sit in the quiet of my office, listening to the sound of her heels carrying her down the empty hall and then the *ding* of the elevator. When I don't hear her anymore, I accept it for what it is.

Ava, for whatever personal demons she's fighting, has closed the door on us.

I shut my eyes and bury my head in my hands, trying to breathe and just feel whatever emotions happen. There's hurt, so much fucking hurt, but a whole lot of sadness too. With a growl of anger, I snatch up a coffee cup from the small table near the couch and launch it against the wall, the sharp sound of shattering china echoing through my office. It takes a considerable amount of restraint not to take one of the chairs near me and beat it into splinters against my desk.

I stand, hands shaking, and grab my shirt, hastily buttoning it back up. I can't stay in this room any longer without going insane. I can still smell her everywhere. My alpha rages inside of me, pressing me to chase after her and drag her home. But I can't.

I bypass the elevator, not wanting any more of her scent, and take the stairs down two at a time. I have no destination in mind; I just know I have to get out of here.

Eventually I find myself in Central Park, with very little recollection of the walk there. My head is finally starting to feel clearer, not that I'm feeling particularly better or anything. I find a bench and sit down, staring out at the trees blankly. After a minute, I pull my phone out and scroll to Ava's contact.

I stare at it, and then before I can change my mind, I block her number. Deleting the contact won't do any good since I have her number memorized, but at least now she can't reach out. Any communication we have from here on out will be coordinated between our offices.

My phone rings right as I'm about to put it into my pocket, Marnie's face flashing across it. "Hello?"

"I was just dusting the crystals, and all of a sudden had the strangest feeling that I needed to call you," she says. "That's crazy, right? I mean, I hope you don't think I'm some weirdo and not wanna talk anymore."

I give a dry, self-deprecating chuckle. "Uh, no. In fact, maybe I need to come buy some crystals, because that woo-woo shit must have some real magic behind it. I really did need someone to talk to."

"What's wrong?" she asks, concern evident in her voice.

"That's an incredibly long story, and probably not one to be had over the phone when I'm still feeling some kind of way about it. But let's just say the situationship I've been trying to figure out is done."

"Oh, Mark, I'm sorry. That's so hard," she says softly. She pauses briefly. "Well, do you want advice, distraction, or someone to sit with you in the suck for a minute?"

I huff out a breath that's almost a laugh. "Honestly, probably the last one. There's not much advice to be given in this situation, and I don't think I'll be easily distracted."

"I can do that," she says easily. "I'm pretty good at sitting with uncomfortable feelings. Occupational hazard of being around all the vibrations from the crystals."

I shift on the bench, rolling my shoulders like I can physically loosen the knot in my chest. "I'm in Central Park. I walked here without really realizing I was doing it."

"Least the weather is nice. Would have really sucked if it was raining or something. Though I guess it would give you the quintessential heartbroken movie moment, standing in the rain looking forlorn."

I laugh despite myself, and though I had said I didn't think she could distract me, I find her doing just that. We talk for a few minutes about nothing important. She tells me a story about one of her customers going on a twenty-minute rant about how they are being stalked by one particularly fat pigeon.

"Do you want some company?" she offers. "You're welcome to come hang out down here at the shop."

I shake my head, even though she can't see it. "I don't think I'm fit to be anyone's company tonight. But I was already meaning to ask you this before my night blew up. What do you have going on tomorrow night?"

"Same old, same old," she tells me. "Why?"

"There's this big, fancy dinner at the mayor's mansion," I say, choosing my words carefully. "I was thinking I should introduce you to my best friend, Adam. He's a reporter and an alpha, and I think you two might hit it off. He'll be there anyway, so I thought maybe you could come as my plus one. If you don't feel each other, there's no pressure. It wouldn't be a blind date or anything."

"You mean I have an excuse to wear a fancy evening gown and meet a pre-vetted alpha that probably isn't a creep? Uh, yes. Count me in," she says with a laugh.

"Okay. I'll pick you up around 6:30."

"Sounds great!"

I smile, despite my still rocky mood. "Marnie, I'm really glad you called. I appreciate it. Tell the crystals I said thanks."

19

Ava

The second Ron opens the door to his and Shelby's brownstone, I fall apart. I burst into tears before I can even form a word. His eyes widen and he glances over my shoulder at Tony, some silent exchange passing between them that I can't see. Whatever it is, Ron decides fast, ushering me inside with his hand at my back.

"Shelby, get down here," he yells, guiding me toward the living room.

Cillian and Rory are on the couch, staring at me like I've sprouted a second head. Ron waves them off with one hand. "Boys, go find something to do."

Rory, the more sensitive of the two, looks at his brother and then back at me. "Is Aunt Ava okay?" he asks, his voice small and worried. The concern in it breaks whatever thin control I had left, and I start crying harder. I want to tell him I'm fine, to apologize for showing up like this, but my brain feels completely short-circuited.

"She's just sad," Shelby says gently as she comes into the room, Aisling perched on her hip. My goddaughter's hair is still damp from a bath, dark curls clinging to her unicorn pajamas, like Shelby rushed straight down without drying her properly. Shelby passes her to Ron without breaking stride. "Take her upstairs, get her settled with Bun-Bun and her story, then start some tea."

She turns her attention to the boys. "Upstairs. Showers and bed. You've got school tomorrow."

"Aw, come on, Mom," Cillian whines.

"Don't sass your mother. I already told you to get out of here, so get to steppin'," Ron says, dad-voice activated as he leads everyone from the room.

Shelby turns to me, opening her arms wide. I press myself between them, sobbing into her shoulder. She rubs long, slow, soothing circles on my back. "This feels like a full omega breakdown," she says softly, her hand never slowing down, "and it has Mark Taylor written all over it, am I right?"

I nod, still unable to speak.

She doesn't rush me, just lets me cry until it burns itself out, until the sobs turn into shaky breaths and sniffles. When I finally pull back, I swipe at my face and manage a weak laugh. "I got snot on your shirt."

She snorts. "I have six kids. This is not the first time someone's bodily fluids have ended up on me." She guides me toward the couch and gives my shoulder a gentle squeeze. "Sit. Breathe. Now tell me what happened."

I sink down into the couch and stare at my hands. "He sent this bogus plea deal for Katie, and I lost it. Went straight to his office to tell him exactly what I thought."

"Right, right, as you do," she says, settling beside me.

"At first, we were fighting," I continue. "Like, real fighting."

"Because of who you two fundamentally are as people," she supplies.

I shoot her a look. "Anyway. We were fighting, and then he just stopped. He told me Harvey had someone in his office send the deal without his approval. That he'd been fighting with him about it for hours."

Shelby's expression softens, but she stays quiet, letting me keep going.

"And then he told me that he's been thinking a lot about the omega laws, and he offered me a real plea deal. No jail time, community service with us. He's going to go to battle with Harvey over it, and it sounds like he doesn't care how it affects his campaign chances."

"Okay," she says slowly. "So how does that land with you here, falling apart on my couch? That sounds like progress. You've been holding back because you didn't trust where he stood."

I swallow. "Well, then we—" I pause, looking to make sure there weren't any small ears listening "—you know. After, he wanted to talk. About us. And he told me he loves me."

Understanding crosses her face, and she gives me a sad, sad smile. "And you panicked."

I nod, fresh tears sliding down my cheeks. "I panicked. And when I got to the door, he told me he couldn't keep doing this. That if I walked out without talking to him, it was over."

"Oh, Ava..." she says, voice thick with pity.

I cover my face with my hands. "I didn't know what else to do! I've never *done* any of this before. I've never had a real relationship or actually said what I'm feeling out loud to a man."

I blow out a breath, which turns into a shaky laugh. "Plus, I think I'm about to have a breakthrough heat. It felt... wrong to be like, 'surprise! I'm actually an omega! Also, I'm going to need you to ride out my heat with me, and I'll probably get knocked up because there's a decent chance my suppressants are failing.'"

She winces and agrees, "I can see how that's not exactly a low-pressure conversation starter."

"Speaking as the only alpha that is aware of this mess, can I add my two cents?" Ron says from the doorway. He's holding a tray with a steaming teapot and several mugs. He sets it down on the coffee table, then looks at me pointedly. "You're being an idiot."

"Ron!" Shelby snaps, slapping him on the arm.

"What?" he says, unfazed. "It's true. I've thought it this whole time, and I'm tired of not saying it because I keep hoping you two will figure it out. You're clearly mates."

"We aren't—" I start.

He cuts me off with a sharp look. "Ava. Yes, you are. It's why you can't stay away from each other, and it's why you had the... incident at the heat clinic." His tone shifts then, less confrontational and more careful, like he knows he's entering dangerous territory. "I hate bringing that up, because I know it was terrible. But your omega rejected that guy because she's already found her mate. That doesn't just go away."

I stare at him, chest tight.

"Look," he says, gentler now, "you can't opt out of your heats forever. And you clearly can't be with other alphas anymore either. So tell him. Give him the chance to take care of you instead of deciding for him."

We sit in silence for a minute. "Ya know," Shelby says, breaking it, "we could write up one hell of an NDA. Maybe combine it with some sort of pre-bonding prenup situation."

Ron blinks at her. "You're joking."

Both of us turn to look at him, dead serious. He studies our faces for a second, then exhales and shakes his head. "Okay, clearly you're not." He rubs a hand over the back of his neck. "Whatever it takes for you to feel safe enough to do this, but it needs to happen." He reaches out and takes my hand, looking deep into my eyes. "I promise you, that man wants to be with you in your heat. And I'd bet good money he won't care one bit about a possible pregnancy. My alpha side never did."

Shelby snorts. "Obviously," she says. "We have six kids."

Ron gives her a look. "You act like that wasn't a group decision. Plus, if you have any more heats, I'd have another baby with you in a heartbeat."

"Don't you place that kind of dark magic on me, Ronan McGregory."

I can't help but laugh at them. The knot in my chest is starting to loosen and unravel. Am I seriously considering this?

Shelby looks back at me, all business. "How close do you think you are to a heat?"

I frown. "I'm supposed to get more suppressants on Friday; I'm almost out. But I don't think they're going to be enough to stop it, and I don't even know if I'll make it that long."

"So," she says, straightening, "we clear your calendar, and you talk to Mark. Tonight."

I shake my head. "Not tonight."

Ron throws his hands up, already gearing up for an argument, but I lift one of mine to stop him. "Let me finish."

He exhales sharply, but stays quiet.

"I need to call my therapist first," I say, forcing myself to stay calm. "And I do want to draft that NDA and the prenup. If this somehow goes south, I want my trust fund and my house protected."

Shelby nods like this is exactly the answer she expected.

"So," I continue, "I'll text him tonight. I'll apologize for walking out, and I'll ask if we can talk tomorrow. When I'm not spiraling and my heat hormones aren't driving the bus."

Ron studies me for a long moment, then sighs. "I don't love the delay," he says finally, "but I'll accept it."

I roll my eyes. "Gee, thanks, Dad, I'm glad I have your approval."

Shelby lifts her mug in a small toast. "Look at that," she says. "Boundaries, plans, and legal documents. I'm very proud of you."

Luckily, I've been with my therapist long enough that when I send a message to her answering service that I'm in a bit of a crisis, she calls me immediately. We talk on the phone for over an hour, going through everything that happened tonight and all of my feelings about it, as well as the plan I put in place with Shelby.

By the time I hang up, I'm feeling considerably better and more like myself. I lift Valentino off my lap, and she gives me a very annoyed meow but settles when I successfully transfer her onto the perch in her cat tree. "Mommy is going to take a bath, drink a big glass of wine, and try to find the courage to text Mark," I croon to her, scratching beneath her chin.

In my bathroom, I flick the lights down to their lowest setting. The marble floor is cool under my feet, the space quiet except for the distant hum of the city outside the windows. I light a few candles along the edge of the tub and the vanity, their reflections bouncing softly off the gilt mirrors and old brass fixtures. Then I turn the taps on the large antique clawfoot tub, the pipes groaning faintly as hot water rushes through them.

It takes a minute to find the right temperature. I test it with my wrist, frowning when I realize it's cooler than I normally like. Not by much, but enough that I notice. Another small warning that my body is already ahead of me.

As the tub fills, I open a drawer in the vanity, pushing past cotton pads and half-used bottles until I find my thermometer. I sit on the edge of the counter and wait for it to beep.

100.7.

I close my eyes briefly. Shit. That's low for an omega fever, but it's climbing,

I open the medicine cabinet and take down the bottle of suppressants, tipping it to count what's left. Not many. If I don't meet Vinny on Friday, I'm going to be out entirely, heat or not. I sigh and shake two pills into my palm, then cup water from the sink to swallow them. When I lift my head, I catch my reflection in the mirror. My skin is flushed, my eyes swollen and red from crying, hair pulled back in a way that says I gave up hours ago.

"Yes," I murmur dryly to myself. "Beautiful. Exactly how one wants to look when telling their mate they love them for the first time."

I pad into the kitchen long enough to pour myself a glass of wine, then return to the bathroom just as the tub reaches the right depth. I turn the taps off and set the glass on the edge of the counter, and I lower myself into the water.

The heat seeps into my muscles immediately, and I sigh deeply. I sink down until the water reaches my shoulders and let my head rest against the curved porcelain. I stay there for a while, letting the warmth and the wine take the edge off the tension still lodged in my body, but finally I can no longer put off the inevitable. I dry my hands on the towel next to my wine glass and pick up my phone.

I open Mark's text thread and chew on my lip as I think of exactly what to say. Being at a loss for words is not something that I experience very often. An apology seems like a good place to start.

"I'm sorry. I panicked. I want to continue our conversation tomorrow. There are things I need to tell you."

I stare at it for a while, gathering my courage, but finally I hit send.

The response back is instant, but not at all what I expected.

Message unable to be delivered

Hurt and betrayal flood my chest, and I sit up so violently that water splashes out onto the floor. He blocked me? Another wave of tears threatens to overwhelm me, and I can feel a panic attack building on the edges of my senses.

I breathe in through my nose and blow it out slowly from my mouth until I feel a modicum of control returning.

Okay. This isn't ideal, but it's not the end of the world. It isn't like I don't see him almost daily. I know where he will be tomorrow night—the mayor's dinner. I'd been invited but hadn't planned on attending.

Looks like my plans just changed.

20

Mark

Marnie isn't quite ready when I arrive to pick her up. It makes me smile because it reminds me of Jess. That is, it makes me smile until I realize it leaves me sitting awkwardly with her father and two of her brothers—all alphas and all glowering at me. It's another bizarre reminder of the alternate reality that omegas live in. The fact that we are in our thirties and I feel like I'm on a high school date is insane. While Marnie might be one of the loveliest people I've ever met, when it comes to this, I'm not sorry we aren't mates.

It's been a miserable day, and honestly, I don't want to go to this stupid dinner. Ava must be feeling as awful as I am, because I received notice from her office that all of our cases for the rest of the week were being rescheduled. I don't think she's ever rescheduled anything in the two years that I've known her. She could be sick, I suppose, which gives me an uncomfortable feeling in my chest to think about, but she'd seemed fine last night.

Marnie appears in the doorway to the living room, interrupting my doom spiral. A skintight red number a la Jessica Rabbit. I hope she and Adam are compatible, because if so, she's about to knock his socks off, and I can't wait to see him gaping like a fish. She's piled all of her hair into some kind of messy updo that reminds me of Pamela Anderson in the '90s. There isn't a red-blooded male alive that doesn't remember and appreciate that look.

I stand and offer her my elbow. "You look beautiful. I was just thinking that I hope you and Adam hit it off, because he's going to lose it over this dress."

She laughs. "From your mouth to God's ears. I'm so ready to find my mate that I don't even care how desperate that sentence makes me sound."

We head out to the private car I'd hired for the evening, and I hold the door open for her. Once inside and alone, she gives me a soft, concerned look. "How are you?"

I give a small shake of my head and a bitter laugh. "I have definitely been better. Bit hungover today, if I'm being honest."

She nods in understanding. "Don't say I blame you. Do you want to tell me more about it, since you said it was complicated? Or would you rather not talk about it at all? I can do whatever you need me to."

I blow out a breath, weighing it. Fuck it. It's over, and even if Marnie tried to stir up trouble by sharing our secret, something I honestly can't picture her doing, there's no proof she could take to the Bar Association anyway.

I fill her in on the details, and to no surprise, she's wonderfully kind and supportive about it all. Eventually I've wrung it all out and we change the subject, spending the rest of the ride to Harvey's chatting easily.

The sound of the car's wheels crunching onto gravel alerts us that we've turned onto the long drive up to the mansion. Old trees line the drive, and the massive old colonial comes into view. Landscape lighting points upward at the house, illuminating the row of large windows, and of course, the American flag flying on display. Everything about it screams old money of New York's elite. Harvey is nothing if not consistent with his branding, even here.

Marnie stops mid-sentence to look out the window, mouth wide as she stares out the window. "It just hit me that I'm actually about to go inside the freaking mayor of New York City's house."

I laugh. "I promise, once you meet him, the wonder will wear off quickly."

A valet opens the door, and I slide out first, turning and offering her my hand. She swallows nervously and then extends her high heel and steps out gracefully. The shoes remind me of Ava, and I fake a smile through the wave of pain that hits me.

We make our way inside, handing our coats over to a worker dressed in a uniform that looks like something housekeeping would wear at a budget hotel. I have to resist rolling my eyes. Can't have the help forgetting their place amongst everyone else in black tie.

"This place is really nice, but it doesn't really feel like a *home*," Marnie whispers.

I shake my head. "I think he mostly stays at Gracie Mansion. I doubt he actually lives here. I'm sure it's something that's been in his family since the Revolution," I whisper back. "Alexander Hamilton's ghost probably chills with the ghosts that haunt this place."

She giggles, and we're ushered into the oversized dining room that was probably some kind of ballroom once upon a time. In the center, a giant table that has to be custom, is set with place settings, and small ivory cardstock tents that tell us where we are sitting. People are clustered in groups chatting, and I spy Adam. He catches my eye and gives me a nod, brows furrowing as he spots Marnie.

"Here comes my friend," I say to her.

"I see him," she says, and I have to keep from grinning at the mildly breathless tone of her voice. I'm not so heartbroken that I can't be excited about the possibility of someone else finding love.

Adam comes over, clapping me on the shoulder. "Hey, brother. You gonna introduce me to your lovely date?"

I smile and take a small step back so they can get a little closer to each other. "Not my date, actually. Just a friend," I clarify, signaling he's free to pursue.

A wolfish grin spreads across his face, and he extends a hand. "Well then, hello new friend. My name's Adam Jenkins."

She slips her hand in his, and I watch as both of them gasp as they touch and catch each other's scent. "Oh," she says, looking a little shell-shocked. "I'm Marnie."

I can't help but chuckle, placing my hand on the low of Marnie's back to guide her to a spot where we can all talk, deliberately riling Adam up just because I can. The look he gives me for touching her could peel wallpaper. The evening is suddenly looking far more fun than I expected.

"Well, isn't this cozy?"

I turn to find Ava standing just behind me. She's wearing a strapless black lace gown that falls all the way to the floor, her hair pulled into a loose side ponytail so the curls spill over one shoulder. It's simpler than what she usually wears, almost as if she got ready in a hurry. For half a second, guilt punches through me, like I've been caught doing something wrong just by standing here with Marnie. Then anger replaces it just as quickly. Fuck that. She's the one who walked away.

Her eyes flick between the two of us, narrowed, brows drawn tight. I expect Marnie to step back to make it obvious this isn't a date, so when she slides her hand around my bicep and instead leans in, I nearly flinch. She tips her chin up, batting her eyes at me with exaggerated sweetness. "Markie-poo, who's this?" she asks.

I hear Adam choke on a sound behind us, but I'm too stunned to respond. Is she doing this on purpose, trying to make Ava jealous?

"Markie-poo?" Ava repeats, fists clenched at her sides. "Are you on a fucking date with this omega?" she hisses.

My shock evaporates, replaced by heat. "I'm sorry, but I fail to see how that's any of your business," I say at the exact moment Marnie cheerfully confirms that we are. I cut a look at her, but she's focused entirely on Ava.

"Less than twenty-four hours, huh?" Ava asks coldly. "Clearly that was a very serious declaration of love."

"Keep your voice down, Ava," I say quietly. "Remember where we are."

"I don't care where we fucking are," she snaps, and for a second, she looks like someone I don't recognize. I've never seen her lose control. Her skin is flushed, and there are a few tiny beads of sweat at the edge of her hairline. I frown despite my anger, remembering that Shelby cleared her schedule. Maybe she really is sick.

I gently pull my arm free from Marnie's hand and take a step closer. "Are you all right?" I ask, genuinely concerned.

Ava glares at me, jaw tightening, and I can practically see her coiling in on herself, gathering venom to strike. Viper, indeed. Hope Marnie understands exactly what she just provoked.

Before Ava can unleash whatever she's about to say, Harvey approaches from the side, clearing his throat to signal his presence. "Ms. Kendrick, I didn't actually expect you to take me up on my invitation," he says mildly. "I hope you and Mr. Taylor aren't planning one of your famous arguments right here in my dining room." His gaze flicks between the two of us, then over to Marnie. There's a hint of amusement there, a smile tugging at the corner of his mouth.

Shit. If he's starting to connect the dots, he'll be like a bloodhound on the trail.

Ava inhales, visibly forcing herself back under control. It takes longer than usual, further testament to how different she is tonight. When she turns to Harvey, her posture has completely shifted. Polite. Detached. Mildly bored. "Of course not, Mr. Mayor. I was simply surprised to see Mr. Taylor on a date with an omega. I thought your particular circle believed they should be hidden away until bonded."

"Well," he draws, "Mr. Taylor appears to have had a change of heart regarding omega rights. I had assumed you were behind that. Still, I must ask, how else is an omega meant to bond if they don't date? If Mark here wants a future in politics, he's well past the age where he should be settling down with a pretty little omega and having babies."

I feel Marnie stiffen beside me, and I watch Ava coil again.

"Yes, of course," Ava says, voice dripping with sickly sweet saccharine. "How could I have forgotten? What else are omegas good for?"

"Your words, Ms. Kendrick, not mine," he quips.

"Mr. Mayor, you have a beautiful home," Marnie says, obviously trying to defuse the situation. "Mark and I were just discussing how old we thought it might be. Has it been in your family long?"

Harvey smiles at her, the kind of smile that makes Adam shift closer with a low growl. Harvey notices. Of course he does. This night is already spiraling, and the last thing I need is him realizing Adam's interest, not mine, lies with Marnie. That would only reinforce every suspicion already forming in his head.

"Why, thank you, dear," he says warmly. "The land itself has been in my family since before the Revolutionary War. The original structure burned down, but this home was built in the late 1800s."

"Mr. Mayor," Adam says smoothly, his earlier territorial instinct buried, "I was wondering if you would be willing to sit with me and give me some quotes for an upcoming article I'm doing."

Adam guides him away, giving me a quick, pointed glance over his shoulder as Harvey prattles on, unable to resist an opportunity to blowhard to the press.

Ava spins on her heel, storming away without a word.

"Go after her," Marnie hisses.

I shake my head. "No. I'm here with you, and I'm not abandoning you to deal with her tantrum."

She rolls her eyes. "If I'm right, you *need* to go after her."

"Right about what?" I ask, genuinely confused.

"Oh my God, alphas are so fucking stupid sometimes! Fine, have it your way."

"You going to fill me in on whatever riddles you're speaking in?"

She shakes her head. "Nope. You two idiots will either figure it out or you won't," she says with a shrug. "Now, let's go save my mate from that horrid mayor."

I grin, forgetting the drama with Ava for a moment. "Mate, huh? So, I was right? You two scented each other?"

She blushes and nods. "I mean, I think so. We obviously didn't get a chance to talk or anything, so I don't know if he felt it on his side, but it seemed like he did."

"Oh, he did. He wouldn't have bristled from me touching you otherwise."

Across the room, Adam is scribbling in a small notepad while Harvey talks at him. He looks up when he notices us approaching, confusion flickering across his face, and I immediately start questioning my choice not to go after Ava. Letting her storm off might have been a mistake.

"Ah, Mark," Harvey says, clearly pleased. "I was discussing my firm stance on crime with Mr. Jenkins here." He glances around, clocking the small audience of potential donors we have nearby, and deliberately raises his voice. "What did you end up deciding with that delinquent omega we disagreed over yesterday?" He looks like a cat with a canary, thinking he's cornered me.

"I sent a plea deal to Ms. Kendrick, and they accepted," I say coolly, borrowing Ava's detached tone and meeting his gaze without blinking. "Time served, a significant fine, and community service. For the record, I don't appreciate you strong-arming my staff into sending a plea deal offer in my name. That was more than a little over the line."

A flush creeps up over the edge of his collar, and I know he's furious that I called him out in front of everyone. Two can play at this game.

"I don't understand why you've suddenly lost interest in prosecuting crime, seeing as that's your entire job," he snaps. "She's a drug addict. The last thing the city needs is more of them on our streets."

"Suppressants aren't drugs," Marnie cuts in beside me, her voice calm but firm. "They're medicine. They're only illegal because we refuse to fund proper research into omega reproduction."

I barely manage to hide my surprise. I hadn't expected sunny, polite Marnie to step directly into the mayor's line of fire like that.

Harvey turns on her, lip curling. "If I want an omega's opinion, I'll ask for it."

"Is that the mayor's official position, for the record?" Adam says dryly, not even looking up from his notepad.

Harvey blinks, clearly startled, as if he'd momentarily forgotten Adam was there at all. "Of course not," he says quickly. "I apologize; that was rude and not how I meant it. I simply believe many omegas lack the nuance to fully understand this issue. That's why we shelter them—for their protection. Heat cycles are natural. Experimenting on omegas with chemicals interferes with nature itself. Our omegas are far too precious for that."

"Menstruation for beta women is natural as well, and yet they have birth control," Marnie challenges.

"Beta women also make up a far more sizeable percentage of the population, dear," he says, condescension dripping from his tone. "As I said, omegas are precious. We simply can't risk it."

I half expect him to pat the top of her head.

"If you'll excuse me, I need to go speak with my other guests before dinner is served," he says smoothly, offering us a tight smile. Before he turns, he gives me one last look, and I can tell that he thinks he's won this round. Maybe he has.

Do I even want to be mayor if I have to sell my soul to men like Harold Harvey for their donations? I really don't know anymore.

21

Ava

Stupid. I am so fucking stupid.

The moment Tony pulls back up in front of the mayor's house, I all but throw myself into the car. Jealousy and betrayal crash through me in equal measure, and even though a distant part of my brain knows I'm being unreasonable, I can't slow it down. My heat has arrived full force, and my omega has seized the wheel. Logic doesn't stand a chance.

My mind won't let go of the image. That blonde bitch wrapped around his arm, fingers digging into his bicep like she belonged there, tilting her face up at him and batting her lashes. *Markie-poo.* The nickname makes me gag. What kind of ridiculous, infantilizing bullshit is that supposed to be?

A cramp clamps down low and hard, stealing the air from my lungs. I groan and fold forward, fists pressing into my abdomen to relieve the pain with counter-pressure.

I have no idea what I'm going to do.

"Do you want to find a clinic?" Tony asks gently, already watching me in the rearview mirror.

The suggestion alone makes my heart race. Panic flares quickly, and I shake my head so hard it makes me dizzy. "No. No, just take me home." My voice comes out strained. "I'll take more suppressants. Sleeping pills. I'll deal with it tomorrow."

"Ava," he says carefully, "we should turn around. You can still talk to him."

"No!" The word comes out too sharp, and I wince immediately, guilt stacking on top of everything else. Tony doesn't deserve that. "I'm sorry. I just... no. He's on a date. With an omega."

"And?" Tony prompts.

"And he's going to smell like her," I snap, the thought making my chest ache. "I can't let him into my nest like that." My voice breaks, tears spilling over before I can stop them. My skin feels overheated and hypersensitive, like every nerve is lit up at once. "If he replaced me that fast, then we obviously can't be mates."

"That's not—"

I don't want to hear it. Whatever reasonable thing he's about to say has no place here, not when my body is screaming and my heart feels flayed open. I hit the button to raise the partition and curl in on myself, knees pulled tight to my chest. It's childish. I know it is. But I'm an omega in heat, and I want to be allowed this. Just for a little while.

Everything hurts. My body. My heart. My pride.

Through the haze, I hear Tony's muffled voice as he calls someone. Shelby, probably. Maybe Jack. I hope it's Jack. Maybe he can get to Mom, convince her to help me push this off again. I don't even care how much she yells if she can just make it stop.

I rock gently, a soft, broken sound slipping out of me as my scent floods the enclosed space. Oranges and deep vanilla, rich and unmistakable, scorched at the edges by stress and pain. The cramps deepen, rolling and tearing, and it feels like my uterus is trying to rip itself apart from the inside. My whole body feels that way. I've been through heats before. They're always painful until I can get a knot. But never like this.

My muscles tense and my body convulses against the seat.

By the time the car stops, the seizure has stopped, but the pain has gone so far past tolerable that everything feels unreal, hazy, like I'm drugged. The door opens and light floods in—too bright, too much, and I curl tighter into myself. I don't want to be out there. Out there is open and exposed. In here, it's dark and contained.

Where's Mark?

Why isn't he here?

I need Mark.

I shake my head weakly, trying to shove the thought away. *No. Mark is with another omega. He chose her. He rejected us.*

Hands touch my skin, and I hiss, instinctively trying to pull back, until a familiar scent cuts through the fog. Muted lemon. Jack. "Christ, Mateo, she's burning up," he says. His voice sounds distant, warped, like it's coming through water. I don't catch Mateo's reply.

I'm glad Mateo is here with Jack.

Maybe he can save me.

Or at least comfort Jack if he can't.

I don't remember getting out of the car. One second I'm folded into the seat, the next I'm cradled against Jack's chest, his arms tight around me as he carries me inside.

Where are we going?

I press my face harder into his shoulder. His scent is familiar and would normally soothe me. But it's *wrong*. So wrong. I need bourbon and leather, not citrus.

Where's Mark?

A sound tears out of me, high-pitched and keening. I don't realize at first that the whine is coming from me, but when I do, I do it louder. Maybe if he hears me, he'll come. Mark can fix this.

Then another scent hits me, familiar and heavy, wrapping around me like a blanket. Home. The tension eases just a fraction. "Nest," I manage, the word scraping out of my throat. My mouth feels dry and swollen, like my tongue barely fits.

"Not yet, sweets," Jack says, his voice tight. Not like him at all. He sounds scared. I should fix that. I should know how. "Mateo says we've gotta get the fever down first. He's gonna give you a shot, okay? Mom says it'll help some. Just till she can get here tomorrow."

Tomorrow.

I won't last that long. It's possible for omegas to die from their heats without an alpha, and I'm definitely alpha-less. I shake my head, panic flaring. "Nest," I cry again, louder this time. He's not listening. Why won't he listen?

Water runs somewhere nearby. Mateo's voice cuts in, sharp and controlled, saying something about the hospital.

"No," I say immediately.

They argue over me, voices overlapping, too fast to follow. I give up trying to understand and close my eyes, surrendering to the pain instead.

Then suddenly, I'm being lowered into water.

It might be lukewarm, but against my overheated skin, it feels like ice. I gasp, lungs seizing. A sharp prick at my elbow follows, then a bitter, metallic taste floods my mouth. Nausea rolls hard and fast.

"I'm gonna be sick," I choke.

Hands move quickly, practiced, rolling me onto my side over the edge of the tub. I retch, emptying what little is in my stomach into the trash can that magically appears. Thanks, random floating hands.

Slowly, the fuzziness at the edges of my vision recedes. The pain doesn't vanish, but it dulls, no longer screaming. I blink and lift my head to find Mateo crouched beside the tub, studying me closely.

"Welcome back to the land of the living," he says quietly. His face shows obvious signs of concern, but he also looks calm and in control. Perks of being a trauma nurse, I guess.

"I'm sorry for puking," I rasp.

He snorts. "Not even the first time this week someone's thrown up in front of me. Least it wasn't on my shoes. I figured you would, given what your mom had me draw up."

"What... was that?" My voice sounds wrecked.

"A frankly bizarre cocktail of hormones, painkillers, and for reasons known only to her, an antacid."

"Are you gonna get in trouble?" I croak. "I know a lawyer."

His mouth twitches. "Your mother assures me she'll handle the hospital end of it. Still, I might have to take you up on that." Then his expression sharpens. "I really think you should go in, Ava. That fever was dangerously high. I think you might have seized once already. This is serious."

"No hospital." I try to sit up and frown when I realize I'm still submerged, my evening gown floating uselessly around me. "You couldn't take the dress off first?"

Mateo rolls his eyes. "Sorry. I was busy keeping you alive and stopping your brother from having a heart attack."

"Where is Jack, anyways?"

"I think he's in the living room, talking to your mom," he says. "She and your dad are catching the first flight back to New York. Wouldn't want to be you tomorrow."

I groan. "I don't want to be me *right now*."

"Come on," he says, already moving. "Let's get you into something dry and comfortable."

He helps me out of the ruined dress and into a robe before depositing me onto the vintage chaise tucked along the wall near the closet door. "Stay here," he orders. "I'll grab you some clothes."

The moment he turns his back, I ignore him and shuffle to the vanity, opening the medicine cabinet and reaching for my suppressants. If I take a few, surely between that and whatever Mom cooked up, I can hold out until she gets here. I tip the bottle, but a sudden wave of vertigo hits, and my fingers fumble.

I watch in horror as the bottle slips and the last remaining pills fall straight down the drain.

I close my eyes and count backwards, forcing myself to breathe. This is not a crisis. I just have to make it to tomorrow. Mom will fix it. I'll just reschedule a pickup with Vinny.

Mateo comes back with a stack of clothes and immediately notices the empty bottle. "What happened?"

"I was going to take some suppressants," I admit. "Figured they could only help whatever you gave me, but I spilled them."

He exhales slowly and rubs at his temple. "First of all, drug interactions are a thing, Ava. You do not mix and match hormones without checking." He sets the clothes on the counter. "Second, I swear you and your brother are going to give me a stroke."

"Don't yell at me," I whine. "I almost died, and I still feel like shit."

He makes a clawing gesture like he's contemplating my murder, then reins it in and steers me back to the chaise. "Let's get you dressed," he says, calmer now. "Then you can crawl into your nest, okay?"

I nod, letting him help me into a soft pajama set. "I figured you're still hot and sensitive," he explains, "so this was the best I could find."

"Thank you, Mateo. Really." My throat tightens. "I'm sorry I'm being such a pain in the ass."

He laughs. "This is nothing compared to your brother with a cold."

As if summoned, Jack appears, phone held in front of him like it's a live grenade. "Mom, here, you can talk to her yourself. Mateo gave her the shot, and she looks better."

"Hi, Mom," I say weakly, glaring at Jack for the lack of warning.

"Ava, what the hell is going on?" Her voice is warm and concerned right now, but I know as soon as she establishes that I'm no longer in immediate mortal danger, that will quickly change.

"Before we get into it," I say dryly, "can you give me the cliff notes on what Jack already told you? I'm a little fuzzy on the details myself."

There's a pause. I hear murmuring in the background. Dad, no doubt.

"Your brother," she says carefully, "said Tony called him saying you went into heat suddenly, were incoherent, and were burning up in the back of the car. You may have had a febrile seizure."

"That does sound like what happened," I agree.

"Do you have any idea why?"

I know a trap when I see one, or I guess in this case, hear one. If I lie and say no, she'll catch me in that. If I explain why, I'm going to get the riot act. I sigh. I don't have the energy to dodge it. And honestly, I want my mom, so best to get it over with.

"I have theories," I admit. "There was an incident with my last heat that I will *not* talk about right now," I say firmly. "And... the suppressants haven't been working like they used to. I've had to double or triple the dose sometimes." I leave off the part that this is almost certainly due to the copious amount of sex I've been having with an alpha who might be my mate.

She's silent for a moment. "And you've been using the same ones?"

"Yes."

"The strongest kind? Formulated through my lab connections overseas?"

Jack grimaces and makes a slicing motion across his throat.

I scrunch my nose up and shut my eyes. "Yes?"

"Okay," her voice is chilly now. "So just to be clear. You haven't had a normal, successful heat in nearly a year, and instead of consulting your mother, a physician who specializes in omega reproductive cycles, you chose to double or triple pharmaceutical-grade hormones at the highest dosage available?"

"Well, when you say it like that," I mutter.

There's a strained choking sound over the line. "Hank," Mom snaps, "talk to your daughter before I say something unforgivable."

The phone shifts. "Peanut," Dad says gently, "you scared us half to death. I don't think I've ever heard Jack that panicked."

"I know, Daddy," I whisper. "I was going to call. The other night. But it was late, and then I got busy, and then everything just... fell apart."

Mom says something sharp in the background. Dad covers the speaker briefly, then returns. "If your fever spikes again, you'll need to go to a clinic."

"Daddy, I can't." The weight of it all crashes down at once, and I start sobbing.

Mom's voice cuts back in. "Jack, give your sister the phone. You and Mateo step out. Hank, tell the flight attendant I need another pillow."

They obey instantly.

A moment later, she exhales, and her voice softens. "Did something happen at the clinic?"

"Yes," I manage to choke out.

"Did someone hurt you?" My silence must be answer enough. "Oh baby, I'm so sorry," she says, tears thickening her voice. "Why didn't you tell me?"

"I didn't want to tell anyone," I sob. "I didn't even tell Jack. Tony picked me up and took me to Shelby's house, so they know, but only because of that. If it hadn't happened, no one would know."

"Okay," she says, and it sounds like she's more thinking out loud than actually talking to me. "If your fever spikes again, you need to take some more suppressants—"

The call drops before I can tell her that I don't have any more. I try to call her back, but it goes straight to voicemail. The plane's wifi must have cut out. Shit.

I come out of the bathroom and hand Jack his phone. "I'm going to lie down in my nest. I feel awful."

Mateo frowns. "What did she say to do if your heat spikes again?"

I give a sharp laugh. "Take more suppressants. Which I don't have. So I'm just going to go to sleep and hopefully stay unconscious until she lands."

Jack and Mateo look at each other, and I can tell they are not in agreement with this plan, but what other choice do I have? I don't have any suppressants. I can't go to a clinic or the hospital, so this is how I have to ride out the next twelve hours.

You could call our alpha, my omega whines.

Except no, I can't. He blocked me. And he's on a date. And I've ruined everything. So, bed it is.

22

Mark

"Is your family going to chase me with shotguns or pitchforks if I let you come home with a different alpha than you left with?" I ask Marnie seriously. After the whole situation with Harvey, the three of us had escaped to a late-night diner for milkshakes. It quickly became apparent that I'm the third wheel, so I'm about to take my leave.

Marnie giggles and looks over at Adam. "I already texted my mom to tell her what happened and that I probably won't be home tonight."

Adam can't keep his eyes off her. I've never seen him like this before. Like a kid on Christmas that just got everything on his list.

"Tell you what, this car is paid up through until 1:00 a.m. You two crazy lovebirds go have fun before you go wherever you're going for the night."

"No, man, we can't take your car," Adam says. It's clearly the same kind of tone you give your grandma when you tell her that you don't *need* the twenty dollars she's trying to slip you without your mom noticing.

"It's fine. Really. I'll get a cab."

Marnie bites her lip and looks at him, and it doesn't take much more convincing. They quickly slide out of the diner booth and head out the door. They're so adorable, it makes my chest ache. It also makes me think about Ava.

Maybe I was too harsh to block her. She obviously came to Harvey's to talk to me, and even though she acted like a brat because she was jealous, do I really have a lot of stones to throw on that one? Did I not literally fuck her on one of her dates and send her back to the table?

All I wanted was some effort on her part. An indication that I mattered, that *we* mattered enough to fight for, and she gave me that.

I chew on my lip and pull my phone from my pocket, staring at her name for a long second before hitting unblock in the contact details. Almost immediately, a text message comes through.

"I'm sorry. I panicked. I want to continue our conversation tomorrow. There are things I need to tell you."

I start to respond and then think better of it. No. I'm done with the text messages. We need to actually speak to each other, not leave any room for misunderstanding. If this is going to happen, it needs to be a real conversation.

I hit call, and it goes straight to voicemail. I frown and hang up without leaving a message. She clearly didn't block me, or it wouldn't have rung through. But Ava never has her phone off. I've texted her at all kinds of hours of the night.

Unease settles in my chest. She did seem different tonight. And she was flushed and sweating like she was running a fever. What if she's actually sick? What if she passed out in her bathroom, phone dead, no one around to notice?

I call again, and the same thing happens. This time, I leave a message. "I don't know if you're just pissed and turned your phone off or if something is wrong, but I'm coming over."

I flag down a cab and give the driver her address, barely registering his nod before sliding into the back seat. The city crawls past the windows, lights smeared and distorted, and my anxiety ramps higher with every passing minute. The driver takes a different route than I would have, cutting across unfamiliar streets, and we hit traffic anyway. Nearly 11:00 at night, and we're barely moving.

I try her phone again. Still off.

I tap the backs of my fingers against my palm, leg bouncing restlessly as we inch along at a glacial pace. "What the hell is with this traffic tonight?"

The cabbie shakes his head. "Think it has something to do with the raids. There's a bunch of them tonight, and traffic is nuts everywhere."

I look up. "Raids?"

"Yeah. Some big, coordinated thing," he says. "Mayor and police commissioner trying to shut down the omega suppressant supply chain. Streets are a mess everywhere."

My stomach drops.

"Bullshit, if you ask me," he adds. "Like we don't have bigger problems than omega birth control. Waste of taxpayer money."

I pull my phone back out and look up what he's talking about. And sure enough, Harvey had announced a sting operation happening tonight with the full force of the NYPD. He must have timed it to release during the dinner party. Prick. Is this my punishment for offering Katie a plea deal?

Joke's on him, I'll offer every single omega without a record. The dealers can be handled on a case-by-case basis. I chew on my thumbnail as another thought settles. Maybe this is why Ava's phone is going to voicemail.

For a second, I feel foolish. Maybe I'm about to show up to her apartment and find it empty because she's downtown with clients. Only, if the raids are happening now, they wouldn't have had time to book everyone and get lawyer calls out, I remind myself.

The cab turns down a side street. Traffic clears for a blessed moment, then locks up again. Red and blue lights flash a block or so ahead, and I let out a frustrated breath. Ava's only a few blocks away now. With this much police presence, no one's going to try anything stupid.

"Hey," I say, leaning forward. "I'm gonna walk the rest of the way." I hand the driver enough cash to cover the fare and a decent tip, since he's going to be stuck in gridlock for a while. He looks relieved.

I climb out, pulling my coat tighter around myself to brace against the chill that has overtaken the city. So much for the beautiful spring weather we'd been having, it's practically like winter again. I walk quickly, cutting down a different side street to avoid the cluster of cops ahead. I step partially into an alley to avoid a very questionable puddle. A low pained groan comes from the darkness.

I slow, debating. Every instinct tells me to keep moving. Ava is my priority. But I can't just leave someone hurt without checking.

I turn back and step into the dark corridor, senses on high alert. I really don't think I'm in danger, but it *is* New York. I catch the faintest hint of a beta, some kind of citrusy lemon with the copper scent of blood. Something about the scent feels familiar. My alpha side surges to the forefront of my mind, urging me forward.

I spy a pair of shoes sticking out from behind a dumpster. They look like expensive sneakers, which is not what I'd expect back here. "Hey," I call carefully, circling just enough to see without putting myself in reach. "You all right?"

Everything clicks at once. I recognize him. Not well, but enough. There's also a deep gash on his forehead oozing blood over his brow and matting his auburn hair. Clutched loosely in one hand are two unmarked prescription bottles full of pills.

I've seen pictures of Jack before, and run into him once at a fundraiser gala he attended with Ava.

There is a police raid on illegal omega suppressants two blocks over, and I suddenly find Ava's brother injured and holding two bottles of pills? Everything about this screams trouble.

"Hey. It's Jack, right?" I ask, already kneeling. "Can you hear me?"

As I wait for a response, I act almost on instinct before I realize what I'm doing. I pull a handkerchief from my pocket, pick up the bottles carefully, wipe them down, and toss them into the dumpster. Guilt flares briefly, then dies. I literally just decided I'd cut omegas some slack. And Ava would never let her brother rot in jail.

Rationalizing? Probably.

I'll live with it.

Jack groans again and blinks, eyes unfocused. "Mark?" His voice is slurred.

"Can you walk?" I ask. I can hear shouts approaching, and it occurs to me that they might be fanning out to look for anyone who ran. We need to get out of here.

"Uh... maybe?" He tries to push himself upright and nearly topples.

"Dammit," I growl. I toss his arm around my shoulders, helping him stay upright. "Come on, I'm gonna take you to Ava's. Do you have your phone?"

"No," he drags out. "Afraid the cops—"

"Stop talking," I snap. "Forget I asked. I'm the district attorney. Don't incriminate yourself to me. I know your sister taught you better."

"I gotta help her," he mumbles. "She needs me."

My pulse spikes. "What's wrong with Ava?" I demand.

"She's sick," he says thickly. "Real sick. I was so scared. Teo helped, but what if it happened again? Mom is in the air still."

I have no idea what he's talking about, but I know enough. I glance down at him, calculating if I could carry him. I'm strong, but he's easily six-three and built like he's carved from marble. Not an ideal situation.

I frown. "Come on," I say grimly. "If she needs help, we need to move faster."

He nods and staggers forward, leaning heavily into me. We make it a block. Then another. Every second feels too slow.

Finally, Ava's building comes into view. Relief hits hard and fast. I guide him toward the back entrance, suddenly thankful she gave me the service elevator code during one of our many secret visits. Dragging a bleeding man through the lobby would probably get more attention than I'd prefer at the moment, thank you very much.

I punch in the code that'll take us straight to Ava's floor. In the light of the elevator, I can get a better look at Jack. He's paler than I'd like, and he already has one hell of a goose egg forming. But I'm pretty sure I learned in some first aid class that swelling out is better than dipping in on head injuries. I think I remember that Jack is married to somebody in health care? Hopefully I can find his phone and call them after I figure out what's going on with Ava.

The elevator dings, and the doors slide open. I adjust Jack, and we step off.

A man steps toward Jack, talking fast and panicked, but the words don't register. Instead, I'm busy feeling like I got hit by a freight train at full speed. The hallway outside the elevator smells like an orange dreamsicle factory exploded. And my alpha recognizes it for what it is immediately. An omega in heat. *My* omega in heat.

"Somebody tell me what the fuck is going on. Right now," I bark.

The sound of it startles me almost as much as everyone else. I've never used an alpha bark in my life. I didn't even know I could. Yet the command snaps through the space, and both of the beta men react.

Jack starts mumbling, but the man removing him from my arms looks at me earnestly. I think he might be the partner of Jack's I was remembering, but my brain is currently a bit fuzzy.

"Ava is in heat," he says quickly. "When I left to grab food, she was asleep in the nest, and Jack was in the living room. When I got back, neither of them were here. Both their phones were. That's all I know."

"What do you mean, she's gone?" I demand, shoving past him into the apartment as if he might be lying to me.

The scent intensifies with every step. Sweet and rich, deeper than I've ever scented her before. If I thought I was obsessed with it before, I'm a goner now. Valentino runs to me, weaving between my legs. I'd normally pet her, but I step over her this time, earning a disgruntled howl for my betrayal.

"Ava!" I yell, even though I have no real reason to doubt what Jack's husband just told me. There's no answer. I spin back to him and Jack. "Did you check with Tony? If she went somewhere, he would have driven her."

"Tried but it went straight to voicemail," Mateo says, settling Jack onto a stool and flicking on his phone flashlight to inspect the gash on his head. "I left Shelby a message telling her to call me back ASAP. I was about to head downstairs and ask the front desk when you all got off the elevator. I don't mean to be rude, but are you Mark? And why does my husband have a head wound?"

I rake a hand through my hair, pacing. My skin feels too tight, my body buzzing with a violent need to move, to hunt, to find my mate.

The word hits me with equal parts horror and absolute certainty. *She's my mate.*

"Hey," the smaller man snaps, sharp enough to cut through the fog. "I need you with us. I know you're on the verge of an alpha breakdown or something, but my husband is bleeding."

I force my attention back to him. "Yes. I'm Mark. I don't know exactly what happened. I found him behind a dumpster about three blocks over. It looked like a police raid was happening nearby."

He goes pale. "The suppressant raid?"

"Mateo," Jack mumbles. "I was just trying to help."

I hold up a hand immediately. "Stop!" I point to myself. "Manhattan DA. Remember?" Why are they so determined to incriminate themselves??

Mateo exhales and nods, then softens as he turns back to Jack. "How'd you hit your head, baby?"

"I was running," Jack slurs. "Tried to dodge a gross puddle. Tripped. Overcorrected. Dumpster won."

Mateo mutters under his breath and starts cleaning the wound. I turn back toward the apartment, fists clenched. "Where would Ava have gone?"

"I don't know," Mateo admits. "I really didn't think she was in any condition to leave. After the seizure earlier—" He cuts himself off, glancing at Jack.

My hands curl tighter. "Seizure?" I grind out.

"S'okay," Jack says weakly. "He knows now."

Mateo mutters something about *HIPAA* and *this damn family*. It's mostly in Spanish, and mine isn't good enough to follow along completely. Finally, he sighs. "After she left the mayor's, she went into full-blown heat in the car. Tony called us. We called their mom. We think her fever spiked high enough to cause a seizure. I got it under control and pushed back the worst of it, so like I said, she was sleeping in the nest when I left."

"Maybe she went to a clinic," Jack says quietly.

Rage detonates in my chest, and I have to place my palms on the dining table and breathe through it.

"She seemed really adamant that a clinic was not an option," Mateo says carefully, eyeing me with apprehension. "But I guess if the pain got bad enough..."

"Why didn't she *tell* me?" The words rip out of me. I want to tear the apartment apart. Tear through the city. No one touches her.

Only, isn't this exactly how Ava operates? She walls herself off. Handles everything alone, even when it hurts her. Especially when it hurts her. I can absolutely see her choosing a clinic over honesty and vulnerability.

My alpha is already pulling me toward the door. "I'm going to go downstairs and talk to the front desk. I can't sit here and do nothing."

I take the other elevator, the one that drops straight to the main floor. The doors slide shut, and the sudden quiet surrounds me, making the noise in my head seem ten times louder. I press my forehead against the cool wood paneling and breathe in through my nose, out through my mouth, trying to get a handle on myself.

I'm overwhelmed. Every interaction we've ever had now makes more sense when viewed in a different light. Yet I also have more questions than ever before.

Did she know we were mates this entire time and chose to keep it buried?

The elevator opens, and I turn immediately, crossing the lobby in long, purposeful strides. An older man with neatly combed white hair looks up from the desk, his expression calm, almost expectant.

"Good evening, Mr. Taylor," he says smoothly.

I slow, caught off guard. "Hello. I'm sorry, do we know each other?"

"Ah, my apologies," he replies. "I know you from the papers, of course. And," he adds, gesturing toward a monitor on the desk, "from our security system."

The screen shows a split feed of the main and service elevators. Not the first time he's seen me enter Ava's penthouse, then.

I nod once. "Right. Well, then you understand why I'm asking. I'm looking for Ms. Kendrick. She isn't well, and she left earlier. Did you happen to see her?"

"Yes," he says without hesitation. "She buzzed down and told me she couldn't locate her phone and asked if I could call her a car."

I perk up. "Did you call her normal driver?"

"No," he answers sheepishly. "She couldn't recall the number, and unfortunately, I didn't have it on file. An oversight that will be corrected, I assure you." He hesitates, clearly choosing his words. "She requested a... particular kind of car service. Which I procured."

For a second I don't understand, but then it clicks. Omega emergency transport. They only employ vetted betas and advertise discretion. I've seen their commercials late at night when I can't sleep.

They typically provide transport to heat clinics.

I let out a sharp breath. "Do you know where she asked to be taken?"

He shakes his head. "I escorted her to the vehicle, but there was an alpha approaching, and I prioritized getting her secured inside. I didn't hear the destination. Though I assumed—"

"I know," I cut in, rubbing at my jaw. "Yeah."

I force myself to straighten up. "Could you buzz her apartment and let her brother know that information? So they're not left guessing."

"Of course, sir."

I turn toward the front doors, my steps slowing as I reach them.

I have no idea what to do now. My mate is gone. In heat and alone. I have no clue where to possibly even start looking, and worse yet, she chose to go to a clinic instead of letting me help her.

Left with no other choice, I flag down a cab and tell them to take me home. If she's in heat, it gives me a few days to try and figure out what the hell to say to her. Or if I even want to talk to her after this.

I have no idea how long it takes to get to my apartment. It could have been the normal twenty minutes or two hours, for all the attention I pay. Memories of the last couple months—the last two years, actually—play through my mind, and I realize how many signs I completely missed. How could I have been so blind?

I pay the driver and head into my building. My clothes must have absorbed her scent at the penthouse, because it's driving me slowly mad. I can't decide if I want to burn my outfit or roll around on it.

I get off on my floor and punch in the code to my door, pushing it open.

The scent intensifies, and my head snaps up. The lights are mostly off, leaving the space dim except for the light coming in from the large window overlooking the city. But I can still make out Ava's form, huddled on the couch, the blanket from my bed wrapped around her like a burrito.

"Hi," she says pitifully.

A lot of emotions cross Mark's face, but strangely, he doesn't look nearly as shocked as I expected him to be. He closes the door behind him and goes to approach me, but I hold up a hand. "Not yet. We should talk first; I think I owe you that. And the closer you get, the more likely you are to lose control."

"I know a good amount already," he says roughly. "Though there are some questions I would appreciate answers to sooner rather than later."

I frown. "How?"

"I just left your penthouse. I found Jack injured—"

"What? Is Jack okay?" I jump up and immediately regret it as a cramp seizes me, making me double over. Mark tries to move again, and I shake my head, breathing through it. "I'm okay. How's Jack?"

"He's fine. It's a long story, but basically, he was trying to get you suppressants, ran from a police raid, and went headfirst into a dumpster. I left him with Mateo."

I close my eyes. Goddamnit, Jack. "Allegedly," I grit through my teeth. I'm still a lawyer, after all. Well, hopefully I can still be one after all of this.

A soft smile tips up the corner of his mouth. "Allegedly," he agrees.

"Okay," I say. "I can pretty well put the pieces together, and the rest, I'll fill in later when I strangle my little brother. How much do *you* know?"

"I know you're an omega. I know you're in heat. I know you apparently had a seizure earlier. And I know you're my mate. What I don't know is how long you've known."

I grimace. He does not sound thrilled with me, and I do not have the energy to fight him. It's taking most of what little I have left to stay planted on this couch and not present for him and beg for his knot. Even that, I figure I only can do for a few more minutes. As soon as I caught his scent, I could feel the edges of my mind going fuzzy.

"That I'm an omega? For the last couple decades."

"You know what I'm fucking talking about, Ava, don't be coy," he snaps. I notice that he's gripping the backrest of one of the dining chairs so hard that his knuckles are blanched.

"I didn't accept it until the day before yesterday. I texted you that I wanted to talk, but you had me blocked, which is why I went to Harvey's tonight. But you were on a fucking date—"

"I wasn't," he cuts me off. "She was trying to make you jealous. I brought her to introduce her to Adam, and it turns out they're mates."

"Oh," I say, suddenly feeling embarrassed and small.

Mark releases the chair and takes a long step toward me. "We still have a lot to talk about, but I don't know how much longer I can stand here without touching you," he says earnestly.

I shiver at the heat in his voice, but I squeeze my eyes shut. Slick starts leaking from me, and I begin to perfume.

"Fuck, Ava," he growls.

"Wait! I have two things left to say, and they're important." I have to take a deep breath between each word to get it out.

"Little cereus, you are fucking killing me here."

I tuck that away to ask him what it means later. "First, um, my suppressants have been failing. That's why I'm in heat. So if we do this, there is a solid chance that I will get pregnant. And I need you to know that I will want to keep it."

"If you think the idea of you swollen with my baby and tied to me forever is a deterrent..." He moves again, hips rolling like a predator.

I swallow. "I just needed you to be informed. One last thing." I hold up my hand again, trying to slow him down. "On the table. It's an NDA, prenup, pre-bond contract I drew up."

That gets him to stop. Mark blinks at me for a moment and then throws his head back, laughing so hard he ends up having to wipe away tears. He opens his coat, pulls out a pen from an interior pocket, and signs the papers with a flourish.

"You didn't even read it," I squeak.

"There is not a single goddamn thing you could have in there that would keep me from claiming you," he says, voice impossibly deep. He's close enough now that I can see when his pupils completely blow. "Are you going to *finally* let me take care of you, little omega?"

"Yes, alpha," I say breathlessly.

He reaches the couch and tugs the blanket away from me. I whine low in the back of my throat, and he grips my pajama top, ripping it open and sending the buttons flying. The cool air is blissful against my feverish skin. I shimmy out of my shorts and lift my arms toward him.

He scoops me up. "I know I don't have a nest. Where do you want to go?"

"Your bedroom," I gasp, pressing my lips to his neck and pushing at his coat. "You're wearing too many clothes," I whine. "I need skin."

"Shhh. Soon, little cereus." He carries me to the bedroom, laying me on the bed before stripping.

A high-pitched, keening whine slips from my lips as I watch him. Another cramp hits me, worse now, like my body knows that what I need is right here but not inside me. I moan in pain. "Mark, please..."

He crawls over me. "What do you need?"

"Your knot. Lots and lots of cum."

"I think I can make that happen," he says with a grin. "But first, how about I take the edge off by eating this perfect little pussy, hmm? I need to see if I love it even more now with your slick."

I nod eagerly, spreading my thighs, rational thought slipping away as the fog of my heat finally slides over me now that I'm safely with my mate.

24

Mark

Clearly I'll need to find a way to block off time in Ava's daily schedule for alone time in her office, because the taste of her slick combined with her full omega scent is the best thing I have ever encountered. As it is, only the thought that I'm going to be able to knot her is enough to make me stop.

I don't think I've ever been this hard before. I have to reach a hand down and squeeze to take some pressure off my knot as I pull myself up from between her thighs.

I can tell she's completely gone into her heat now. Her eyes are unfocused, and the only rational words I've heard her manage in a while are "more," "please," and "knot." She's the most beautiful thing I've ever laid my eyes on. Her hair is fanned out across my pillow, breasts heaving as she tries to catch her breath, thighs and pussy gleaming from her slick and my attention.

She whines and reaches for me, but I grip her hips and roll us so that I'm lying on my back. "The first time we ever fucked was in this bed, and you took control and rode me. Seems only fitting that this first time be the same, don't you think?"

I don't know how much of that she fully catches, but she scrambles onto my pelvis quickly, and with no fanfare, sinks me inside of her. I have to hiss through gritted teeth to not come immediately. She'd always been what I considered wetter than most of the betas I've slept with in the past, but nothing compares at all to the way it feels to slide into her slick-coated heat.

Ava moans, lifting her knees so that she's able to plant her feet firmly on the mattress and lift herself up and down my shaft at a frenzied pace. She leans down to kiss me, and I cradle the back of her head with my hand as my tongue meets hers.

"I'm not gonna last long if you keep that up, baby," I growl against her lips.

"Knot," she whimpers, doing a little figure-eight motion that has me seeing fucking stars.

I want her to finish again while I'm inside her before I'll allow myself the indulgence of knotting her, so I move my hand to the front of her throat, easing her back up to a sitting position as I lightly choke her. I slip my other hand between us and find her clit. She's an absolute slut for that combo. I have to hold back a chuckle as I remember teasing her about that not long ago at the courthouse.

Pressure builds as my knot starts to inflate, so I press my thumb harder against her, letting the movements of her thrusts grind the sensitive little bundle of nerves against it. "Come for me, Ava," I moan, hoping she does so I can.

It only takes another moment, and her back arches, her entire body shaking as she does. The end of her hair tickles my shins as I push my hips higher, pushing my knot inside her. As I feel it lock into the spot that only omegas have, I shout, and Ava screams. My orgasm overwhelms me, and it feels like her pussy milks the cum from my body.

I tug her down so she can sprawl on my chest, which makes my knot shift inside her in a way that has us both moaning again. I press soft kisses over her temple, rubbing circles along her back. She lifts her head to look at me, and I'm pleased to see that she's a little more focused.

"Hello, little cereus. Welcome back. Did a good knotting help you come back online?" I ask with a grin.

"Mmmm, a little. What does that mean, by the way?" she purrs, rubbing her cheek against my chest hair like a cat scenting its favorite toy.

"Cereus?"

She nods.

"Oh." I blush a little. I hadn't really thought I'd ever call her that out loud. No point in closing the barn door after the horse has already escaped. "It's technically the genus name for a cactus that only blooms at night. A beautiful and rare thing to behold. And... it's always seemed fitting in my head for you and us."

She lifts her head again, and I'm distressed to find her bottom lip quivering and her eyes welling up with tears. My pulse speeds up. What did I do wrong? "Baby, what? Did I say something upsetting?" I ask quickly.

"No. I'm just still really hormonal, and that's incredibly sweet," she says with a sniff.

I genuinely have no idea how to act with a soft and gentle Ava that cries over pet names. It makes my chest ache in the best ways to see the side of her that no one else gets to.

I kiss her forehead, splaying my hands across her ass to adjust her further so I can cuddle her better. I consider telling her I love her then, but I can't quite make the words come out. The first time wasn't particularly well-received, and I don't feel ready to take that step again. Not yet, at least.

"How are you feeling, by the way?" I ask gently, feeling like that is a safer conversation path at the moment. Which really says a lot about how much we still have to work out. "Did you really have a seizure?"

"My mom seems to think so. And I guess it makes sense. I..." She trails off. "I think there was a moment where I genuinely thought I might be dying. Thank God Tony called Jack, who had a functioning brain cell for a moment and called Mom."

The shot of fear that goes through me feels like ice shooting through my veins. I could have lost her tonight, and I would have never known any of it. Her being an omega, us being mates.

It spurs my alpha side, and I growl—a genuinely primal sound—as I roll her over, pinning her beneath me as I grip her wrists and hold them firmly over her head. I grind my cock into her until I feel my knot completely firm back up. "You don't get to leave me. Not ever, do you fucking hear me?" I ask her roughly.

"Oh, god," she gasps.

"Say it, Ava. Tell me you aren't going anywhere." I roll my hips as much as I can while still locked inside her, and she makes the most adorable little squeak. If I wasn't half out of my mind at how close I came to never having her in my life, it would have made me smile.

"I'm—oh," she moans, "—not going anywhere."

"Ever," I demand.

"Ever," she agrees.

Rut. Claim. Bite, my alpha demands.

So I do.

My teeth sink into the top of her left breast, right over her heart. A sizable portion of it will show in the types of revealing clothing Ava tends to wear, but she can cover it easily enough if she needs to in court.

There's the briefest moment of panic where I wonder if she'll reject the bond. Worry that I should have asked first. Except she'd brought a fucking prenup pre-bond contract for me to sign. Surely that shows intent on her part?

She doesn't reject it, and suddenly my senses are filled with... Ava.

It's impossible to describe. I can't hear her thoughts so much as I can feel what she's feeling, and right now, it's awe and love. All of my earlier possessive anger at the idea of losing her dissipates like fog under a sunny morning.

"I love you," she moans against my lips.

"I love you, too," I answer, pressing my forehead to hers.

***

I'm aware that I'm far too jealous to genuinely consider pack life. However, after thirty-six straight hours of Ava's heat, I'm beginning to wonder if one man can truly keep up. She's generally lucid for about twenty to thirty minutes after I knot her, but then if she doesn't fall asleep, the cramps and brain fog returns.

We've been resting for a few hours, spooning with the lightest, softest sheet I own tossed over our bodies. Anything else has been deemed too hot and too scratchy. I don't know if all omegas are this high-maintenance during their heat, but I suppose that's really not much of a shock considering how high-maintenance she always is.

I float back to consciousness to find her grinding her ass against my cock. Even with exhaustion starting to weigh on me, it's not a bad way to wake up.

"Alphaaaaa," she whines. "Please..."

I don't think I'll ever get tired of hearing her call me that. I had always found it kind of tacky when alphas and omegas referred to each other by their designations, but something about the way it slips from her luscious lips gets me every time.

"You need to come again, little cereus?"

She nods eagerly.

"The next time you go into heat, I'm getting some toys so I can fill both of your holes at once," I whisper hotly in her ear. I glide my hand over her side, nearly in a tickle, enjoying the way goosebumps follow the path. Then I ease my fingers between her thighs, coating my fingers in her slick and guiding them back to press against her ass.

Ass play isn't something that we've done before. Probably because it requires a certain level of vulnerability that Ava was not previously capable of. But since we bonded, I have discovered that my mate is, for lack of a better term, quite the little anal slut. Or at the very least, she is when she's in heat. It'll be interesting to see if that holds true later.

Just in case it doesn't, I'm going to use it to my advantage now.

I slip one finger in, and then two, curling them slightly as I move them in and out of her tight hole. "You okay?" I ask her gently. She just moans and presses her ass harder back against me.

I'll take that as a yes.

"Rub yourself," I command. "Get your hand nice and covered in your slick and then reach around here and stroke me while I finger your ass."

I increase my tempo, easing a third finger in. She's whimpering, moving her head restlessly as she plays with her pussy. "You gonna come for me, Ava? Just from rubbing that greedy little nub and me stretching you open? Dirty thing."

She stiffens, and I can feel the rhythmic pulsing of her orgasm in the way the ring of muscle tightens and squeezes around my fingers.

"Oh, good girl. Now what was the second part you're supposed to do?" I question.

She reaches for me. Her drenched hand wraps around my cock, coating it in her slick. I groan a little, bucking my hips against her. Finally, I think it's enough, and I push one of her thighs forward with mine and press my tip where my fingers just were.

"Come on. Wiggle back onto it. Show me that you want it, or I'll take it away," I say, nipping at her neck. Yeah, right. Like I have any hope of ever denying her.

She whines and starts rocking her hips until the head of my cock slides inside. She's so fucking tight—well, everywhere, but definitely back here. I moan and push forward, meeting the slight bit of resistance until the muscle relaxes and I'm able to sink in fully.

I fuck her like that for a while, letting her get acclimated to the shallower thrusts from us being on our sides. Once I think she's stretched enough for more rigorous play, I slip out briefly, earning a whine and a pout from my greedy omega. I playfully swat the top of her pussy with my hand. "Patience, Ava. I'll be back inside you soon enough."

I roll her onto her back, shoving a pillow under her hips and bringing her legs up onto my shoulders. "I want to watch your face while I fuck this tight little ass."

She smiles wide and reaches up to grip her thighs and widen herself further for me. I give her a wolfish grin in return and guide my cock back inside of her, but just the tip.

"You want it?"

She nods.

"Want it hard and rough or loving?"

She bites her lip, debating. "Rough," she says finally.

"Good choice. Go back to rubbing yourself. I want to see how many times I can make you come without touching your pussy."

25

Ava

I open my eyes, and for the first time in days, my head feels clear and my skin is no longer on fire. I'm sore, of course, and... sticky, but no longer in heat. Mark is asleep beside me on his stomach, with one arm draped across my middle and the other wedged beneath his pillow. There are dark smudges beneath his eyes, and his hair is sticking up at the craziest angles.

Poor guy looks like he's been through it. I smile softly and brush a lock of hair off his forehead. He doesn't even stir. *Wonder how long he'll sleep.*

I wiggle out from beneath his arm carefully, easing off the mattress and making my way to the bathroom. I desperately need to pee, brush my teeth, and take a shower. In that order.

After I wash my hands, I look in the medicine cabinet to see if he still has the toothbrush and toothpaste I used when I was here last weekend. God, is that all it's been? It feels like significantly longer than a week has gone by since I showed up here drunk.

Thankfully, he hung on to them, and I grab them before closing the cabinet. I get a good look at myself in the mirror, and I'm not looking any better than Mark. Although, the healed bond mark on my chest is a nice touch.

I run my fingers over it lightly before pressing them to my lips as I try to contain a happy squeal. I never thought I'd have one of these, and despite all the obstacles we will have to face in the near future as we navigate everything, I can't deny how happy I am.

I quickly brush my teeth and turn on the hot water. As I'm stepping in, Mark enters behind me. "You're lucky I could smell you still, or I'd have thought you were running."

I laugh. "Maybe after a shower. I'm disgusting."

"Uh, maybe never," he deadpans. "You promised, and you're a bonded woman now. I'll go all caveman on you and drag you back by your hair." A grin threatens at the corners of his mouth.

"That sounds really kinky, but I gotta be honest with you, sex is genuinely the last thing I want at this moment," I say, dipping my head back under the spray and letting it run over me.

"Oh, I don't know." He watches me through the glass shower doors. "Might not be so awful," he says, eyes traveling up my body. He's nude, and I can clearly see that part of him is still somewhat interested.

"If you don't at least let me get clean and feed me first, I will literally claw your eyes out," I warn.

He laughs. "Fair enough."

He finishes up his own pre-shower necessities and then slides in beside me. We've actually done this a fair number of times before. Mostly silently, of course. But sometimes when you have sex multiple times in one night, you need a shower in between. I reach for the bottle of my shampoo that at some point had magically appeared, like my favorite energy drinks in the fridge. Just another thing I had willfully ignored because I didn't want to face what it might mean.

"When did you buy this to keep here?" I ask, squeezing a large dollop into my palm.

"A couple weeks after we started, I think?" He flushes slightly and rubs the back of his neck. "I had this random thought in court that your hair wasn't shiny and soft-looking, and I realized it was because you'd showered over here the night before. So the next time I was at your place, I looked to see what you used. That shit is ridiculously expensive."

It's my turn to laugh. "Yes, it is. I don't think I ever properly thanked you." God, I am stupidly in love with this man.

"I can feel what it means to you in the bond," he says quietly.

"Good. And when the idea is a little more appealing than it currently is, I'll show you in other ways too." I stand on tiptoe and kiss him gently.

We finish showering, and I strip the bed while Mark works on ordering us something to eat. Since I don't have any clothes with me, I snag a button-down out of his closet and toss it on. "Hey babe, can I use your phone to email Shelby?" I call loudly. "I need to tell her where I am and see about getting some clothes."

He leans against the doorframe. "If the alternative is keeping you here in my shirt like that, then the answer is no." He holds the phone out to me, and when I reach for it, he grips my wrist and pulls me to him.

He kisses me thoroughly, almost reverently, until I'm breathless and beginning to lightly perfume.

"The code for my phone is 051291," he says, pulling away finally.

"Just going to give me that so easily? What kind of lawyer are you?" I tease.

"The same kind that signs contracts without reading them, apparently. I have nothing to hide. Plus, how else are you going to learn my birthday?" He flicks my nose and heads back to the kitchen.

I unlock the phone and open his email, quickly drafting one to Shelby telling her I was with Mark and I'm feeling much better. And that I was in desperate need of a supply drop as soon as possible.

Almost instantly, it rings, and Shelby's name flashes on the screen, with "Ava's EA" in the company section of the contact. It makes me smile for some reason.

"Hello?"

"I like how you email me that like I didn't already figure out where you were," she says with a laugh.

"How?" I ask, settling crisscross applesauce on the bed.

"I knew you wouldn't have gone to a clinic like Alfred had Jack and Mateo believing. Which really only left one spot. Though I did cross-reference the route the car service took you to verify."

"Shelby, I think the word you meant to use instead of *cross-referenced* is *hacked,*" I say dryly, "since I can't imagine they gave that information up willingly. Though if they did, I am going to have a field day taking them to court."

"Psh. Whatever. If Mark goes across the hall to Mrs. Choi, she has a bag for you with some clothes and toiletries."

I scrunch my face in confusion, and almost as if she can see me, she continues. "You all weren't exactly subtle with your heat. When I came by, she was practically guarding the elevator and making sure no one approached Mark's apartment."

"Are you kidding me?" I ask, embarrassment making my face heat.

She laughs. "Nope," she says. "It's cute, though. I explained who I was and gave her the bag."

"Yeah, but that means she knows..." I trail off, chewing on the edge of my thumbnail. "In the last four days, I've gone from a handful of people knowing my secret to, like... ten."

"Ava, babe, I know we drafted an NDA for Mark, but I think you're going to have a very hard time keeping the lid on this one now that you're bonded. I mean, I'm assuming you are."

"We are," I admit. Anxiety churns in my stomach, and I close my eyes. I wish I could have stayed in my little bubble with Mark for a while longer.

"Hey," she says softly. "Do you want me to come over and we can start brainstorming? You always feel better when you have a game plan."

"Yes, but I think I want to do it at home. This heat has been wonderful, but riding one out without a nest has me feeling some kind of way."

She makes a sympathetic sound. "I bet. And being freshly bonded, you'll want him in it quite a bit. You two won't be able to stand being apart for very long for the next couple of weeks."

I glance at the time. "I think Mark just ordered us food. So maybe meet me at the penthouse in like... three hours?"

"Of course."

We hang up, and I come out to the living room. "Apparently, your neighbor has a bag of my clothes and has been playing heat security."

"Mrs. Choi?" Mark asks, brows furrowed.

"That's what Shelby says."

"Guess we were sorta loud, huh?" He chuckles, seemingly nonplussed by it until he sobers again. "You feel anxious through the bond. What's wrong?"

"I think the bubble popped," I say quietly. "I didn't have any real control over your neighbor finding out, or even the beta driver that drove me here, and it's crashing in that we have to go out in the real world tomorrow and deal with everything."

He comes around the couch and gathers me in his arms. "And we will face every bit of it together. You're right, though—we do need to have some serious conversations."

"Shelby is going to meet us at the penthouse in a few hours to start making battle plans."

He presses a kiss to my forehead. "Suppose that's first on the agenda of conversations, hmm? Where do we want to live?"

I try not to stiffen and to keep a mature, level head to have an open discussion about this. Of course Mark wouldn't automatically want to give up his apartment. Yet the idea of leaving my penthouse and my nest when I'm already feeling this vulnerable and exposed makes me extremely anxious.

He laughs. "I'm kidding, little cereus. I like this place well enough, but I have no real attachment to it. Your place is larger, and I'm assuming you own it instead of renting, right?"

I nod.

"So, yours makes the most sense. Though you will have to concede *some* closet space to me," he says.

There's a knock at the door, and Mark drops his arms from around me to go answer it. I have the strongest urge to hide, and even though I know it's just habit, it's something I'm going to have to work on. I don't want Mark to ever feel like I'm ashamed of us, because I'm *not*. It's just that a lifetime of hiding doesn't magically get better overnight.

He stands in the doorway talking for a few minutes, and I stand on tiptoe trying to peer around him. Except he fills the frame, and I can't see a thing. Finally, he turns and kicks the door shut behind him, juggling what looks like a large donut box and one of my overnight bags.

"Food and supplies from Mrs. Choi," he says, holding both up. The scent wafting from the box has my interest. He opens the box, revealing neatly lined rows of what appear to be round rolls of bread. Inside the lid of the box, there's a labeled grid.

"What are those?" I ask, perching on one of the chairs.

"I'm about to change your whole life," he says with a grin. "These, my dear, are called a kolache. This half of the box is filled with sweet fillings like apple, blueberry cream cheese, and chocolate hazelnut. The other half is savory, like sloppy joe, breakfast burrito, and uh—" He looks at the grid. "—mac 'n cheese."

"That's a lot for just the two of us," I say, chewing on my bottom lip.

"I wasn't sure what you'd like, so I ordered a variety." He cocks his head to one side. "Where're you at in that head of yours?"

I sigh. "I'm anxious and feeling out of control. And..." I hesitate, but we're bonded now, which means no secrets, so I continue, "I'm in recovery for an eating disorder. I haven't had a relapse in several years, but feeling like I do right now is a trigger I have to really fight to overcome."

There's no judgment or pity on his face, just concern. "How can I help you feel less anxious? Or support you in general with this?"

"Talking about it helps. And I think once we get home, I'll feel a little less on edge. Shelby said part of it is that we are newly bonded and I'm away from my nest."

"Then let's go. Get dressed. I'll pack a bag, and we can take breakfast with us."

"Just like that? No arguments?"

He sets the box on the table and kneels in front of me. "Ava, I guarantee there are plenty of arguments in our future. Probably even today, since you have a tendency to make me want to strangle you on a regular basis. But when it comes to stuff like this, my job is to be whatever you need me to be."

A few hours later, the intercom buzzes beside me. "Ms. Kendrick, you have several guests wanting to come upstairs, including your brother and Ms. McGregory," Alfred says.

Several? I push the button to respond, "Uh, sure, let them up."

Valentino jumps off me since I dared to shift my lap, turning to glare at me with airplane ears and a swishing tail. I sigh. I had just gotten her to stop scream-meowing at me for being gone, even though it was clear that Jack and Mateo had taken care of her.

"You want me to get the door?" Mark asks from where he'd been working on his laptop at the end of the couch with my feet in his lap.

I shake my head. "No, I've got it. I'm sure I'll have a million questions to answer."

When the door opens, I find that Alfred was correct. It is several people: Shelby, Ron, Jack, Mateo, and... my parents. "Jeez, Shelby, you couldn't have warned me you were bringing a welcoming party?"

"Sorry, boss. Soon as I let Jack know that I'd heard from you, it sort of spiraled from there," she quips.

My mother pushes to the front and clasps her hands on my cheeks, looking over me as if she needs to verify that I'm alive. She hugs me tightly and then pulls back to look at me some more. "I could murder you for scaring us like that. Flying across the ocean thinking my daughter is on the verge of death, and we get to New York and nobody is sure where you are?"

I grimace. "I'm sorry, Mom. I wasn't exactly all that lucid, and Mark said that Alfred filled Jack and Mateo in that I was safe, at least."

At the mention of his name, she releases me and steps around me to stare at Mark, hands on her hips. "Yes, I have things to say to Mr. Taylor, too," she says coolly.

Swell. This should be fun.

26

Mark

The woman staring me down looks so much like my mate that I nearly have to blink to make sure I'm not seeing double. Her hair is the same shade of red as Ava's, only with streaks of an ash-toned blonde along her temples and through her part. I also recognize the same coiled serpent energy. She means to dress me down—for what, I'm not exactly sure.

"Hello, Dr. Kendrick. I'm pleased to finally meet you," I say smoothly, rising from the couch and extending my hand to shake hers.

She eyes it warily. "Do you care to explain to me why you left one of my children with a bleeding head wound and then disappeared with my other for days, leaving us with no idea where she was?"

Fucking hell, she even *sounds* like Ava.

Luckily, I have plenty of experience with this particular subspecies of viper.

"I left Jack with his husband, who is far more skilled in healthcare than I—"

"You don't have to answer that, Mark. Mother, dial it down a notch. If you want to be mad at anyone, sounds like it needs to be me or Jack," Ava cuts in, hands on her hips in a mirror image of her mother. "By the way, Jackson, don't think you and I won't be having a conversation about your stunt," she adds.

"Oh my God, I was only trying to help. One of my clients is a dealer, so I reached out—"

"Shut the fuck up, Jack," Ava, her father, and I say simultaneously.

The tension eases a little as everyone except Dr. Kendrick bursts into laughter.

"Lawyers," Jack says, with a dramatic roll of his eyes.

"I cannot defend you if you want to blab to the cops," Ava says. "But I know you only meant to help. I'm glad you're okay." She goes over to him, throwing her arms around him for a tight hug.

"Mark isn't the cops," he grumbles, but squeezes her in return.

"Close enough, Jack."

"Rest assured, I am mad at you, Ava Lynn," her mother says, arms crossed and reminding everyone of the original issue. "All of this could have been avoided if you hadn't been risking your health by doubling or tripling up on your suppressants for no damn reason. So you almost get your brother arrested—"

"I didn't almost get Jack anything! I was asleep in my nest when he took off on his half-brained mission," Ava says loudly.

"Wait a minute, what does she mean you were tripling up on the untested illegal suppressants?" I ask at the same time Ava speaks up, my own arms crossing as I glare at her.

Overlapping the both of us, Jack protests, "Now, hold on!"

"That's enough, everyone," Ava's father says, and the room immediately quiets. Despite being a beta, I have a feeling he's a "speak softly, carry a big stick" sort of man. Real alpha energy.

"Suzanne, it seems to me that Mark here kept our son out of jail and most likely saved our daughter's life by helping her through her heat. Ava, you should have at least left a note and not scared everyone half to death. Jack, you could have been less... Jack about that. So everyone knock it off." His voice remains steady and on the quieter side, but the effect is noticeable.

"Sorry, Dad," Ava and Jack both mutter.

"Now then," he says, walking towards me and extending his hand, "Shelby made it sound like it's basically a done deal that you're our new son-in-law, so welcome to the family, chaotic as it is. I'm Hank Kendrick."

I can't help but smile at him as I shake his hand with a firm grip. "I honestly wouldn't have expected anything less from the family that produced Ava. She's a force of nature."

Dr. Kendrick clears her throat. "Not to break up this touching moment, but I need a blood sample from Ava to compare her hormone levels now that she's finished her heat. See if we are out of the woods, along with... other things." Her voice still carries a distinct chill. I get the impression that she's retracted her fangs because of Hank, but she's still going to take a while to warm up to me.

"Like if I'm pregnant?" Ava asks, and I feel myself freeze. I know she'd mentioned that it was likely, but I didn't think we'd find out this soon. And I hadn't truly thought about it.

A baby? Nine months from now? God, it'll probably be a little spitfire redhead. The thought isn't unappealing by any stretch. I wonder how many I can convince her to have. My own little army of mean-ass gingers.

Her mother sighs. "Possibly. Omega hormones work differently than beta pregnancies, so in theory, I should be able to pick up traces of the hormones, particularly if you conceived at the beginning of your heat. But there's no way to know how your overuse of the suppressants impacted things."

She turns back to me. "And how will you react, hmm? In regard to my daughter's career and finances," Suzanne says quietly. "Especially in regard to your political aspirations."

I chuckle, shaking my head.

"I fail to see what's humorous about the question," she says coolly.

"I apologize, Dr. Kendrick. It's only that the majority of your questions were covered by the pre-bond prenup your daughter made me sign."

"That's my peanut," Hank says proudly.

"As far as my political future, I've found in the last few weeks my interest in that has been waning. I only ever wanted to change the city, and now..." My voice quiets as I look at my mate with a soft smile. "Well, I'm beginning to think I might have more of a background role supporting the most capable woman I know."

Ava comes closer and squeezes my hand.

"We haven't fully had a chance to talk about it yet, but I think if a baby is in our near future, I likely won't run for reelection. It's easier for me to take on the brunt of childcare; what Ava does is too important. I can transition back to private practice and take on limited cases."

"You don't intend to make her play a traditional omega role?"

"Nothing about Ava is traditional. I don't see why we should start now," I reply.

By the time we shoo everyone out of the penthouse, we've had dinner and come up with a game plan for how to handle the fallout from our relationship going public, and I can feel the reduction in anxiety from Ava's side of the bond. She's still feeling a little weak after her heat, so I take care of cleaning up the kitchen while she relaxes in the nest.

I lean against the doorframe, looking in on the only room of the penthouse I'd never been allowed into before. It's a cozy space but, much like the omega it belongs to, looks expensive and luxurious. The colors are muted champagne, bronze, and white, with various textures of fur and silk. One of the walls is nothing but a massive window overlooking the city, only with a special tinting that Ava can darken with a remote.

"May I enter your nest, little cereus?" I ask quietly. I don't remember a lot from biology class, but I do know omegas are very territorial about their nests.

She lifts her head from the pillow she'd burrowed into and turns to me. I'm dumbfounded by how gorgeous she is. Will she ever stop taking my breath away? She's fresh-faced, in a shirt she'd quickly stolen from me despite her closet with enough clothes in it to outfit a small army, and her hair is piled into a messy bun. Of all the looks I've seen this woman in, this is easily my favorite. Well, tied with when she's naked, I suppose.

"Yes, please," she says, making grabby hands toward me.

"Clothes on or off?"

"Off, but toss them here so I can mix them in," she says, shifting some blankets around.

"Wait a minute," I say with a laugh. "Are those my ties? I've been looking for those! I thought I was going crazy."

Her cheeks flush. "Most of them you just forgot. I only stole like... two. Maybe three."

I shake my head and strip as instructed, handing her the discarded items. I wait patiently while she moves things around, fluffs them, and adjusts some more. I have no idea why; I can't see any sort of difference, but her nose is scrunched up in the most adorable look of concentration, the tip of her tongue sticking out between her lips. Finally, she seems satisfied and motions for me to come onto the bed.

"If I'm naked, only fair for you to be too," I point out as I slip beneath the pile of blankets.

"Is this a ploy to get into my panties, Mark Taylor?"

"If I ever *don't* want into your panties, I want you to promise to have Tony take me 'round back and shoot me."

She giggles and tugs my shirt off along with the sports bra she'd been wearing.

I pull her body to mine, amazed at the way my muscles relax as soon as our skin is touching. "Fuck, that's better. I know it was an important evening, but I was starting to feel like I was going to climb out of my skin if I didn't touch you soon."

"Side effect of the bond. I am a little nervous about the next few days," she admits.

We had ultimately decided to contact the bar association in the morning and report that Ava was an incredibly late-presenting omega and we had bonded. It was rare, basically unheard-of in someone's thirties, but her mother seemed confident that she could produce the necessary bloodwork documentation to prove it.

Shelby believed that with the correct strings pulled with the press, it would be easy enough to spin it into quite the fairytale romance. An explanation of why we'd always fought like we had. Which, honestly, was the truth—the best kind of lies usually were. Ava would reassign any of her open cases in my borough, and hopefully, that would be the end of it.

Unfortunately, it meant that we would no longer be working against each other, so how much time we'd be able to carve out together during the day was questionable.

I tickle my fingers lightly down her side, pressing my lips to her forehead. "We'll figure it out. Once we make the official public announcement after we talk to the bar, people will be more understanding of us needing to see each other and touch frequently."

"Were you serious about the baby stuff?" she asks quietly. A complete shift from what we'd been discussing, so obviously something she'd been chewing on for a while.

"Yes."

"You really don't want to run for mayor anymore? I'm not going to ask you to give up your political aspirations," she says, propping herself up on her elbow, cheek pressed to her palm. "We could hire a nanny."

I sigh. "I've always wanted to be a dad. I just never really pictured what that looked like before, because I could never see myself getting married. I didn't think I'd ever find an omega and never felt much of a pull to any 'betas' before you," I say, poking her. "Faced with the reality of a possible baby now, though, I don't think I want a stranger raising them for the long hours that we both sometimes work. I'm... excited about the idea of parenting, if I'm being honest."

"A stay-at-home alpha is certainly a new one. You're going to catch a lot of shit about it."

I shrug. "Ask me how much I care. If I'm not running for mayor anymore, I no longer have any desire to impress any of those stuck-up assholes. The only opinion I care about is yours. Will *you* respect me less if I stay home with our baby?" It's a genuine question, I realize. I hadn't considered that Ava might view it as emasculating. A bit of panic surges through me, and she must feel it, because she cups my cheek and kisses me.

"No, Mark. I wouldn't respect you less. In fact, I find it incredibly sexy. Something about a man who is secure enough in his masculinity to embrace more 'submissive' roles is hot. Maybe I'll talk you into it in the bedroom too," she says with a grin.

It's nothing I've ever fantasized about before, but the sudden mental image of Ava in a black leather teddy and stockings makes my cock twitch.

She fake gasps. "Did I just feel a surge of desire, sir?"

I blush. "Maybe. I've never thought about it before. But the idea isn't... unappealing."

Ava bites her bottom lip. "Wow. Well, it isn't on my end, either. Maybe we should do some toy shopping soon. Ease into certain things." She pushes on my chest until I roll onto my back, and she straddles my hips. She still has her panties on, but a large wet spot is showing on the cotton where slick is beginning to leak from her.

Her perfume fills the small space of the nest, and I groan. "Please tell me you've recovered enough that you're interested in sex again."

"Now that I'm thinking of pegging my big, strong alpha mate, I'm definitely interested in sex again," she says, slowly grinding along my length.

"Fuck, Ava, you can't just say things like that out loud," I rasp, embarrassment and desire filling me in equal parts.

She laughs and leans down to kiss me, gripping my wrists and holding them above my head like I've done to her in the past. It's crazy how different everything feels now that we are bonded. It's like I'm comfortable enough with her, with us, to let down guards I didn't even know I had.

The idea of switching who's trading off who's in charge in the bedroom?

Sounds kinky. I'm in.

27

Ava

Four hours since I last saw Mark.

Not that I'm counting or anything. I definitely didn't start noticing after the second hour that my patience was wearing thin and my body was staging a full-scale rebellion. The courthouse air feels stale and wrong, like it's been recycled too many times. My blouse clings in places it shouldn't, and the waistband of my skirt feels too tight even though it isn't. Everything is also itchy.

It's the same restless, prickly discomfort I get before a heat. The only thing that will help is wrapping myself in Mark's scent.

This new bond nonsense is no joke.

I shift my briefcase into my other hand and glance down the hallway, hoping Mark will appear just from the pull of me thinking about him. If the bond is any indication, he is also getting restless and crabby. We need to go home.

The meeting with the ethics committee from the New York State Bar Association went exactly how I knew it would—exhausting. They accepted our proposed path forward. The reps from the NYSBA listened, nodded, and asked their questions. They weren't thrilled that they were forced to take us at our word regarding our relationship timeline, but there was little else they could do.

It doesn't bother me nearly as much as it bothers Mark. He and I *weren't* technically dating before this weekend. Maybe it's the defense attorney in me, but I've always had more patience for those kind of white lie technicalities.

Apparently, they are going to review our past cases against one another to ensure that another lawyer could not reasonably decide we had pulled our punches. I have zero fears of that. Fighting each other in the courtroom was practically our foreplay. All our past clients will be notified, and it does open up the chance for attempted appeals on the cases I lost.

I'm not going to lose any sleep over it. If I lost, it was because the police had properly done their job and they had my client dead to rights.

My neck aches from tension, and I roll it slowly, wincing when something pops. Mark should be done soon, hopefully. Just have to make it a little longer.

I tire of restless pacing and drop onto a bench along the wall. I dig my phone out of my briefcase and start answering emails, even though I know I'm only halfway reading them. Every few seconds, my attention drifts back down the hallway.

Patience has never been my strong suit.

My phone vibrates in my hand, and I realize I've been staring at the same email for a full minute. The screen lights up with a picture of my mom and me at the beach, both of us squinting at the camera, hair whipped into chaos by the wind. Not that we lingered outside for long—our skin isn't exactly made for the sun.

Nerves flutter in my gut, and I debate letting it ring for half a second. She's almost certainly calling to discuss my bloodwork results.

It's childish, I know that. Ignoring the call won't change anything. Either my life is about to flip upside down because I'm pregnant, or the suppressants did enough damage that it didn't take at all. Both options sit heavy in my chest for different reasons.

With a quiet groan, I swipe to accept. "Hi, Mom," I say, forcing lightness into my voice. "Bloodwork, I presume?"

"Hello, sweetie," she says warmly. Almost too warmly. That never bodes well. She'd still been fairly chilly when she left the penthouse yesterday. I knew it came from a place of fear; didn't make it less annoying, though. "Yes, I just finished running all the numbers. It's actually quite fascinating. The way your progesterone levels are interacting with the—"

"Mother," I interrupt, pinching the bridge of my nose as I stand and start pacing again. "Non-science speak, please."

She laughs softly. "Right. Of course."

I shift the phone to my other ear, balancing it between my shoulder and jaw, and nearly collide with a man coming around the corner. I mutter an apology automatically and keep moving.

Out of the corner of my eye, I notice someone approaching. Tall. Dark-haired. Another lawyer, probably. Half the men in this building look the same at a glance. Suit. A long coat draped over one arm. Nothing remarkable.

Yet something about him makes the fine hairs along my arms lift, prickling with awareness. My steps slow without me quite deciding to do it.

"Ava?" my mom prompts. "Are you still there?"

"Yeah. Sorry." I swallow, forcing myself to breathe. "Listen, can I call you back? The signal in here is awful, and I want to actually focus on what you're telling me."

There's a pause on the line. "Is everything all right?"

"Yeah. Totally fine," I lie, even as my gaze locks on to the man drawing closer. "I just don't want to miss anything important."

"All right," she says, though she doesn't sound convinced. "Call me soon."

"I will."

I end the call before she can say anything else and shove my phone into the pocket of my skirt. My pulse is loud in my ears now, every beat thudding harder. The man's eyes are on me, so intense it makes my skin crawl.

I don't make it more than a few steps.

A hand clamps around my elbow, fingers digging in hard enough to hurt. Something solid is shoved against my ribcage, and it shocks a gasp out of me.

"That's a gun pressed into your side," a voice growls near my ear. "If you scream or try anything stupid, I'll shoot you. Keep walking."

Fear washes over me, and for a moment I want to send it through the bond, my instincts screaming for Mark. But then a new fear quickly replaces it. If Mark feels this, he will come running. Bursting out of his courtroom. Gunshots in a crowded courthouse flash through my mind in sickening detail.

I shut the bond down, as best I can. I don't know if I'm doing it correctly. It's still so new and fragile.

"Listen, sir, I don't know if you know who I am," I say quietly, "but I can help you out of whatever mess you've landed in that makes you think this is a good plan. I'm a *really* good lawyer."

He barks a short laugh. "So everyone says. And yet, my brother's rotting in a cell because you were too busy fucking the DA."

My body stiffens as my mind tries to race through all the possibilities. I have no idea how he knows about me and Mark, since we haven't gone public other than to the NYSBA, and something tells me this guy isn't exactly close with many attorneys.

Think, Ava, damn it. A brother. A case you lost against Mark.

That narrows it down considerably, but not enough. I could ask for more information, but would that set him off further?

"I can promise you this," I say carefully. "If your brother was my client, I did everything I could to get him acquitted." He jams the gun into my side again, harder this time. "But... maybe I missed something. Appeals exist for a reason. We can go back to my office and look at—"

"You're not going anywhere," he snaps. "You're going to pay for what you did. And after that, I'm coming back for that piece of shit DA."

Oh god, Mark.

He sounds crazy. When I glance at him, I notice the haggard stubble along his jaw and the wide, bloodshot eyes. Is he on drugs? That's going to make it a lot harder to reason with him, and I have to de-escalate this situation.

He keeps pushing me down the hallway, and I try to think of where he might be taking me. There's a back exit where they move defendants in and out from the jail for their trials. It's getting late enough in the day; it probably doesn't have very many people near it.

We pass the door to the courtroom where Mark is, and it swings open. For a heartbeat, hope surges. Then falters. Instead of Mark, Henry steps out, dressed in a bailiff's uniform. I forgot he sometimes picks up shifts over here to help pad out the retirement fund. His familiar face nearly breaks me, and I have to fight to keep from sobbing.

"Ms. Kendrick," he says, "good to see you. I heard you were out sick. How're you feeling?"

His eyes flick to the man beside me. His posture stays relaxed, but his hand drifts closer to his belt. Close enough to his gun, but not so obvious it will immediately draw attention.

The man beside me stiffens. "Oh, much better," I say brightly. Too brightly. "Must've been the flu."

"That particular flu's a doozy," he agrees, and I swear he's being careful with his wording. Did Mark tell him I'm an omega, or did he figure it out? Not that it matters now, I suppose. "My wife used to get it a few times a year. Always needed help getting through it. Did you have anyone taking care of you?"

"Nah," I say lightly. "Tough single gal, remember? All I needed was my stuffed tiger." Please let him remember Mark's nickname and recognize something is afoot. I don't want Mark busting out here and causing a recreation of the OK Corral, but I also don't want to be alone with the guy holding a gun to my ribs. "Anyway, I've gotta run. My new client and I need to go over some facts of his case."

"Mm-hmm. Yes, ma'am," Henry agrees, eyes looking over me and then back to the man beside me. "You're lucky to have such a great lawyer, sir."

"Yes, very lucky. If you'll excuse us," he says curtly.

We start walking again, and every step away from Henry feels like tearing something loose inside my chest. God, I wish I knew if this fucker actually had a gun.

"How did you manage to get that past the metal detectors?" I ask once we're further down the hall.

He snorts. "You'd be amazed at what you can 3D print these days." He jerks his head toward a side corridor. "Turn right."

How does he know the layout of this building so well? I do, but I'm here nearly every day. In fact, I recognize the hallway he has us turn down. Supply closets and camera blind spots. The location of more than one reckless tryst between me and my mate.

"I thought you wanted to leave," I say, slowing. "That's not the exit."

He cocks his head, and his grin is wide and wrong. It reminds me of the Joker, and the thought is so bizarre it almost makes me burst into a fit of nervous laughter, but his next words dry my throat as if I'd swallowed sand. "I told you. I'm handling you first."

I open my mouth to plead with him, but the sharp blare of the building alarm cuts me off. Bright pulses of light illuminate the hallway from the emergency flashers at the top of the hallway. "This is not a drill. Everyone shelter in place." A voice blares over the speaker. "This is not a drill. Shelter in place."

His grip loosens, and panic flickers across his face. "No, no, no. He said he would handle the cops. He promised!"

I don't know who the hell *he* is, but I'm not about to waste my opportunity. I wrench free and hurl my briefcase at his head with everything I've got. I spin and run.

Only my goddamn heels betray me. My ankle rolls. Pain shoots up my leg as I stumble. Something hard slams into my temple. My vision blacks out around the edges, and I can't hear anything anymore other than the blaring of the alarm, which sounds much further away than it did.

28 Mark

If this defense attorney doesn't wrap it up soon, I might be the one facing charges. Their strategy appears to be boring the jury into a coma and hoping for a mistrial. The last four witnesses have all given nearly identical accounts, each from a slightly different angle—none of which actually help their case. What the hell are they thinking?

It's also possible I'm just getting cranky.

I bounce my leg under the table, fighting the urge to tap my pen. Even the judge looks like he's struggling to stay awake. At one point, I'm almost positive I saw him jerk upright as if he had nearly nodded off. The jury isn't absorbing any of this, and honestly, neither am I. Surely he will call for a recess soon. I can't believe he hasn't yet. Maybe because he's new?

Suddenly, a sharp burst of fear slams into me through the bond. It's so intense and unexpected that I drop my pen and hit my knee on the bottom of the table. I squeeze my eyes shut and breathe through my nose. The fear disappears almost as quickly as it came, but it still leaves me unsettled. I try to tell myself it was nothing; maybe Ava saw a spider or a rat. Yet that doesn't feel quite right.

I spot Henry standing off to the side, whispering with a new bailiff who had just entered. Maybe he's about to take a bathroom break. I pick up my pen and scribble 'Please check on Ava' on my notepad, motioning for him to come my way with a tilt of my head. It's a bold move on my part, but at this point, I don't care. We're going public after today, and Henry probably already suspects. She would have run right past him the other night after our fight, crying and smelling like me. There's no way he didn't notice that.

Henry glances at my note, gives a sharp nod, and slips out of the courtroom. The pressure in my chest eases slightly. I trust him. He will make sure she's all right until I can get out of here.

Finally, after another few minutes, the defense wraps up with their current witness. I'm on my feet before they can call another. "Your Honor, may I request a sidebar?"

He nods, and I approach the bench. "I believe the jury has reached their limits for the day and are not fully absorbing information. Could we possibly have a recess?"

"Yes, Mr. Taylor, I believe you're correct," he says quickly. He sounds almost relieved. It's mildly annoying that he didn't just call it himself, but I let it go. At least we are finally getting some freedom. "Ladies and gentlemen of the jury, we will be breaking for a recess. We will return tomorrow at," he pauses to consult his calendar, "12:30 p.m." He bangs the gavel.

Everyone starts gathering their things, conversations filling the room. Just before anyone has a chance to leave, the alarms blare to life. The jurors freeze, wide-eyed and anxious. The bailiff is pressing a finger to his earpiece. His face goes pale. Panic surges through me. Something is wrong, and I just felt a spike of fear from Ava.

I have to get out of this courtroom.

I spin and take large strides to the door, but the bailiff blocks my path. "Mr. Taylor, we have shelter-in-place orders."

"I don't care what orders you have. I need to check on my mate," I growl. My voice is rougher than I would normally ever dream of being at court, but I cannot find it in me to care.

"Mr. Taylor, return to your seat," he says firmly. "If you don't, I will be forced to restrain you."

My mouth opens, ready to tell him he can certainly fucking try, but Henry slips back in through the doorway. As soon as he sees me, he raises his hand in a placating gesture, and I *know*. I don't need to hear whatever he's about to say.

"Let me out of this fucking room, Henry."

"Mark, security has this, and NYPD is en route. If you go charging out there, you'll put her in even more danger," he says gently.

Normally, I like Henry. I really do. Right now, though, my alpha is screaming at me to get past him and/or rip his head clean off his shoulders. My mate is in danger, and he is *in my way*. "What would you do if it was Grace? How can you ask me to sit here and do *nothing*?"

He winces. "I know. Believe me, I do. But please, listen to my forty-plus years of experience. Let the experts handle this."

"The police force hates her, Henry!" I yell, fear erasing every ounce of rationality I have left. "You want me to leave her safety to them?"

He studies me for a long moment, lips in a straight line and jaw tight as if debating with himself. The alarms are still blaring, and I can hear some of the jurors and spectators crying softly, but nothing matters to me just then except Henry and the woman—my woman—in danger past the doors. I clench my fists, and it feels like every muscle in my body is coiled like a spring, just looking for a reason to pop.

Finally, he sighs. "All right. You can come out with me into the hallway and down to the command center. But you stay behind me and do exactly as I say. Otherwise, I'm going to taze your big ass. Understood?"

I nod, not trusting myself to speak.

He presses his earpiece and notifies someone that he will be walking out of courtroom five's door with one other unarmed individual. Once they respond, he nods at me and then unlocks it.

We step out into the hallway, where several police officers are gathered with a group of armed guards. One officer is hunched over a laptop, monitoring a live feed from the building's security cameras. I can't see enough from my vantage point to spot where Ava is on the screens, and the knot of anxiety and fear in my stomach only tightens.

"Tell me what happened," I say roughly.

Henry's expression is more serious than I've ever seen. "When I came out the door, Ava was walking past with a man at her side. He had his hand firmly on her elbow and was standing much too close. Given what I know about you two, it immediately struck me as off. Then she mentioned needing a stuffed tiger when she was ill this weekend, and I knew she was signaling for help. Since I'm assuming she was in heat this weekend?"

Nausea forces acidic bile into my throat. I give a terse nod, closing my eyes to get myself under control before finding the strength to speak again. "Do we know who he was? Where did they go?" I ask quietly.

"NYPD is running facial recognition now. He's an alpha, that much I could tell, but not anyone I recognize. The good news is, they're still in the building."

I grit my teeth. "Do we think he targeted Ava specifically, or was she just a random woman he took hostage?"

Henry shakes his head. "We're not sure yet. But we will get her back, Mark. I promise."

The guards and police give us quizzical looks when we join them. I can practically feel the unasked question hanging in the air. They want to know what the hell I'm doing out here. I ignore it, leaning forward to get a clearer look at the camera feeds.

"Where is she?" I ask the guard closest to me. He looks familiar. Nick something, maybe.

He points to one of the squares and clicks to bring it into a larger view. "Best we can tell, she's in the hallway by the storage closets. We don't have eyes on her yet, but he's paced through there a couple of times."

"There are several blind spots over there," I say, more to myself than to him, as my gaze tracks the empty stretch of hallway. "She must be in one of them. We're positive she didn't get away from him?"

He nods and splits the screen, fingers moving quickly over the controls to pull up recorded footage. Ava appears, turning the corner with the man pressed tight against her side. His grip looks brutal, like he's afraid she'll take off if he loosens it. She's probably going to have bruises. My jaw locks. A low sound rumbles out of my chest before I can stop it.

The room goes quiet. A few of the men glance at each other. Henry steps closer, voice low. "Mark. You gonna be able to keep it together? We can't handle an alpha losing control right now. She can't afford us having to split resources to babysit you."

I shake my head and suck in a breath through my teeth. "I'm *fine.*"

Footsteps approach from behind us. Two men and a woman join the group, each in black tactical vests with NYPD ESU patches. The largest of the men is armed with an assault rifle strapped across his chest in a way that speaks of complete ease and familiarity with the firearm. The other man, I recognize immediately.

"Lieutenant Mulligan," I say. "I'm glad to see you."

And I am. I've worked with ESU before. There's a saying in New York—when we need help, we call 911; when the cops need help, they call ESU.

"Mark," he says, studying me carefully. "Why are you here?" There isn't any judgment in his tone. Not yet, at least. Right now, he's just assessing how I fit into the equation.

"Ava and I are bonded," I say quietly. The reaction is immediate. Heads snap up, and everyone's eyes widen. "It's a very recent development," I add.

He pinches the bridge of his nose. "You're telling me you're an alpha with a fresh bond, and your omega is being held hostage? Who the fuck let him out here?"

Henry clears his throat. "I did, sir. It was that or he caused a scene in one of the courtrooms."

"Jim, I'm handling it," I say. "But that's my mate. Every one of you knows you'd be the same way if it was yours. I can help. I know that hallway. I know Ava. Please," I beg.

He exhales slowly. "Can you track her scent?"

"She wears some pretty heavy-duty neutralizers," I say, thinking it through. "But if she's scared enough, it should bleed through. If that's the case, yes, absolutely."

"Get him a vest," he snaps to the nearby officers. Then he looks at me. "If you weren't trained in ride-alongs, I wouldn't even consider this. And I swear to God, I'll shoot you myself if you force my hand."

I nod. The good ole boy system worked in my favor—this would never have worked for most people. I don't have time to feel badly about it. A vest is shoved into my hands, and I strap it on quickly, fingers not quite steady.

An officer to my right is holding a tablet. He clears his throat without looking up. "Lieutenant, we have a probable ID. Appears to be Joseph Simmons. Extensive record. Most recent charges were drug distribution and weapons violations."

My stomach drops. The name is familiar. "Does he have a brother named Christopher?"

The officer taps the screen a few times. "Yes. He's at Rikers."

"Then he's targeting Ava directly," I say. I might be sick. "She was the attorney on that case. I won, but it wasn't the charges I'd hoped for. We suspected mafia ties, because it didn't make sense how he could even afford her firm, but we could never get proof."

"Then we assume he is armed and dangerous," the large officer with the rifle says.

"How the fuck did he get through security?" I snap, then immediately clamp my mouth shut. "Sorry. I'm terrified and angry."

"It's a good question, but one we have to figure out later," Jim answers. "Let's move."

We advance down the hallway, stopping short of the corner. "Can you scent her?" he asks me quietly.

I close my eyes and try to focus. "Yeah," I say, after a second. "It's hard to detect over the scent of so many alphas. I can't feel her through the bond, though." My throat tightens around the words.

"She's probably blocking," he reassures me. "Don't assume the worst."

The female ESU officer kneels and extends a small mirror on a pole, angling it just enough to see past the corner. "Subject is pacing. Appears agitated and is talking to himself. I have eyes on Ms. Kendrick."

Relief floods me instantly, only for my stomach to recoil at her next words.

"She doesn't appear conscious. She's seated on the ground. I believe she's bleeding."

A vise-like pain clamps around my heart. I dig my fingernails into my palms until the skin breaks.

The officer inches the mirror back and straightens, careful not to expose herself. "Mr. Simmons, my name is Alicia Anderson, and I'm with ESU," she says loudly, keeping her tone empathetic and warm. "I can hear you moving around back there. I'm not here to hurt you. I want to understand and help so nobody gets hurt today."

A harsh laugh echoes off the tile. "Bit late for that. The bitch is already bleeding, and you all won't let me leave here alive."

My pulse pounds in my ears, and Jim's hand grips my arm.

Alicia doesn't react to his language. "I'm hearing that you believe this ends with you dead. That sounds like you feel trapped," she says.

A scoff. "I am trapped. None of this went how he said."

"Who?" she asks.

Silence for a moment. "Doesn't matter. Someone who should know how things work here. The cops were supposed to be handled. You all weren't even supposed to show up."

Jim shifts beside me.

"You're saying you were promised protection," Alicia says. "And that didn't happen."

"I was supposed to take her out the back and handle her, then slip back in to take care of him when he went looking for her. It's all wrong!" His voice sounds high-pitched and crazed, and it terrifies me.

"Hey, Joseph, it makes me nervous how you sound right now. We don't have to talk about that. Can you tell me what happened to Ava?"

"She tried to run," he says defensively. "Threw her damn briefcase at me and bolted, so I reacted."

I don't know if I can do this. My body feels like it's on fire. My vision is blacking out around the edges with rage.

"How did you react?" Alicia asks.

A pause. Then, quieter, "I hit her. With the gun. She dropped."

"Thank you for telling me," she says. "I can help better if I understand. Where exactly did you hit her?"

"Her head," he mutters.

"Is she still breathing?"

The silence is deafening, and my whole body starts to shake.

"Joseph, stay with me. I'm worried about her bleeding out if we don't address it," Alicia says. "That will only make everything harder on you. If you let us help her, that goes a long way to showing the DA you aren't a monster and can only make things better for you."

He laughs again. "Yeah, right. He's fucking her. Did you know that? It's why she lost my brother's case. Too busy being a whore. So, what do you think he'll do to me?"

"I can't say what the DA will do. But if you're right and they have a relationship, I'm sure he would be more concerned with her safety over anything else. So let's see if she's still breathing, yeah? We can work together from there."

We hear footsteps and the rustle of fabric. Ava groans. It's low and pained, and our bond flares back to life. My knees nearly collapse under me. "She's alive, but in a lot of pain. Please let me talk to him, Jim," I whisper. "I won't attack, but I can make promises that Alicia can't."

He stares at me for a moment and then looks to the negotiator. She shrugs, and he gives me a tight nod.

"Joseph, this is Mark Taylor. If you want to be angry with anyone, you're taking it out on the wrong person. I'm the one that prosecuted your brother. And I promise, she did not make it easy on me," I say loudly.

"Oh, bullshit," he snaps. "You expect me to believe she fought you for real and then went home with you at night?"

"We just bonded this weekend. I don't know where you got your information, but we are pretty well-known for hating each other." The lie slips easily off my tongue. "She is a late-presenting omega, and that's the only reason we realized we are mates."

"That's not what I was told," he fires back. "He didn't say anything about her being an omega. Just that you two were fucking. None of this makes sense." His voice is taking on a panicked whine, and I don't know enough about these situations to know if that's a good or a bad thing. I look to Alicia for guidance.

"I'm hearing a lot of fear in your voice, Joseph," she says. "I think that maybe whoever told you all these things might have been using you for their own gain. Don't let someone have that kind of power over your future. Let us help her and you. This can end peacefully."

"I don't want to die, and I don't want to go back to jail," he shouts.

"Joseph, all I care about right now is Ava's safety," I say truthfully. "If you let them help her, I give you my word that I'll do everything in my power to help you. But hurting her more doesn't protect you from anything. It just guarantees you never get to explain who set you up."

He's quiet for a while. "Okay, I'm going to come out."

"That's great, Joseph," Alicia says. "I need you to put the gun on the ground and kick it over here first, okay?"

There's a thud, and then the gun slides into view. It isn't shaped like a normal pistol; instead, it's made of some kind of hard, white plastic.

"That's great. I'm so proud of you for working with us," Alicia says warmly. "Now, I need you to walk forward with your hands on top of your head. Nice and slow, okay?"

Footsteps echo down the hall, and Jim grips my arm again as the man comes into view. The warning is clear, but despite my burning desire to reduce Simmons into nothing but a puddle on the floor, I meant what I said. Ava is my top priority.

They get him down to his knees and handcuffed, and I yank free from Jim's hand and race around the corner. I slide to the floor and scoop Ava up to my chest.

"Are you okay, baby? You gotta be okay," I beg her.

"Mark? My head hurts," she whines.

"I know. We're gonna get you fixed up. I'm right here. You're safe, okay?"

29
Ava

Mark has me gathered onto his lap like I'm some kind of porcelain doll.

It might not be too far off, considering the side of my head definitely feels like it might be made of broken china. A paramedic is walking down the hall toward us, and Mark starts to growl low in his chest. She freezes and shows us her hands.

Shit. He's going into an alpha guard.

"Alpha, I need to touch her to check on her and help. I thought she was a beta. Is my information incorrect?" Her voice is a touch nervous, but she remains calm. More so than most would be.

"I'm an omega," I say weakly. "We're newly bonded, so he's... a little extra at the moment."

She nods. "That's good to know, there are different medication interactions. I still need your alpha to stand down before I can treat you, though."

"Mark," I say gently. "Let the nice lady help my head. It really hurts." I cup his cheek with my palm. "You don't have to let me go, but she has to touch me, okay?"

He closes his eyes and buries his nose into the side of my throat, but finally nods. "Sorry, yes, help her. I'm still coming down from everything, I think," he says into my hair, but loud enough she can hear him.

She nods in understanding. "It's all right. Pretty common thing when omegas are hurt. Most of the doctors at the hospital are alphas, though, so you'll need to keep it under wraps there, or you'll get a hard nap from the happy drugs."

I shake my head quickly, but then groan as pain lances my temple. "No hospitals. Please. I have some fairly intense medical trauma."

She frowns. "Well, I can't make any promises that you won't need one, but let me check you out first, okay? My name is Katrina, by the way."

"Hi, Katrina. My name is Ava," I respond. "My brother-in-law is a trauma nurse at Weill Cornell. I have access to care at home, if that matters."

"Well, it certainly doesn't hurt." She glances at the wound on my head. "The bleeding has mostly stopped, so I'm going to check your vitals before I clean it, okay?"

"Yes, that's fine."

"Can you tell me when your last heat was?" she asks as she unwraps the blood pressure cuff from my arm and jots the numbers onto a notepad from her pocket.

"It ended yesterday morning," I say quietly. "There's a chance I'm pregnant, but it's too early to really be sure. My mom called just before all of this happened, and she was going to tell me my results, but..." I trail off.

"Are you cramping or have any sort of pain?"

"No, ma'am. Well, none in my belly. My head is killing me."

Katrina shines a small flashlight at my eyes and has me follow it. Seemingly satisfied with my vitals, she starts cleaning the blood off my forehead. I hiss despite myself as she presses an antiseptic wipe against the wound. Mark lets out another low growl from behind me.

"Easy, big guy," she says without looking up, unbothered. "I'm almost finished."

She rummages through her bag and pulls out butterfly closures. The sting sharpens as she draws the edges of the wound together, then dulls as she applies the bandages. "There we go," she says. "You're going to be okay. Though you'll probably have a nasty-looking goose egg for a while, and I wouldn't be surprised if that eye turns a little black."

I exhale in relief, and I feel some of the tension ease out of Mark as well.

"My main concern is a concussion," she says, meeting my eyes. "I don't see anything here that requires an immediate ER visit, unless your symptoms worsen or you just want to be evaluated. Your brother-in-law knows concussion protocol, and he can walk your alpha through what to watch for once he has you safely back in your nest and he can think a little clearer."

I smile. "I promise he's normally not like this. It's all just very new."

She squeezes my hand gently. "You have someone who loves you. That's a good thing." Her tone softens a touch. "I do want you to follow up with an OB as soon as possible. Just to be safe."

"So, I can take her home?" Mark asks, sounding mostly like himself.

"Yeah, but you're going to want to talk with the police about the best way to do that. I know you'll want to carry her out, and I'm certainly not going to stop you. We don't have *that* many paramedics. But I imagine it will be like chum in the water to the sharks outside, considering who you two are."

Katrina packs her supplies back into her bag before giving me one last smile. "I always said I thought you two had a thing for each other. Nobody fights like that unless there's some chemistry there."

Mark carefully stands, cradling me against his chest bridal-style. I wrap my arms around his neck and lay my cheek against his shoulder.

"Lieutenant Mulligan, can I take Ava home? Someone from the precinct can come take her statement tomorrow, but she needs rest now," he asks someone that I don't bother lifting my head up to look at.

The sound of his voice and his scent soothe me, and I close my eyes against all the brightness.

I must have dozed off, because the next thing I know, the dull roar of people beyond the door jerks me awake. "Keep your head down, little cereus," Mark murmurs. "I've got you."

"Mr. Taylor! Why are you carrying Ms. Kendrick?"

"Are the reports true? Are you two bonded?"

"Ava, how long have you secretly been an omega?"

Question after question is lobbed at us. I hear the police surrounding us and telling the reporters to back up. I can hear the clicks of the flashes on the cameras, and I'm grateful Mark told me to keep my head in his shoulder, because I can't even begin to imagine how painful all the light would be.

"That's her car and driver right over there. Help us get to him, please," Mark says to someone. I press my face closer to him, whining. I should care more about people seeing me this vulnerable, normally I would. But I just can't seem to bring myself to care. God, I want to be home and in my nest.

"Thank you, Tony," Mark says quietly, easing me into the car seat through the open door. "Keep your eyes closed, Ava, and scoot just enough to let me in."

I do as instructed, curling back into his side immediately once he's settled.

***

"Before we do this," the woman in front of me says, pausing just outside the conference room, "I need to ask you something plainly." She tucks a strand of hair behind her ear, holding a slim folder against her chest, the seal of the New York Attorney General stamped neatly against the front. "Do you actually want to be in here?"

Mark rests his hand against the small of my back. He has the bond shut tight enough that I can't read him clearly, but I know he isn't thrilled—hadn't been since I'd agreed to the request from Harvey's attorney in the first place.

"I do," I say.

She studies me for a moment and then nods.

Joseph Simmons' statement had been a bombshell. He claimed someone identifying himself as being from the mayor's office contacted him and told him Mark and I had been sleeping together during his brother's trial. It hadn't taken much nudging for Joseph to draw the rest of the conclusions on his own. That I'd thrown his brother's case. That the solution was to remove both me *and* Mark at once. Along with assurances that he could do so cleanly with no police involvement.

It wasn't enough to incriminate the mayor directly. The word of a convicted felon against the mayor of New York City. However, it was enough to get Tony and Shelby on his tail, and once those two grab a thread, it tends to unravel pretty quickly. I don't think the CIA could keep secrets from them if they were determined enough.

After Simmons' arrest, Harold had immediately gone on the defensive. Before the story about me and Mark officially broke with our statement about our relationship, someone was fanning the flames that we'd been involved for months.

What saved us was that we'd already met with the NYSBA, and there was no evidence anyone could find of us having anything to do with each other outside of court or public events. Our circle had been tight by necessity. And any stragglers... well. I'm not entirely sure how Tony handled them, and I don't want to know. He told me I didn't need to worry, and I trusted that.

Once we started digging into Harvey, the information came fast. Phone records. Burner phones. Payments routed through shell nonprofits that funneled money into consulting fees and "community outreach" accounts. Far shadier things than just this attempt on my life.

A lot of it wasn't clean enough to use outright. Some of it had been obtained through methods that would never survive a courtroom challenge. But it was enough to convince the attorney general that there was something real there. Enough to get a warrant.

What ultimately led to his arrest was the delay.

ESU hadn't been called immediately when I was attacked, despite protocol for an active hostage situation inside a courthouse. That alone raised red flags. Then came the proof that Harvey had paid off one of the courthouse officers earlier that morning.

The only reason Lieutenant Mulligan's team had shown up at all was because Truck 1 had been monitoring radio traffic and caught enough irregular chatter to get uneasy. Otherwise, things could have gone very differently.

Harvey had been quietly arrested last night, which was a surprise. I'd have thought the attorney general would have eaten up the chance for the press, since Mark's office was forced to recuse themselves from the entire investigation.

I'm not sure what Harvey hopes to gain from this proffer session. Damage control, maybe? I'm too curious to not show up and find out for myself.

We step through the conference room door. Inside, a long table dominates the space. Harvey is seated next to several attorneys—his, no doubt. A pitcher of water sits untouched in front of him. His jacket is draped over the back of his chair, and his tie is loose around the neck. Overall, though, he doesn't look frantic or angry. Still as cool as a cucumber, and it makes me want to rage at the unfairness of the entire system.

His eyes land on me briefly, then wander over to Mark. There's a flicker of something there, but it's gone before I can catch it. Hate? Envy?

Mark pulls out my chair and waits for me to sit before he takes the seat beside me. He folds his hands on the table and regards Harvey coolly. I wonder if the mayor is aware he's in mortal danger. I've seen my mate in almost every stage of angry he is capable of, usually at me, but I've never seen him this calm. It's like the eye of a hurricane.

"Ms. Kendrick. Mr. Taylor," Harvey says, "thank you for coming. I was hoping we could all sit down and discuss this and come to a mutually beneficial agreement between us and the attorney general."

The prosecutor, Maria Gonzales, clears her throat and presses a button on the recorder in front of her. "For the record, this is a proffer session with Harold Harvey, current mayor of New York City. Mr. Harvey understands the limits and protections of this agreement."

He nods.

"And you understand," she continues, "that statements made here may guide further investigation, even if they are not directly admissible."

"Yes."

She clicks her pen. "Then let's begin. Mr. Harvey, can you explain why Joseph Simmons believed he was acting with political protection from your office when he entered a New York City courthouse with a weapon?"

Harvey exhales slowly and shakes his head. "I don't know Mr. Simmons beyond what I read in the paper about his attack on Ms. Kendrick. I certainly wouldn't put much stock in the word of a violent criminal trying to leverage Mr. Taylor's political aspirations to reduce his own potential charges."

He folds his hands together on the table, posture composed. "People say a lot of things when they're desperate. That doesn't make them true."

Gonzales doesn't answer right away, just makes a note on the pad in front of her. "I understand that," she says evenly.

"For the record, we're not asking you to validate Mr. Simmon's credibility, merely to explain his belief."

Harvey's mouth tightens. I like this woman; she's good.

"I cannot begin to explain what a criminal believes," he replies, "nor should I be expected to."

"Of course not," she says. "But you do control what your office communicates, do you not?" She pauses, waiting to see if he'll respond. When he doesn't, she continues. "Let's talk about the days leading up to the incident. Did anyone from your office contact Mr. Simmons through intermediaries after Ms. Kendrick left the dinner party at your house?'

"No."

She nods, as if she expected that answer. "Did anyone from your office discuss Ms. Kendrick with outside parties in that same period?"

He glances briefly at his attorney, then back. "Of course we did. Ms. Kendrick is constantly in the press and on the NYTV channel that my office runs. I don't see how that's relevant."

"It's relevant because your chief of staff exchanged twelve calls with a number later identified as a burner phone," the prosecutor says calmly, "the majority of which occurred directly after a call with you. That phone was later recovered from Mr. Simmons."

Harvey's attorney stiffens. "We object to the characterization—"

She scrunches her nose and curls her lip. "This is a proffer, counselor. I'm outlining the scope of our inquiry. There are no objections here." She looks back at Harvey. "Did you authorize those calls?"

"I did not. And I knew nothing about them," he answers.

She makes a thoughtful sound. "Let me be clear about where the state stands. I believe we have sufficient evidence to pursue charges including conspiracy to commit official misconduct, bribery, obstruction of justice, conspiracy to intimidate an officer of the court, and several related counts."

She meets Harvey's eyes squarely. "What I don't yet see is what you believe you can bring to the table in this meeting."

Harvey leans back in his chair and folds his hands. He glances at his attorney, then returns his attention to Gonzales. "Perspective," he says. "Context."

"Context doesn't matter in criminal court, Mr. Harvey."

He scoffs. "Of course it does. It especially does in the moving parts of politics. Nothing is linear. There isn't an order, an action, and a consequence. It's not that neat."

"So your position," she says, "is that multiple individuals independently decided to intimidate or possibly even kill a defense attorney, compromise courthouse security, and delay emergency response, all in ways that conveniently benefitted you."

He shrugs.

The prosecutor studies him for a moment. "And what are you offering in exchange for us accepting that framing?"

"I'm willing to give up information on the alphas pulling the strings on the omega rights issue that Ms. Kendrick is so passionate about, if she agrees to stand down as the injured party and not pursue charges." His eyes lock on to mine as he speaks.

She turns to face me for a moment before looking back at him. "You're proposing to trade information about political actors for immunity from consequences tied to a violent felony?"

He smiles, and it's clear he thinks he's just placed a temptation on the table we won't refuse. "I'm proposing to make this useful for everyone. Ms. Kendrick gets to protect the cause she claims to care about. You get possible convictions of some very big names. I get this reframed."

I shake my head. "You genuinely believe that omega rights are a bargaining chip. You're disgusting."

"I think," he replies smoothly, "that movements survive on compromise."

Mark's hand tightens once against the table. That's the only warning. "No," he says quietly. "This meeting is over."

Harvey lets out a short laugh. "You're recused, Mr. Taylor. You don't get to—"

Mark is on his feet instantly, his chair toppling backwards. "I am her *mate,*" he snarls. "You assumed her passion and her status made her open to negotiations. Worse yet, you viewed her as fucking expendable."

Harvey jerks back in fear before catching himself, masking it with practiced boredom. "I assumed she'd care about results," he says. "And that you'd appreciate the leverage to help your campaign."

Mark gives a bitter laugh. “I’m not running for mayor.”

Harvey blinks in surprise.

I stand, linking my fingers with my mate. “What you failed to account for,” I say evenly, “is that I don’t need anything you can offer to bring these men down. You think I don’t already know who profits from keeping omegas in their place?”

He looks at me now, really looks.

“My family is just as wealthy as yours,” I say with a laugh, “and I’ve been fighting this battle long before you ever learned my name. You have nothing of value to me.”

The prosecutor closes her folder. “Mr. Harvey, your offer is noted. And rejected.”

“You’re making a mistake.”

“No,” Mark says, guiding me toward the door, “you made that a long time ago by underestimating me and Ava.”

His voice follows behind us, stripped of its polish. “You could have changed things.”

I pause, just long enough to look over my shoulder. “I am changing things,” I say. “You just won’t be around to see it.”

EPILOGUE

Mark

Fourteen Years Later

"Mr. Kendrick-Taylor, the senator's office is on line three," my assistant announces over the intercom, and I frown. What is important enough that a text or voice memo wouldn't have sufficed?

I pick up the receiver. "Shelby? What's wrong? Is everyone okay?"

"Yes, sorry. Nothing like that," she says quickly. "I'm just juggling a lot of last-minute changes, and it was easier to call you while I sort the rest out."

This only deepens my confusion. "What changes? I thought we were all driving back to New York tonight?" God, please do not let the president be calling a special session. The kids have been counting down the hours until they can get home and put up the tree at the penthouse. We've all settled into DC well enough, but it's not where our roots are.

"Yes and no. Everyone is leaving tonight, except Ron and I will take the girls to Jack and Mateo's. Tony will drive you and Ava separately."

I pause. "Why?"

She sucks in a breath. "You're in for a bit of a surprise, big guy. Are you sitting down?"

Now I really don't like where this is going. "Spit it out, Shelby, before you give me a stroke."

"Ava is going into heat."

Some powerful emotion fills my stomach. Not sure if it's excitement or dread, though. "Shut up. She hasn't had a heat in over seven years. We're done."

"Apparently not. She's running a fever, her scent is exploding, and she's being an even bigger pain in my ass than usual. She flat-out *refuses* to even consider having her heat at the brownstone nest. All her babies were conceived in New York. Hence all the juggling."

I pinch the bridge of my nose. That sounds exactly like my mate.

Shit.

Another baby. I mean, I adore my trio of little vipers, but I'm pushing fifty. Starting all over?

"I can call Suzanne," Shelby offers gently. "I know she's said suppressants aren't safe for Ava anymore, but there have been so many advances in birth control."

"No," I say immediately. "Nothing like that. I won't risk her health just because I'm having a minor midlife crisis about diapers, midnight feedings, and being eligible for retirement when this kid is still in high school. It's exciting. Just... terrifying."

She chuckles. "Hey, maybe you'll finally get a boy."

I snort. "At this point, I don't even know what I would do with one. My lot in life is to be surrounded by redheaded girls that bully me."

"Especially since Amelia presented as an alpha."

"Yeah, no joke," I say, shaking my head. "All right. When and where do I need to be?"

"Here at the office in an hour. Tony is picking up the girls and heading this way as well."

I blink. "He's going to allow someone else to drive the girls somewhere? That sounds made up."

"You laugh, but he's being a bigger pain than Ava about it," she says dryly. "I explained that either someone other than him drives Ava while she's vulnerable and in heat, or Ron drives the girls. Those are the options."

"I mean, *I* can drive us back to New York."

She laughs. "You *are* wildly out of practice. I suspect you're going to be a little busy in the back seat to be of much use behind the wheel."

Oh. Right.

My cock stirs at the reminder, as if my body just remembered all the fun that comes with a heat.

"Okay, I'll see you in an hour. Give my omega my love."

When I arrive at Ava's office in the Hart Senate building, it's far emptier than usual. Shelby must have let the rest of the staff go home early, either for the holiday break or because of Ava's heat. Regardless, it's blissfully quiet in a place that is normally organized chaos. One junior aide remains, and she's busy packing up her laptop bag. I recognize her as the omega that Ava had recruited straight from Georgetown. The first omega congressional staff member for the first omega congresswoman. What Ava has accomplished in the last decade or so has been nothing less than extraordinary.

"Hello, Mr. Kendrick-Taylor," she says with a smile. "Mrs. McGregory and the senator are in her office with your girls."

"Thank you, Dakota. Happy holidays and safe travels if you're leaving the city."

She shakes her head. "No, I'm a local, so not very far to go at all. Same to you, though it sounds like you're going to have a happy holiday indeed," she says with a laugh.

I open the door to Shelby's chief of staff office and I find the chaos that was missing. Amelia, our oldest is in a chair as far as humanly possible away from her two younger sisters, playing on her phone. She's always been our bossiest and most stubborn, but her recent presentation as an alpha has thrown it into overdrive.

Olivia, our middle daughter and easily the wildest of the three, is busy holding something above Charlotte's head.

"Hello, baby vipers. Let's maybe tone it down several notches," I say gently, setting my bag down on a table near the door. I ruffle Amelia's hair and she wiggles away while making a face, which only makes me grin. "Olivia, give your sister back her toy. Where's Mom?"

"She's in her office with Aunt Shelby. Amelia told Mom that she stinks, so she sent all three of us out here to wait for Uncle Ron," Olivia informs me eagerly, never one to miss an opportunity to rat out her big sister.

I cut a look at my oldest, who at least has the self-awareness to look sheepish. "I didn't mean it like that. It caught me by surprise. I never smelled mom's scent like that before, and my nose is so much more sensitive now."

"Commenting on people's scent is rude in general, and you know that. Doing so when an omega is going into heat would be like a boy calling you disgusting for being an alpha," I chide.

"I know. I told her I was sorry. I don't think she was too mad. More that those two were getting on her nerves," she says, pointing at her sisters.

"Were not!"

"Were too!"

Thankfully, Ron picks that moment to open the door. His practiced dad—and now grandpa—eye quickly takes assessment of the situation. "Oy! Can it. Let's go tell your mom bye and hit the road. If you guys can keep from fighting for thirty whole minutes, we'll stop for ice cream on the way."

We all head into Ava's office. It's a large, vaulted room, with a partial wall in the center that has cutout openings to a smaller space Ava uses as a makeshift nest when she needs it. The American flag and the New York state flag bracket either side of a large portrait of Eleanor and Franklin Roosevelt. Ava liked to say that Eleanor should almost be considered the first female president with as much as she helped FDR, so she deserves just as much recognition.

My mate is sitting at her large desk underneath, and her scent is intoxicating even at a distance. I stay back by the doorway, not wanting to respond too much to it in front of our children. She catches my eye and gives me a bashful small smile, and I can feel her anxiety through the bond. I silently shake my head and send love and happiness her way.

I see her shoulders relax, and she opens her arms. "Give me a hug goodbye, girls. I'll see you in a few days," she says. "Well, Amelia, you don't have to," she adds quickly, and I can tell that her feelings *are* hurt a little by Amelia's offhand comment.

I glance at my oldest to see how she'll respond, but she steps forward and hugs her mother. "I *am* sorry, Mom. My nose is just sensitive," she whispers.

"It's all right, baby, I understand. I bet it is intense when you've never smelled it before. It'll be gone when I see you next, okay?" Ava presses a kiss to her forehead and releases her, before pulling the other two into hugs.

They say their goodbyes to me before Ron and Shelby usher them out the door. I can hear Amelia and Olivia already starting to argue as they head out. So much for ice cream.

I turn back to face my mate and crook a finger at her. "Come here, you."

"Nah, you come here. Or does my perfume not lure you in anymore?" she responds, jutting out her chin with a fake pout.

"Must not be too far into your heat yet if you're still being a brat." I grin and close the distance between us. I pull her out of her chair and into my arms, burying my nose against her throat and scenting her. I hadn't ever thought I'd get to smell this particular flavor of Ava again, and I intend to savor it and commit it to memory this time.

"You sure you want to try and get back to New York? You feel very hot, and your perfume is pretty strong," I ask against her skin. "The brownstone is closer." Not to mention that the sooner I get inside of her, the happier my cock will be.

"All my babies were conceived at home in New York. I'm not changing that now. You can get me off as many times as possible in the car, but don't you dare knot me until we are at home in my nest." Her words are demanding, but her voice has a needy omega whine pitch to it.

"Don't know why you're being bossy. Like you don't turn into a greedy little submissive when you're in heat," I growl, nipping lightly at her throat.

Ava shivers. "Yeah, well, I'm not fully in heat yet. But I mean it. It's... important to me."

"I know, sweet cereus. Only New York-bred baby vipers at our house. I won't knot you until we're home. No matter how many times you beg me to, because we both know you will."

She swallows, and her eyes have a glassy look that tells me keeping that promise and making it to the penthouse is going to be difficult. My scent and proximity has ramped up her heat, and my alpha side is responding in kind.

Tony knocks at the door, and I breathe a sigh of relief. Just a few more hours and I can fuck her into the mattress. In the meantime, I think I'm going to indulge in my favorite snack until we get there.

***

Nine Months Later

I stare in awe at the tiny creature wrapped tightly like a burrito in the small bassinet beside Ava's bed. It doesn't matter that this is my fourth time doing this, it always takes my breath away. His lips make a small sucking motion, and I can't help but grin. Probably dreaming about mama. "I get it, I dream about her a lot too, buddy," I whisper.

"He's perfect," Ava says quietly.

I glance over at her. "You're supposed to be resting. You comfortable enough?"

She nods and sits up with a wince. "I'm fine. That was the easiest labor I've ever had. Wonder if that means he's going to be an easy baby."

"From your mouth to God's ears. We're too old for another spitfire." I grab the pillows and adjust them behind her back.

"I almost feel bad keeping everything so quiet and peaceful in here and then subjecting him to the chaos at home," she says with a laugh. "Can you hand him to me? I need to wake him up to nurse, it's been a few hours."

"That alone says he's an easier baby then his sisters. I don't remember ever having to wake them up to feed them." I pick him up gently, smiling as he purses his lips in annoyance and cracks an eye open. He lets out a soft, squeaky sigh, then settles against my chest, his warmth seeping through the thin hospital blanket.

"Yeah, yeah," I murmur, rocking him softly, "we're interrupting your beauty sleep. Better get used to it, your sisters will do it more than me."

Ava huffs out a quiet laugh, reaching for him. I place him carefully in her arms, cradling his head until he's settled at her breast. I love watching how her entire posture softens the second he touches her. No matter how exhausted she is, or what she's gone through, she's always soft and gentle with our babies.

He stirs, rooting instinctively, his tiny hands flexing against her skin. She guides him with practiced ease until he latches on. She runs a finger along the downy red hair along his scalp. The room grows quieter somehow, like the whole world has agreed to pause for just this moment and let us enjoy the new life we've created.

I sit on the bed, just watching them. It's perfect. *She* is perfect.

"You did good," I say, hoping the reverence and gratitude I feel for her is coming through clearly over the bond.

She glances over at me, one eyebrow lifting. "Pretty sure I did more than *good.* This is one grade-A perfect baby."

I grin. "He is. You did incredible. As always. Have you decided on a name yet?"

Since we were fairly confident that this was our last baby, Ava had wanted to be surprised by the gender, even though we'd all been sure it was another girl. We hadn't even considered any boy names.

She sighs and looks back down at him. "I was thinking something like Grant. But I can't decide on a middle name that isn't too much next to Kendrick-Taylor."

"What about Thomas? After my dad?"

"Grant Thomas Kendrick-Taylor," she says, testing it out. "It's a mouthful, but it flows nicely." She grins. "Yeah, I think that works. What do you think, Grant?"

He makes a small sound of contentment.

"I think he approves." I press a kiss on her forehead and then the top of his head, breathing in his soft baby scent. "Are you ready for me to call Jack and have him bring the girls over, or do you want some more blissful silence?"

"Guess he's got to get used to it sometime."

I head toward the door out into the hallway, since the cell signal inside the room is abysmal. Before I step out, I turn and look back at her, and my breath is taken away by the perfect picture she makes holding our child.

“Hey, sweet cereus,” I say softly. When she looks up at me, I smile. “I’m so fucking glad I insulted you on television. Best contempt of court I ever earned.”

Her laughter follows me out of the room.

Thank You
For Reading

ACKNOWLEDGEMENTS

Completely changing genres was more than a little nerve-wracking. However, the basis for this story came to me in a dream, and once it gripped me, it wouldn't let go. With that being said, it never would have made it to print without the help of many others.

To Junie, for cheering me on and making this book one of the most beautiful things I've ever held in my hands. I hope this was a good show out of the gate for your "thoroughbred".

To Tess, for seeing my vision in my head for the cover illustration.

To Hannah and Cassie, for being excellent alpha/ beta readers. I'm sorry I measure commas with my heart.

To Ana, for taking the three possums in a trench coat rough draft I gave you and making it into something magical.

Lastly, and as always, my husband. I don't know if all writers are lucky enough to live with their muse, but I am. Thank you for listening to hours and hours of storyline as I fi gured out the world of Ava and Mark. Hell, I even yapped about their children. I will love you in this life and the next.

ABOUT DANI

Dani is an indie author that debuted in February 2025 with her romantasy novel Embers of Fate.

Ever since she got pulled into the principal's offi ce for writing love stories instead of doing math, she's been obsessed with writing about love and magic.

She lives in Missouri with her husband, two teenagers, and far too many animals. By day, she tries to change the world in the non-profi t sector. By night, you'll probably fi nd her with head in a book or writing.

DANI LOUGHARY

AUTHOR

Website

DaniLoughary.com

Instagram

@DaniLougharyAuthor

Reviews from the early readers of Motion to Claim

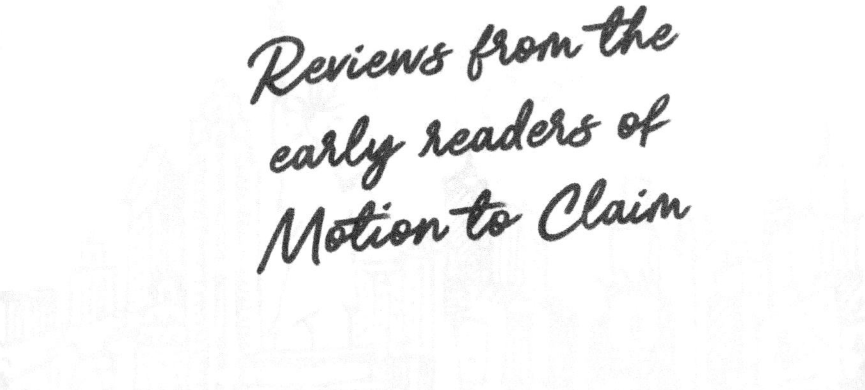

I really loved everything about this book. It was an easy, engaging read. The trial aspects kept me interested, the relationship kept me invested and the side characters added to the story without ever feeling overwhelming. I also really appreciated the omega storyline. It felt like an allegory for real-world issues and marginalization. It added an extra layer to the story without ever feeling too heavy-handed.

Only Here for the HEA

@OnlyHereForTheHEA_

I DEVOURED this book. Once I got started I was hooked trying to fi gure out what was going on. And for as fast as I read this book at no point was I bored. I defi nitely didn't predict what was going to happen in the end plot wise at all. It was full. It was eventful. It was enemy-to-lovery. And most importantly it was well written.

Bcgor Books

@Bcgorbooks

This book balances heat, emotion, and tension really well. The buildup is just as satisfying as the payoff, and when they fi nally choose each other, it feels both powerful and deeply emotional. If you love enemies to lovers, omegaverse dynamics, strong FMCs, and high-tension relationships that evolve into something real, this is absolutely worth picking up.

SmutGremlin

@SmutGremlin

Ava is that girl - sharp, intimidating, and completely untouchable on the surface, but with this quiet softness underneath that just makes you want to hold her a little closer. and Mark? I was seated for every single one of his POVs. the way he meets her fi re without ever diminishing it - if anything, he admires it - made their dynamic that much better. you can feel how much he respects her, even when they're at odds, and it just adds to everything simmering between them.

Vaeh

@VaehsReads

Their road to discovery is a wild ride! I loved seeing how the MCs peeled back their layers to reveal wonderful, supportive people, especially Mark. He is an Alpha, but his support of Ava is unwavering, and so refreshing. I felt that parts of this story were a commentary on the current status of life. If that's the case, well done! The pacing was even throughout the book, and I never had the sense that it was too slow. It did seem full, in a complete way.

Kate

@NurseLadyReads

I truly loved this one—and I can't even fully explain what pulled me in, but I was HOOKED! I just needed to keep reading to see what would happen next… and honestly? That's my favorite kind of book because I wasn't expected to be so into it where I have to put my others down. Enemies-to-lovers can be hit or miss for me, but THIS ONE?? It hit; It wasn't dragged out, but gave just enough tension to have me rooting for that HEA the whole time.

Julissa

@JulissaReviews

This is one of my fi rst lawyer romance and I love the enemies to lover with the DA and defense attorney angle. Also I love Tony and his side comments about "You need a gun...Guns faster..." I think I laughed out loud so much I had to put the book down. This was an amazing book and was the light hearted standalone I needed! Highly recommend for my dark romance girlies if you need a fun short cleansing read! I will defi nitely be adding this to my shelf to read again!

Bailey

@BaileyReadsNow

Made in the USA
Coppell, TX
20 June 2026

82573526R00204